SENTINELS OF TZURAC

ZARKWIN'S REVENGE

JAMES RAVEN

Published in 2015
by James Raven
www.jamesraven.com.au

Typesetting by Publicious Pty Ltd
www.publicious.com.au

Cover design by Bruce Hart

Catalogue-in-Publication details available
from the National Library of Australia

ISBN: 978-0-9871243-3-3

ACKNOWLEDGEMENTS

For her relentless help in editing my novels and for her continuous strong support and encouragement of my writing, I would like to express my deepest gratitude to my partner Julie.

I would also like to sincerely thank Bruce Hart for his wonderful creative artwork in designing the 'Zarkwin's Revenge' book cover.

I am also grateful to those readers who encouraged me to write the sequel in the 'Sentinels of Tzurac' series.

CONTENTS

PRISON LIFE

SUDDENLY, the pitch-black room was flooded with an extremely bright light emanating from the ceiling, accompanied by the persistent noise of an over-amplified clanging bell. Then a moment of dead silence reigned before the room was drowned in a low, repetitive monotone voice. *'All prisoners vacate cells within 3 minutes... All prisoners vacate cells within 3 minutes.'* Every day for the past five years of his life-term incarceration, Jackson Jensen had tolerated this same irritating wake-up call.

He stirred reluctantly from his prison bunk, running his fingers through his tousled hair, waiting for the next routine direction to be broadcast. A tall and wiry man, now in his early thirties, with an olive complexion and thick dark hair, Jackson had changed little in appearance over the years. Standing in his grey prison-issue pyjamas and surveying his all-too familiar surrounds, it was only his dark brown eyes that burned more intensely than ever.

Like all the cells in this massive complex, Jackson's small lockup was bland, totally secure and indestructible. It was windowless; the entire prison building being housed below the planet's surface and extending vertically three hundred feet below the ground. And it was encased by three six-inch-thick, titanium-reinforced concrete walls, the fourth wall a solid, sliding, titanium exit door operated by the Control Room on the second level.

As the titanium door slid open, the next message sounded. *'All prisoners vacate cells... All prisoners vacate cells.'* Jackson stepped onto the open walkway outside his lockup and joined the stream of lookalikes wiping the sleep from their eyes as they were herded to the shower blocks by black-uniformed prison guards. The walkway opened onto a huge, central, circular core, eighty feet in diameter, channelling natural light into the complex and providing a clear view of the walkways on the floors above and below where close on two hundred male inmates were all doing the same.

"Morning, ladies! Lovely day!" Jackson called sarcastically to the guards, as he always did.

The prisoners' working day started at 06.00 hours. Emerging from their morning ablutions in bright orange prison-issue overalls, they were escorted to the prison cafeteria to be fed a tasteless porridge. By 07.30 hours they were ready for their day's labour – rostered, if lucky, for general maintenance, internal transportation or kitchen, laundry and library service and, if not, for the dreaded task of mine labouring.

Located on the remote and inhospitable planet, Terra Upsilon, the penal colony had been established to isolate and contain Earth's most dangerous offenders, those with violent tendencies who could not be rehabilitated. The prisoners provided the manual labour for the only other activity on the planet – the underground mines – working in filtered-air caverns deep below the planet's surface. Terra Upsilon was being mined for essential raw minerals by Earth's Mining and Engineering Resource Industrial Company, MERIC.

There was nowhere to run or hide. The surface of the planet was subjected to destructive sandstorms. Breathing apparatus and heavy protective clothing could shield the wearer for short periods of time, but silt-covered skeletal remains scattered on the planet's surface were constant reminders of desperate or foolish prisoners who had attempted to escape while on mining detail.

Wherever they were, in the mines, in their cells or throughout the prison complex, the prisoners were under constant surveillance. They were scrutinised by security cameras and monitored by bar-coded micro-chips implanted in the nape of their neck and hard-wired into their nervous system. If a prisoner strayed outside their designated area, the multi-functional chip automatically delivered a sudden electrical jolt causing excruciating pain. Using a device on their utility belt, the guards could also trigger an electrical shock to curtail unwanted prisoner behaviour. The prisoners were captive and controlled.

As Jackson began his catering shift, he joked to the others working the ovens, "Just another day in Paradise."

***

As a prisoner, Jackson was unique. He wasn't a hardened low-life like most of them. In fact, he was quite the opposite – an intelligent, well-educated professional and former corporate director who had been imprisoned for conspiracy and murder.

While biding his time on Terra Upsilon, Jackson had continued to be ever-vigilant, keeping a constant eye on Earth's current affairs by watching the latest news on the monitors in the Recreation Room. He maintained a sharp mind, spending some of his free time in the prison library digesting information, studying spacecraft design and operations and keeping up to date with the latest techno-advancements and industrial developments on Earth. He also maintained his physical fitness through regular use of the prison gym. He kept his body toned, honed his fencing and martial art skills and developed his boxing prowess.

In the face of gang rivalries amongst the prisoners, Jackson had managed to gain a position of safety and high status. He adapted his business acuity into street-smart cunning, making a lucrative enterprise from contraband. He dealt in drugs, cigarettes, alcohol, small-bladed weapons, confectionery and luxury food items smuggled into the complex from visiting transporters. Jackson's personal bodyguards watched his back while he conducted 'business' with the inmates and prison guards.

The prison warden, Commissioner Daniel Davies, who had been in charge for some seven years, was aware of Jackson's smuggling operations. But, turning a blind eye, he used Jackson's influential status to keep him informed of what was happening amongst the prisoners and to assist him in keeping relative peace. In turn, Jackson used Davies to extract information about planned prison activities that might affect his business dealings. Commissioner Davies often invited Jackson to his office for an 'informal chat'. And, this morning, Davies had something of importance to relay to Jackson, summoning him from his kitchen duties.

If Jackson wasn't the typical prisoner, then the Commissioner wasn't the typical 'Company man'. He was rather short in stature and quite rotund, reflecting both his over-indulgence in confiscated food contraband and a lack of physical exercise. But he was a stickler for protocol. He dressed in the corporate charcoal uniform, his blazer adorned with black-velvet collar and cuffs and studded with silver buttons at the front. His uniform was immaculately clean and well pressed and his black leather boots were spit-polished to a shiny, glazed finish. He kept his black hair cropped short and parted to one side and he was always clean-shaven, exposing his anaemic moon-face. He was constantly peering over his half-rimmed, wire reading glasses which he wore habitually and he spoke in a high-pitched tone in short, sharp bursts of sentences, sounding as though he was always in a hurry.

Seated at his glass-panelled desk, Davies continuously shuffled papers from his desktop to one of four neatly-stacked trays on his left or from these trays to neat piles on the desktop. Nothing was ever orderly enough for this fastidious man, which was an annoying distraction for visitors trying to engage him in conversation. Perhaps this anal-retentive quality was one of the criteria the Prison Board sought in a prison administrator destined for isolated penal colonies? Under the command of a warden who was precise to the point of pedantic, all would run efficiently. And, for a warden who was busy attending to his own obsessive needs, the seven-year tenure would pass more quickly.

"Yes, yes, come in, come in," said Davies when the alert chime was pressed by the guard at the armour-plate door. Activating the entry control from his desk, Davies rose to his feet as the door slid open. "Sit down, Jackson. Tea or coffee?"

"A glass of your single malt thanks Dan," said Jackson, provocatively.

"Don't be ridiculous Jackson," replied Davies, taking the bait. "We don't run a hotel here. This is an institution for criminals who have forfeited such privileges."

"Yeah, yeah, alright Commissioner, stop the lecturing. Why don't you sit down and tell me why I'm here?"

Davies followed Jackson's instruction unconsciously and, when seated, beamed at Jackson like a Cheshire cat. The smile was uncharacteristic and Jackson was curious.

"Alright, Dan. Why are you looking so smug and happy with yourself?"

"Guess what year this is Jackson?" asked Davies, eagerly.

Taking his time and pretending to ponder in thought, Jackson decided to play the cat-and-mouse game to amuse himself and to frustrate Davies. Jackson knew Davies could be just as cruel as he could be friendly and he didn't want to change Davies' mood to one of retaliation. Jackson had learned just how far he could tease him without causing a mood swing, keeping Davies squirming like a worm on a fish hook.

"This is the fifth year of my incarceration," replied Jackson with tempered sarcasm, "and I don't think it's anything to smile about Davies, unless you intend releasing me for good behaviour."

Davies leaned forward on the table, resting his chin on clasped hands, "My, we are in a humorous mood today, aren't we?" He paused momentarily, relaxing back in his chair before smugly announcing, "No Jackson, this is the year I retire."

Jackson was taken completely by surprise. He was usually aware of everything that happened in the complex but he hadn't seen this coming. While his mind raced with myriad thoughts, he maintained a poker face, giving nothing away to the Commissioner. Jackson listened intently as Davies continued his gloating.

"I'll be departing this isolated hell-hole to return to the real world, leaving the scum behind me. I can tell you this; your new master will not be as lenient or tolerant as me. *He* won't let you get away with the use of contraband or briberies and there'll be no liberties."

Jackson didn't stir at Davies' words. He knew Davies was right. A replacement taskmaster would undo the 'business' network he had taken years to establish, and a new Commissioner might also change prison systems in a way that would set him back years in his plans of escape. Jackson was focused on working out a way of extracting the information he needed to use the Commissioner's arrival to his advantage. He leaned back casually in his chair and placed his hands behind his head.

"So Dan, when do we throw the farewell party and pop the champagne? After all, we've been through a lot together and I've enjoyed our rather unique business relationship. I think I'll miss you and I'm sure you'll miss me."

"No Jackson," said Davies with a look of disgust, "I won't miss you or your sarcasm, but I'll have a small farewell celebration with some of the guards the day before I leave. You'll be invited of course, just to give you a taste of what you'll never have again."

"I'll need to consult my diary to see it doesn't clash with my other social engagements," joked Jackson, hoping to pry from Davies the time of the farewell event.

Without thinking, Davies played right into Jackson's hands. "I'm sure you won't be busy on Sunday night Jackson and I'll have my guards escort you personally to the party."

It was just the information Jackson needed. *Seven days. Perfect!* He maintained his cool façade. "Thanks for the invite Dan. So, who's the new Commissioner?"

Davies answered with a wry smile. "Captain John Tanner, retired ex-army officer from boot camp, chosen specifically for his successful methods of churning out mean and lean, disciplined soldiers. The Board felt this place needed some smartening up and Captain Tanner won't tolerate the crap you lot have been giving me and my men over the last seven years. He's just what the doctor ordered to give you low-life's a dose of your own medicine. He *won't* be bribed or threatened. No Jackson, you're in for a rude awakening and so are your cell mates. And I think this ends our conversation for today. So you can tell your buddies they'd better be on their best behaviour when my replacement arrives or they'll wonder what's struck them."

"Thanks for your consultation and pearls of wisdom, Dan," responded Jackson, sarcastically. "I'll pass on your advice and I'm sure my colleagues will comply with your thoughtful considerations. And what should I wear to this special black tie occasion you've planned? My tux?"

"Just wear your same old smarty-pants Jackson, they really suit you," said Davies. "Guards, escort this worthless prisoner back to his cell!"

As Jackson rose from his chair, the two guards seized his arms and removed him from Davies' office, Jackson grinning smugly to himself. *My window of opportunity has finally arrived, even if sooner than expected.*

***

In his former life, Jackson Jensen had been not only a corporate director but also heir to the MERIC empire. But, while being groomed to take over his father's company, Jackson's lust for power had got the better of him. Following MERIC's discovery of the powerful resource Xytrinium on Planet Terra Iota, Samuel Jensen wanted to declare the finding immediately to Earth's governing body, the World Assembly, and accept their direction about how it should be used in mankind's best interest. Jackson was frustrated by his father's 'archaic' protocols, wanting exploitation of the potent resource for MERIC, *and* for himself.

His attempts to take over the Company were hampered by a MERIC engineer, Kyron Shield, a man Jackson despised as his father's confidante. In a ruthless and cold-hearted rage, the selfish and extremely determined Jackson arranged not only for attempts on Kyron's life, but also for his own father's death. When his father was killed in an 'accident', Jackson took control of MERIC, determined to govern all mining operations and hold the World Assembly to ransom.

However, Kyron proved a difficult target, surviving Jackson's hit-men and exposing Jackson's conspiracy as well as his involvement in Samuel Jensen's murder. With the help of elite Tzuracian 'super soldiers' called Sentinels, Kyron saw Jackson captured, sentenced and banished to Terra Upsilon for the rest of his life. Jackson seethed with jealousy when he learned Kyron Shield not only had Sentinel blood, but also had been bequeathed ownership of MERIC.

Five years in prison had fuelled Jackson's bitterness. As he watched the expanding progress of what he believed was rightfully *his* company, he became determined to escape and return to Earth to exact revenge and reclaim his inheritance. He also became obsessed with the notion of finding a source that would give him the power necessary to match Kyron Shield and his Sentinel allies. He had learned the key to the Sentinels' enhanced powers and extended lifespan was DNA infusion with Xytrinium. Jackson realised if he were ever to overpower Kyron Shield he would need to find the long-lost formula and infuse himself and an army of faithful followers.

Jackson had been devising a plan since his arrival on Terra Upsilon.

Over time he had built up an army of loyal supporters among the prisoners and guards, promising he would lead them to freedom and give them the elixir of life. He hand-picked fearless prisoners experienced in combat – misfits from all walks of life including ex-military, deserters, mercenaries for hire and trained assassins. All were physically fit, shared a hatred for government authority and needed no excuse to fight. One by one, Jackson recruited them, convincing them it was only a matter of time before an opportunity to escape would come.

He also befriended some of the prison guards who had previously worked as his security officers at MERIC. Having rewarded them well at the time, Jackson now regained their loyalty. With their cooperation he gained access to the blueprints and schematics of the Control Room's operating systems. He monitored the internal operation systems as well as the arrivals and departures of supply ships, ore and prison transporters. Secretly, he studied blueprints of the prison complex and guard rosters. He also had a tech-savvy ex-terrorist, called CT, work covertly on developing portable devices to temporarily disable the deadly, implanted micro-chips. CT's devices would permit the chips to be momentarily disabled before being permanently deactivated from the Control Room.

Over years of careful planning and painstaking development, Jackson had almost perfected his plan of escape. Now, with a more ruthless Commissioner set to take charge within the week, Jackson had no choice. He had to bring the escape plan forward and take full advantage of what might be his one and only opportunity.

THE PLAN

Back in his cell before lights out, Jackson worked overtime on his escape plan. He had a sleepless night formulating the stages in his mind and, the following morning, he began to put the pieces of his plan into action.

The first step was to ensure he and his followers could be free of their implants come Davies' party and, to do so, he needed assurance from CT the devices he'd been working on could be ready within the week. It was no easy matter to disable a micro-chip. Tampering with the implant simply amplified the pain, and the only way to temporarily disarm a micro-chip was by delivering a precise micro surge of electricity directly to it. The electrical charge needed to be calibrated perfectly because an overload caused brain haemorrhage and death within seconds. The success of Jackson's plan hinged on CT's confirmation that the devices were functional and the number needed could be delivered in time.

Nicknamed CT or Circuit, Jackson's would-be accomplice was an electronic whiz and a combination of madman and genius. His life sentence to the far-flung Terra Upsilon had been punishment for his association with an international terrorist group which had systematically assassinated almost half the members of the World Assembly. Six years on, CT still threatened to finish the job, if given half the chance. Forever expanding his knowledge base in the hope of escape, CT was always reading the latest developments in technology, bio-mechanics and robotic engineering. There wasn't an electronic device he couldn't pull apart or put together again and Jackson knew CT would be more than eager to assist in his plan.

With a lightweight frame and allergies to dust and smoke, CT was unable to work in the mines and instead had been placed in charge of the library. It was the perfect vocation given his keen interest in books and his talent at troubleshooting and fixing faults in the prison's computer systems without needing to call in the specialists. In this lucrative position CT had become central to the distribution of contraband and a close business partner of Jackson. He concealed smaller items in purpose-built books he included amongst items to be checked out to prisoners. In return, he took a percentage of the takings or was owed favours.

Being on roster that morning to deliver the guards' morning teas, Jackson was able to catch up with CT in the library. While the two guards on duty there were busy getting their coffee from the mobile dispenser, Jackson took the opportunity to chat to CT on the pretext of borrowing a book.

"How's things CT? Keeping you busy?" asked Jackson in a deliberately loud voice, guiding CT along the reception counter while pretending to browse the books on the shelf behind.

"Yeah Jackson," responded CT in his boyish voice, "but things could be better."

Jackson dropped his voice to a whisper as soon as he was out of earshot of the guards. "Things *are* going to get better, and within the week CT. Don't say anything, just listen. I don't have much time. Davies is retiring and his replacement arrives next Monday. This is our chance to escape and I already have a plan. I know I'm not giving you much time, but I need you to make up fifty-five of those de-activating zappers for the gang. And they need to be ready by Sunday night. Is it possible? Can you manage that?"

"Anything to escape this hell-hole! Sunday night is cutting it fine JB, but I'll make damn sure they're ready in time. Trust me!"

"I also want several small explosive devices with remote-control activation to be placed strategically in the Control Room. I need to knock out all the communications inside and outside the complex when we leave this stinking planet. Can you manage that as well?"

"Yep, no problem," replied CT with a wicked look. "I've been waiting a long time to show off my real skills."

"Thanks CT, I'll fill you in on the whole plan later. Just keep it under wraps and tell no-one. Stay cool. Now, hand me that book over there so the guards don't get suspicious."

Jackson grabbed the book from CT and headed back to the mobile dispenser, the guards unaware of the significant conversation that had just taken place.

Jackson's next port of call was the Guards Room located on the second floor next to the Control Room adjoining the Armoury. *En route*, he engineered a distraction by knocking several cups from the dispenser onto the floor. While the prison guard was distracted by the noise of shattering china, Jackson deftly slipped a note into the pages of his library book. The cryptic note, which he had prepared the previous night, held instructions for Sergeant Stoltz, the ex-MERIC security officer in charge of the guard roster. In readiness for an escape, the message asked for a loyal prison guard to be in the Control Room on Sunday night and for other complicit guards to be in attendance at the Commissioner's farewell party.

At the Guards Room, four guards, including Stoltz, converged on the dispenser, keen for their morning coffee. As Stoltz reached for his, Jackson deliberately bumped him, almost spilling the hot cup of coffee he had in his hand, while drawing attention to the book he was carrying.

"Watch it, you clumsy idiot!" yelled Stoltz with a thick Austrian accent. "Get out of my way."

"Sorry Sergeant, it was an accident, don't hit me," said Jackson, pretending to cower and humble himself before Stoltz. The other guards laughed with amusement.

Most of the inmates as well as the prison guards were quite fearful of Sergeant Stoltz who had a reputation as a hard-nosed, no-nonsense military man. With no prospect of further promotion on the planet, and his shore leave cancelled on two consecutive occasions, Stoltz was a frustrated officer who couldn't wait to depart Terra Upsilon. After five years of working out in the gym, the solidly-built Austrian was known for taking his frustration out verbally and physically on the prisoners; on occasion, badly beating several of them. But Stoltz had been treated well by Jackson when in the employ of MERIC and when Jackson promised to extend Stoltz's life with the DNA treatment and offered him passage off the planet, he secretly joined Jackson's gang.

"Give me that book you swine!" shouted Stoltz. He wrenched the book from Jackson's hand and swiped the back of Jackson's head with it, acting out the role play perfectly.

"Yes, alright, Sir, take it, it's yours. Just don't hit me again," cried Jackson, feigning fear.

"Get out of here you miserable excuse for a man, before I decide otherwise."

"Oh leave him alone Stoltz!" cried out one of the other prison guards. "He's not worth the trouble."

"Yeah, you're right," responded Stoltz, tossing the book on his desk as Jackson continued on his rounds. The message had been delivered.

Next, Jackson needed to know the exact time of the Commissioner's farewell party. Perhaps there would be a note to that effect on Davies' desk? When Jackson and his escort arrived at the Commissioner's Office with morning tea, Davies was caught slightly off guard. His back was turned to the glass sliding door while he was trying to find something in the bottom drawer of his filing cabinet. In his haste to turn around he knocked one of his neatly-piled stacks of papers onto the floor, flustering him even more. Waving his hand for Jackson to enter, he ordered one of the prison guards to collect the papers from the floor.

"What is it Jackson?" the Commissioner blurted out impatiently. "I'm very busy sorting out this office before I depart and *you* are interrupting my schedule."

"Calm down Dan, I've brought you morning tea with your favourite *petite gateaux*."

Davies couldn't resist sweet, rich food and his attitude changed immediately. "Sit down and join me Jackson and tell me what the gossip is amongst the inmates now the word is out on my imminent departure."

Jackson was quick to pull up a chair. "Well Dan, most of the prisoners are happy to see the back of you. But some are saying they're probably better off with the devil they know than the devil they don't. I didn't tell them the new 'boss' is ex-military with an agenda to 'whip these boys into shape'. Otherwise you may have a riot on your hands before you leave."

While the Commissioner was indulging in a cream-layered delight, only half-listening to what Jackson was telling him, Jackson scanned the desk. There was no sign of information on the farewell party. Just as Jackson began to think he would need another approach, the prison guard placed a bundle of Davies' spilt papers back on the desktop. And there on the top sheet was the time and date circled in red: 7.00 pm, Sunday 14th. *Too easy*, he thought.

The Commissioner swallowed an overfilled mouthful of cake before responding, "Good thinking on your part, Jackson. But I don't have time to talk today. Guard, see Prisoner Jensen on his way."

Jackson rose from his chair, keeping his back to the Commissioner as he strolled out the door escorted by the watchdog guard. A cunning smile came across his face as he offered his parting words, "Thanks for the pleasure of letting me join you for morning tea, Dan. It's been *most* illuminating."

***

Jackson seized any available opportunity the following day – in the showers, in the kitchen, in the laundry and in the gymnasium – to spread word of the escape plan to his gang of prison followers. At lunch in the mess hall Jackson sat inconspicuously with CT at a distance from the other inmates. While keeping a watchful eye on the roaming prison guards he gave CT more details.

"The party starts at 19.00 hours so all the de-activators need to be with our gang members before then. The remote control explosive devices should also be ready to fix into place once we're in the Control Room. How's it progressing CT?"

"I've had to improvise with some of the bits and pieces JB, but I'm on track and I'll keep you posted."

"Thanks, CT, it's going to be a hell of a party. You bring the girls, I'll bring the wine."

"You're on," said CT with a grin.

While counting the days, Jackson spent every opportunity secretly reviewing flight charts and calculating navigation paths to his intended destination, committing these to memory. He deduced the ship coming from Earth would have just enough fuel to get him and his followers to the chosen planet but he trusted no-one with this critical information.

Four days from countdown Sergeant Stoltz advised Jackson the duty rosters were in place for Sunday night and he was ready to release the cell doors of fifty selected prisoners at exactly 19.30 hours. CT was still working to meet his tight deadline when Jackson gave him more explicit instructions.

"You need to get those zappers to the gang before Sunday afternoon with instructions on how to use them. They must be de-activated just before the cell doors open at 19.30 hours so the prisoners can overpower the guards without warning. If the implants are not disabled in time, the guards will be able to use their remote control pain switches and put us out of business."

"Can do, JB. Here's yours." CT discreetly handed Jackson a small, dark-grey tube resembling an old-fashioned, thumb-click ballpoint pen. "All you do is place the tip of the tube on the bar code on your neck and press the thumb-click down for three seconds. No more, no less. The electric zap will feel like an ant bite just for an instant. Simple, but effective."

"Well done CT. Ingenious design and small enough to smuggle in our boots."

All was going according to schedule. The sense of impending freedom was surging throughout Jackson's whole being and he knew exactly what he would do with his freedom and who would pay for his imprisonment. Jackson was on a mission. Escaping was only the beginning. Everything now depended on timing.

THE ESCAPE

IT was Sunday evening and Jackson's head was buzzing with anticipation, his body alert with adrenalin. He'd been unable to eat his last meal in captivity, instead playing with his food while counting the minutes until his plan unfolded. His gang was primed for action – his loyal guards in the Control Room, and his selected fellow prisoners poised with CT's ingenious 'zappers'. Jackson paced anxiously back and forth in his cell, until one of his favoured guards appeared at the cell door at the pre-arranged time.

"You ready Mr Jensen?" asked Officer Harris, knowing what Jackson's answer would be.

"Never more ready Harris. Should be a great party, one I'll remember for the rest of my *free* life."

Harris unlocked the door, both men chuckling as they made their way to the second level Amenities Room.

The tinted plate-glass door slid open to a sound-proofed room filled with floating, coloured balloons and decorated with fluorescent-yellow streamers. Some old-time music was playing loudly, Jackson recognising the tune as 'Auld Lang Syne'. *How appropriate and how hypocritical,* he thought. In the middle of the room was a long wooden table covered with a starched, white-linen cloth, cluttered with a dozen plates filled with lavish amounts of savoury finger-food and sweet cakes. There was a half-emptied bottle of cheap champagne on the table and an unopened bottle was cooling in a chrome ice bucket near an empty chair.

"Welcome Jackson," shouted Davies in a muffled voice from

the far end of the table, while forcing a cream-filled pastry into his already-bloated mouth. With a large white napkin stuffed clumsily into the front of his shirt collar, Davies was living up to his gluttonous reputation. "Glad you found the time to join my celebration."

"I see you've raided the supplies, again, Dan. Why am I not surprised?" Jackson sneered.

"Shut up Jackson. They're not yours to worry about. Besides, how often do we get the chance to celebrate farewells when no-one leaves this god forsaken hell-hole unless it's in a pine box?"

Jackson had to bite his tongue: *Wish Davies was leaving that way.*

Judging by Davies' over-confident, slurred speech, it was obvious the Commissioner was slightly inebriated from the champagne he'd already guzzled. The six guards on duty in the room, who had clearly not been invited to celebrate with him, stood watching Davies with contempt.

"Come and sit over here next to me," invited the half-intoxicated Davies, waving to the vacant chair.

Jackson declined the offer. "No thanks, Dan, I have more important matters to attend to."

"What are you talking about Jackson? It's my party. Sit down and behave yourself before I have my guards instil some respect into you."

"*Your* guards?" said Jackson, chuckling. "I'm sorry to inform you Dan, but you've been living an illusion over the last few years thinking *you* were in control of this establishment. These are *my* guards and they take orders from *me*."

Davies was taken back. "Don't be a fool Jackson. Guards! Place this prisoner in confinement and relieve him of all privileges." All eyes were on Davies, the guards standing fast. "Did you hear my orders? Do as I command you, *immediately*, or you'll all bear the consequences."

"Shut up Dan. Harris, cuff him and gag him before he does something stupid. We need him in one piece, so try not to damage the goods. And someone turn off that *bloody* horrible music!"

In a blasé manner, Jackson reached for a champagne glass and poured himself a drink from the open bottle. "Okay men, pour yourselves a glass too," he said, pointing to the other bottle in the ice bucket.

Raising his glass, Jackson turned to his men, "I propose a toast. Here's to our freedom and the spoils we deserve." He took a mouthful of champagne and then flung his glass to the far end of the room, just missing Davies. The missile shattered loudly against the wall. The guards mimicked Jackson with great delight.

Davies was livid. "You'll pay dearly for this Jackson! They execute rebellious prisoners who buck the system." Before he could say anything else, Harris gagged Davies with tape, clapped cuffs on his hands and raised him to his feet.

"Right you guys," said Jackson "let's head to the Control Room. Keep a look out for any of Davies' guards just in case they escaped the clutches of our fellow prisoners."

Jackson assumed his gang members on the other floors had been freed from their cells, taken charge, and were now on their way to the Control Room as planned. But as the door slid open from the Amenities Room, he heard yelling and laser fire coming from the floors below.

"What the hell's going on?" said Jackson, turning to his men. "Harris, you and Walker take the Commissioner to the Control Room. Tell Stoltz to lock down the door to the Guards Room to stop the rest of Davies' guards from getting out. You others come with me to the Armoury. And keep your heads down!"

Rushing out the doorway, Harris and Walker bolted right, bundling Davies between them, while Jackson and his men sped in the opposite direction, reaching the Armoury fifty yards further along the corridor. One of Jackson's guards hastily punched the keypad and the door slid open.

"Grab some firepower," ordered Jackson, "and follow me to the service lift. No time to waste."

This was the first time Jackson had been free to venture inside the Armoury. He'd seen the blueprints of the layout but had no idea of the quantity and types of hardware stored there. He was amazed with what confronted him – two large rooms the size of the Gymnasium with floor-to-ceiling metal shelves stacked with every conceivable assault weapon. Row upon row of high-tech laser handguns in various power sizes were neatly arranged in numbered racks and there were laser rifles and an assortment of attachments that fired pulse bolts,

EMP harpoons, flash bombs and shard dispensers. There were also weapons stencilled with foreign names Jackson couldn't even pronounce. Several shelves were packed with large wooden boxes of ammunition, gamma flares, night vision equipment, flak jackets and combat fatigues.

"Holy shit!" Jackson exclaimed. He realised, with this arsenal, Davies and his guards were well armed to contain any riot.

Buckling a dual-holstered leather belt around his waist, Jackson wrenched two medium-sized pistols from their racks, activated them, and tucked them snugly in their holsters. Then he donned a black, laser-proof flak jacket. The four guards followed his actions, also shouldering several laser rifles. Spying micro-communicators in an open container on the closest shelf, Jackson grabbed one and plugged it into his left ear. Depressing the switch and hearing a static signal, he attempted to contact the Control Room.

"Stoltz, it's Jackson, can you hear me?"

The device crackled loudly in his ear before a familiar accented voice responded. "Ya, JB, I hear you. Where are you?"

Jackson replied with urgency. "I'm in the Armoury with my guards. We have a situation out here. Tell me what you see on the cameras!"

Stoltz responded immediately. "Your gang members have left their cells as arranged and have captured two of Davies' guards. But they're pinned down on the seventh level. The other guards who were on duty have assembled on the fourth level, blockading the lifts and stairwells, and are firing down on your team through the central core. Harris and Walker have just arrived with the Commissioner who's been secured and I've locked the door to the sound-proof Guards Room to avoid Davies' guards from hearing the commotion."

"Good Sergeant. Patch me into the guards on the fourth level. I don't want to be heard over the PA system. The last thing I need is to start the other prisoners rioting."

Jackson heard a click in his earpiece and then Stoltz's voice. "You're live, JB."

Peering slowly over the four-foot metal railing, Jackson could see the guards on the fourth level near the lifts. He spoke calmly but firmly into his micro-communicator. "You guards on the fourth level, this is Jackson Jensen. I have control of the Armoury and your Commissioner is in custody. I suggest you surrender yourselves to avoid getting killed."

Without a word, one of Davies' guards spun around, looked up, and fired a laser blast in Jackson's direction. It ricocheted off the guard rail, just missing Jackson's arm. The diversion gave the other guards on the fourth level time to dive for cover and start firing in the general direction of where Jackson and his men were stationed. Squatting low and out of sight from Davies' guards, Jackson yanked his earpiece out while gripping his pistol in his right hand.

"Stupid fools!" he muttered turning to face his guards. "We need to stop these guys before they create any more problems. Benson, go into the Armoury and find something to take them out with one hit."

"Okay JB, I know exactly what to get. Back in two minutes."

No sooner had Benson entered the Armoury, than he reappeared, smiling, with an attachment fixed to his laser rifle. "This mini EMP grenade will knock out anything breathing within a twenty-foot radius, rendering it instantly unconscious. No blood, no collateral damage." Benson sounded excited at the prospect of using the weapon.

"Okay, Benson, give it your best shot," ordered Jackson.

Peering carefully over the rail, Benson raised the weapon, aimed and fired. The missile smashed into the wall just above where Davies' guards had set up their defence. There was a high-pitched sound lasting a few seconds before everything went dead quiet.

Getting to his feet and surveying the result, Jackson gave a wry smile, patted Benson on the back, and started shouting orders to the forty gang members on the seventh level below. "Okay men, this is Jackson, you can come up to the Control Room now. The threat's been eliminated."

When all were present in the Control Room Jackson addressed the unruly group who were revelling in their new-found freedom. "Listen up you lot!" he shouted above the noise. "Pay attention and we might be lucky enough to get out of here and off this stinking planet."

The ruckus subsided allowing Jackson to talk at normal volume while giving directions with his hands. "Once our chip implants are permanently disarmed, I want half of you to go to the Guards Room to round up any of Davies' guards who are still sleeping peacefully.

The other half are to go and collect the guards who are sleeping – not so peacefully – on the fourth floor. Secure them all in the empty cells. Make sure you change into the guards' black uniforms, arm yourselves with their pistols, and wait back in the Guards Room until further orders. Remember you'll need to look and behave like real guards so as not to raise any suspicions when the landing party arrives tomorrow morning."

Jackson turned his attention to the captive Commissioner, who was standing restrained by two ex-MERIC guards. "Harris, tie Commissioner Davies to that chair in the corner out of everyone's way. As much as you'd all like to kill him, I don't want anyone going near him. I need him to talk to the incoming transporter in the morning. He's an essential part of our plan to hijack that vessel. Do I make myself clear?" Jackson's men nodded in agreement, muttering curses under their breath.

Jackson waited until last to have his own chip permanently disabled and then headed to the Guards Room, where he couldn't discard his prison overalls quickly enough. He changed into a clean, pressed uniform, slipped on a pair of knee-high boots and a smart-fitting leather jacket, all in black, and completed the outfit with two laser handguns, one strapped to each thigh. A black guard's cap, embroidered with the emblem of an American golden eagle, reassured himself and the others he was captain of this mutinous army. With his followers all dressed in black prison-guard uniforms, Jackson felt that escape was imminent.

Leaving his new army to prepare themselves for the morning, Jackson returned to the Control Room to check everything was running smoothly and that CT had planted the explosive devices as arranged.

CT smiled as Jackson approached. "Almost done, JB. These babies are goin' to make a great fireworks display. Hey, nice outfit with the matching jacket and cap."

"You like? This is my little black after-five number. It's a real killer." They both chuckled at Jackson's humour. "Let's hope these explosives do the job."

CT cut in before Jackson could finish. "No worries, JB. The communications will be out of action for a month or more."

Davies mumbled something from under his gag, his flustered face turning red while he struggled awkwardly with his restraints.

Jackson grinned. "Yes, yes Dan, just be patient, you'll have a front row seat for the whole show."

Turning his attention to the screens on the control panel, Jackson punched in some commands. Up flashed the incoming ship's manifest. It showed the names and photo-IDs of the replacement Commissioner, Captain John Tanner, and his entourage of four dignitaries and six security officers. It also displayed the scheduled arrival time as 09.00 hours.

"CT, do you know how to operate the controls to open the hatch for the entry of the transporter into the complex?"

"Child's play, JB."

"And what about the voice commands to direct the craft?"

"No, haven't read the manual yet, but I can always use the backup-operator who usually does this job."

"Well, we'd better locate him just in case."

Over-hearing the conversation, Sergeant Stoltz intervened. "Jackson, don't worry, I can handle that part of the operation. After all, I've been stuck in this bloody Control Room for the last five years and something useful has to come out of it."

"Excellent! I knew I could rely on you Sarge. Now boys, I'll leave you to it. I'm going back to the Guards Room. Get some sleep if you can and I'll see you at 08.00 hours tomorrow. And Sarge, disarm that bloody morning alarm and let the other prisoners enjoy the sleep-in."

"With pleasure, Captain," replied Stoltz.

***

Jackson woke, excited, at exactly 06.00 hours. He was more than ready to put his plan into action, 'Do or Die'. Still in his new uniform Jackson sprang from his bunk, with more vigour than at any other time during his five-year incarceration. The new man slipped on his leather boots and leather jacket, strapped on his side-arms, and donned his guard's cap. This time he was all dressed up with somewhere to go. "Right,' he said aloud, "Now to get the others moving."

The Guards Room was large enough to house fifty double bunks and Jackson's men were still asleep, oblivious to the fact the morning alert hadn't sounded. He picked up one of the guard's heavy, black truncheons and started hammering forcefully on one of the steel-framed bunk beds, shouting loudly over the clanging. "Rise and shine! Rise and shine! Move your butts and get in line! We have work to do."

After waiting a minute for his men to rouse, Jackson continued. "Listen up men! You're to take directions from Evans while I'm in the Control Room. I don't want any stuff-ups. Everyone's to play their part so we all get off this stinking rock. Keep your cool and we'll all get what we deserve. Understood?"

Still half asleep, his men responded with a groan, a nod or a hand gesture.

Jackson turned to Evans. "Evans, you being an ex-guard and knowing your way 'round this place, you're temporarily in charge of this lot. Get them up and feed them some coffee. We don't have much time to organise ourselves. After they've had their caffeine fix, assign them to their positions around the docking bay ready to surround our visitors when they arrive."

"Okay, JB, I'll make sure they're ready by 08.00 hours," replied Evans, efficiently, as Jackson strode out of the room.

"Morning Stoltz, everything ready to go?" called out Jackson as he entered the Control Room to see Stoltz standing at the caffeine dispenser.

Surprised by Jackson's sudden appearance, Stoltz almost choked on the sip of coffee he'd just taken. "Morning JB. I've been tracking the new Commissioner's transporter since 06.00 hours. It'll be docking at 09.00 hours as expected."

"Have they communicated yet?"

"Yeh JB, they asked for verification of the co-ordinates which I signalled back as confirmation."

"Good, everything's going according to plan."

Davies began mumbling loudly under his gag while frantically writhing about in his chair, trying desperately to shed his restraints. Jackson paced towards him and raised his hand, pointing a finger inches from Davies' face. Davies fell silent and stared at Jackson with fear in his eyes, the reddish pigmentation of his face draining rapidly to a pale sickly white.

Jackson spoke to Davies in a low threatening tone. "I'll make a deal with you Dan. If you behave yourself, I'll remove the gag and release you from the chair. You can settle yourself with a cup of coffee to be ready to talk on the screen to the new Commissioner. However, do anything wrong to anger me or raise any suspicion in the new boss and I promise you a slow, painful death using a very sharp serrated-edged blade. The first cut will be to remove your testicles. Do we have a deal?"

Davies' eyes widened. Perspiration droplets wept from his brow and trickled slowly down the side of his temples as he nodded frantically in agreement.

"Harris, cut the Commissioner free from the chair and take him over to the coffee machine. Take off his gag but leave his hands cuffed. He's got five minutes to finish his coffee before you sit him at the console to talk to the new Commissioner on screen."

"Okay JB," replied Harris who was already on the move with a combat knife in hand.

"And keep a sharp eye on him just in case he attempts something stupid!" commanded Jackson, sternly. "Stoltz, what's the status on the transporter?"

Stoltz checked his console screen to track the ship's distance, speed and time of arrival. "The transporter's five thousand klicks away and will be here in thirty minutes, JB."

"Good. Get hold of Evans to see if all the others are in position on the first level."

Stoltz tweaked the Comms switch on the console. "Evans, report in."

There was an immediate response. "Evans here. What's up?"

Jackson, who was now standing beside Stoltz, spoke into the console. "Evans, this is Jackson. Have you organised the men into their positions?"

"Yes JB, they're in position, armed and ready to act."

"Well done. Set their pistols on 'stun' and give them orders not to fire on anyone, including the new Commissioner. We might need them for hostages if anything goes wrong. Take out the escort guards only if they decide to start firing their weapons. Have your men all been issued communicators? And are they switched on?"

"Yes, JB."

"The craft should be arriving in about 20 minutes. Make sure your men remain out of sight until the ship has landed and all the passengers have disembarked. You know what to do then Evans. Okay?

"Okay, out."

Davies finished his coffee, but as Harris was escorting him to the console, Davies couldn't contain himself. "They'll hunt you and your gang down Jackson, like the dogs you are. You'll be back in permanent solitary confinement and wish you were dead by the time they're finished with you."

Unfazed, Jackson responded in a low threatening voice. "If you don't keep your mouth shut Davies, you'll wish you were dead. Sit down and start mentally rehearsing your welcome speech. Don't say another word. Harris, remove his cuffs but don't put your knife away just yet and stay very close to the Commissioner to 'assist him' with his speech. The rest of you, take your positions on the consoles. Stoltz, what's the situation with Commissioner Tanner's ship?"

"They're entering the planet's outer atmosphere and have decelerated. Ten minutes before they land. They're in range for us to lock on the traction beam."

"Transfer the visual to main screen Stoltz," said Jackson "and connect us to their bridge to start guiding them in. Davies, as soon as Captain Tanner opens dialogue, start your welcome speech. Don't stuff up or I'll be removing your tongue before I remove your testicles! Okay Stoltz, activate screen communication."

As Jackson positioned himself out of view, a figure dressed in the familiar charcoal-coloured corporate suit appeared on the screen seated at the bridge. He was surrounded by six armed security officers and his stone-cold, chiselled face with short-cropped, black hair and dark empty eyes was staring directly into the screen.

Davies forced a smile and uttered the first words, his throat parched through a combination of fear and nervousness. "Captain Tanner, welcome to Terra Upsilon Penal Colony." Davies paused, clearing his throat and taking a deep breath while reaching for the glass of water at the side of his console. He glanced sideways at Jackson before continuing. "I hope you had a pleasant, uneventful journey. We're guiding your craft to the landing dock with our traction beam so we request you power down your craft's thrusters and we'll do the rest."

Tanner gestured to one of his crew to follow through with the request and then responded in a low monotone voice, devoid of emotion. "Thank you, Commissioner Davies for your welcome and concern. You and your prison guards can refer to me as Commissioner Tanner as I'm no longer in the army and have been promoted to the rank. Yes, the trip was uneventful with the exception of an unsuccessful Blader attack." Jackson stirred on hearing Tanner mention the Bladers.

Davies continued. "We'll greet you at the docking station as soon as you have landed. All preparations are in place to accept your post and the guards have been briefed. See you soon Captain, I mean Commissioner. Out."

Stoltz closed off communications and the screen went blank. Davies had turned pale and was sweating profusely, anticipating what Jackson might have in mind for him next. He gulped down the rest of his glass of water for temporary relief.

"You did very well Davies," said Jackson, patronising him. "Harris, bind the Commissioner's hands and escort him to the cells."

Davies pleaded desperately in a high-pitched voice. "Please, Jackson, don't throw me in with the other prisoners. You know what they'll do to me."

"You deserve everything you get Davies and a taste of your own medicine."

"They'll kill me, Jackson, please I beg you! I have a family."

"Alright Harris, throw him into one of the empty cells and let him fret over what the inmates might do to him after they're all released. When that's done, join the rest of the men at the docking bay. Stoltz, where's the incoming craft now?"

"It's half a klick from docking and will be here in five minutes, JB."

"Okay, tell Evans to get the men prepared and hold their position until I give the order. I'll be greeting the party personally when they disembark. And tell them not to shoot the pilot if they see him."

"Aye, aye, JB."

Just as he finished speaking, the main screen flashed on, showing the ship landing in the docking bay. Jackson was impressed to see it was a Deep Space Transporter (DST) built using Tzuracian technology with fully-equipped armaments, hyperspeed thrusters powered by Xytrinium crystals, and stealth capabilities. This Assault-class battleship designed for long distance, high speed voyages was almost invincible to Blader assaults.

"Okay men, follow me," Jackson ordered.

All the gang members in the Control Room, including CT and Stoltz, filed in behind Jackson and made their way via the internal transporter to the docking bay on the first level. The ship had shut down and the newcomers were already disembarking from the open hatch down the ship's ramp. Commissioner Tanner raised his right arm in a formal salute and Jackson responded.

Then, as Jackson approached the party he signalled Evans to make his move. Within seconds, Jackson's men surrounded the party with weapons drawn and aimed at the newcomers. Tanner's escort guards attempted to draw their weapons in response, but Evans fired his pistol, stunning one of them and forcing the others to raise their arms in instant surrender.

"What are you doing?" exclaimed a surprised Tanner.

"Welcoming you, Commissioner, to this *hell-hole* of the Galaxy. I'm Jackson Jensen, leader of this rebellion and you're *my* prisoners. Evans, collect their weapons and bind their hands. Tanner, how many pilots are there? And where are they?"

"I don't have to answer to a convict like you," Tanner replied indignantly. "I know what you are Jackson, a low-life who should've been executed. I've read your file."

Jackson responded by drawing his pistol from its holster and pointing it squarely between Tanner's eyes, barely an inch away from his forehead. He spoke in a restrained, low voice. "If you know what I am, then you know what I'm capable of. I've got nothing to lose. What about you Tanner?"

"You're very persuasive Jackson." There was urgency in Tanner's response. "I ordered the two pilots to hold their positions at the Captain's Helm."

Jackson returned his firearm to its holster. "Wait here with your men Evans, secure the area, and then send some of them to find the pilots still on board. Be careful, they could be armed after witnessing on the visuals what's just happened. Don't kill them as we may still need them to fly this craft. Sergeant Stoltz, as soon as the Captain's Helm is secured, familiarize yourself with the controls and the layout using the data on the computers. CT, you accompany the Sergeant to disconnect the craft's homing devices and check out all the languages stored on the computer. I'll be back soon."

All three acknowledged Jackson with a casual salute and he responded with a quick flip of his right hand from the peak of his cap. *I could get used to this,* he thought.

As Evans and his men began to secure the area, Tanner again spoke abruptly to Jackson. "Where's Commissioner Davies? I demand to speak with him."

"You're in no position to demand anything Tanner. Dan's currently indisposed but anxious to see you to discuss the situation. If you'll just follow me, we'll take you and your entourage to your luxury suites," said Jackson, tongue-in-cheek.

As Jackson and his men approached the fourth level where the other prisoners and Davies were locked up, they heard a terrible commotion coming from the cells. The inmates were going berserk, bashing cups and plates on the metal doors of their cells, screaming profanities, tipping their bunks over and throwing them against the internal walls. While Tanner tried to shield himself from the noise by cupping his ears with his bound wrists, Jackson tapped his earpiece to contact Evans.

"Evans here. What is it?

"This is Jackson. What cell is Davies in?"

"Number 417, Captain. We've located and secured the pilots without any trouble. They were happy to co-operate after the treatment they got from Tanner – said he was an arrogant son-of-a-bitch."

"Yeh, I got the same impression. Okay, out."

"Harrison, do you still have the master key card to these cells?"

"Sure do."

"Good. Throw Tanner into the same cell as Davies, 417. The two Commissioners have some catching up to do. Throw the rest of his entourage separately into any of the other empty cells, but body search all of them first for any communicators they may be carrying. When you've finished, you and the others meet on the landing bay. We'll be casting off in twenty minutes."

"Aye, Captain."

Back on board the craft, Jackson checked to see everyone at the Helm had completed their tasks. "Stoltz, what can you tell me?"

"One of the pilots, a female, is requesting to join our rebel army and says she will get us anywhere we need to go. Her name's Pam Dawson, Flight Lieutenant, first class. She's the daughter of one of the ore transporter pilots. She has a grudge against her employer, ASPECT, and is sympathetic to our cause. She was keen to show me the diagnostics and schematics of the craft."

"This is good news. An insider from ASPECT with information we can use," said Jackson, obviously very interested. He knew the Aero Space Program for Colonization and Transportation worked in alliance with MERIC. "But instruct her to stay clear of the others. No telling what these half-crazed animals will do after years of female deprivation. I'll be warning them of the consequences if they lay a hand on her. She's under my personal protection. What about the other pilot?"

"Captain Newman wants to stay here. And he'd be a problem if we forced him to come with us."

"Alright, have Evans escort him to the cells with the others and remind Evans there's only ten minutes remaining before take-off. I need to talk to CT to see how he's progressing. You have your orders."

"Okay JB."

"Thanks Stoltz, and stay on the communications console."

CT was working on one of the consoles at the Helm as Jackson paced over to him. "CT, what's the status?"

CT was excited to tell Jackson all about the craft. "The status is JB, you've got yourself a prize with this beauty. This battleship has state-of-the-art technology. I've read the schematics and she's equipped to take on any war craft that I've ever studied. She has cloaking, sound damping, full pulse shielding, superior weaponry, hyper-thrusters and self-repair engineering."

"Excellent, CT. It's good to know we're fully equipped to deal with any enemies who come our way. But what about the detonation set up for the explosives you planted in the Control Room? Are we set to go?"

CT leant over the console and grabbed a black metal box about the size of a cigarette packet. Three tiny globes were set in a line across the top with a silver button under each globe. "All you have to do is press each of these buttons," he said with pride. "The globes will light up red and within milliseconds the charges will explode. The signal will reach up to half a click away. They'll have no communications, incoming or outgoing, for at least a month. All the cell doors will also be released. I'd like to see how the Commissioners deal with the angry mob of inmates on a rampage."

Both men laughed raucously.

"Well done CT. We'll detonate the charges when we've cleared the landing bay."

Jackson lowered his voice to a whisper. "Did you have a chance to find out what languages are stored in the system? I want to know if the ship has Treldarian dialects, spoken by the Bladers."

CT whispered back. "Treldarian? There's nine hundred languages including I think around forty Treldarian dialects. Why do you ask JB?"

During his time in prison, news broadcasts had alerted Jackson to the activity of ruthless Blader pirates who targeted Earth's cargo transporters to steal Xytrinium. For years Jackson had toyed with the idea of persuading the Bladers to join forces with him in the fight against the Sentinels and for possession of Xytrinium. Jackson decided if he ever escaped he would attempt to contact them, hopefully without getting him and his army killed in the process. It would be a high risk move, but he had nothing to lose.

"I don't want to inform the others of my intentions until we're in deep space, but my plans are to invite the Bladers to become our allies. Together we'll have a better chance of eradicating the Sentinels and taking control of the Xytrinium supplies and reserves."

CT was sceptical. "What makes you think those marauders will want to join us in *your* cause JB?"

"Because I'll promise them the elixir of life, infusion with Xytrinium. How could they refuse that enticement, CT?"

CT was even more sceptical. "Sounds good. Only one problem JB. You don't *have* the formula."

"Don't worry CT, I'm working on it," Jackson said confidently. "I'll discuss my strategy with you once we're on our way. As soon as we've left the orbit of Upsilon I want you to start sending out a message in Treldarian dialects. I'll discuss later what the message might say, but let's get out of here first."

By now Jackson's men had arrived back on board the ship and reported all was going to plan. Jackson was ready to set the course for their destination. But when he turned to Dawson to give her instructions, he was momentarily taken with her beauty. This was the first opportunity he'd had to take a close look at his new pilot. She was about thirty years of age, had long, silky, chestnut hair tied back in a ponytail, steel blue-grey, melting eyes, a cute nose and soft, moist lips. Judging by what he could assess from her seated position, she also had a slender physique. Jackson was mesmerized and it wasn't simply lust after five years of being without female company.

CT saw what was happening and tugged on Jackson's arm to snap him back into the present. Jackson instinctively brushed CT's arm away as if it was an annoying insect, but when CT pulled harder, Jackson suddenly realised where he was and the urgency of his mission. He cleared his throat to speak.

"Lieutenant Dawson," he said in a serious tone, trying to cover his embarrassment, "sorry for staring but it's so nice to see a friendly face after so long. Welcome to the fold. Chart our co-ordinates to the planet Terra Iota, and check the energy reserves to ensure we can make the distance. Then take us out of here."

"Aye, aye, Captain." Dawson smiled, knowing there was more to Jackson's stare than he admitted. She replaced the Comm-set in her ear and swivelled her chair around to focus on the controls at the console and the small clear screen suspended at head height. Her hand darted across the console, her nimble fingers stabbing several buttons. Lights flickered rapidly on the screen and coloured graphics appeared in unison on the console monitor, revealing tech data on gravity, propulsion, fuel mix, star nav-charts, compass readings, oxygen levels and more. She nodded to Jackson, confirming all was well.

The thrusters sprang into life, levelling off at a roaring pitch. Although cushioned by insulation, the noise resounded throughout the fuselage as the heavy craft began to lift effortlessly through the open hatch to the surface of the planet. The ship tilted and turned slowly starboard changing direction to cruise out of the planet's orbit.

Jackson signalled CT to ignite the charges. Through the portals on the right side of the craft CT as well as the rebels on the deck below witnessed three small explosions destroying the Control Room of the complex they hoped never to see again. CT smiled with satisfaction at a job well done and the men cheered loudly and spontaneously, raising their fisted arms upwards in a sign of victory. It was a small symbol of defiance against the establishment and a celebration of their new-found freedom.

The intercom crackled and a familiar voice of authority stilled the noise of the rabble. "This is JB, or should I say, your Captain speaking. Welcome aboard our newly acquired ship which I've appropriately christened on behalf of us all, the 'Jolly Roger'. You have just experienced your first taste of freedom and adventure. Enjoy! But remember men, *we're on a mission.*

"Until we reach our first destination, I expect you to maintain your skill levels using the holographic chamber on board. We expect to encounter Sentinels and we need to be prepared. We'll be on rations to conserve our food supplies and anyone caught pilfering will be executed. Further, anyone attempting to interfere with my pilot, Lieutenant Dawson, will be subjected to a slow, painful death. You are the few I chose for your elite skills and your loyalty. I expect you all to behave as soldiers, fighting on the same team with the same purpose. So, conserve your energy, keep your weapons clean and serviced and enjoy the ride. We're at war and you *will* be rewarded for your dedication to the cause as promised. Out!"

The craft accelerated to hyperspeed and, within seconds, disappeared into the darkness of space.

OLD WOUNDS

THE intercom buzzed on what had formerly been Samuel Jensen's office desk on the thirtieth floor of the MERIC Building in New York City. The penthouse window behind the new CEO seated at the desk displayed a breathtaking view of clear blue skies and clean buildings sparkling in the bright sunshine. It was a scene in stark contrast to the polluted environment and carbon-coated skyscrapers that Samuel Jensen had been accustomed to five years ago, before Earth's first encounter with the Tzuracians. Since joining the Federation of Planets and with the assistance of advanced Tzuracian technology, the atmosphere had been transformed dramatically, making Earth once again a clean, liveable planet.

A tall, well-built man with wavy, short-cropped fair hair and steel-blue eyes, dressed in the MERIC corporate grey suit, reached for the intercom. "Yes Lauren, what is it?" asked the softly spoken voice.

"May I see you Kyron? The matter is most urgent."

"Yes, *please* come in."

Within seconds, Kyron Shield's secretary, Miss Lauren Blake, appeared in the office with a very concerned look on her usual smiling face. Now in her early forties, she was still of slender build and pleasant appearance with short, dark hair. She looked smart dressed in her standard, dark-grey corporate trouser suit.

Kyron motioned for her to sit in one of the burgundy leather armchairs while he moved from his desk over to the matching leather couch. Over the last five years of working closely together, the two had developed a close relationship, talking freely about most things, be it business or personal. "So Lauren, what's this all about? You seem quite worried."

"I've just received a message from my father. He's been informed by the Assembly of an escape that occurred two weeks ago from the penal colony Terra Upsilon." Lauren's father, General Blake, was the Chief of Airforce at ASPECT.

Kyron raised his eyebrows, puzzled. "Escaped? How could anyone escape from a high-tech security prison located on a planet light years from nowhere? Prisoners sent to that place never escape. That's why they're sent there."

Lauren started to explain. "According to my father, they captured the new Commissioner on his arrival and locked him up with his security escorts, then commandeered his ship. The fifty inmates were led by…"

"Jackson Jensen!" cut in Kyron.

"Yes!" said Lauren in surprise. "How did you know?"

Kyron shook his head in disgust and frustration. "Only *he* would have the dammed determination and mastermind to organise such a daring operation. Jackson has nothing to lose and everything to gain. I well remember the hateful expression on his contorted face when he yelled his last threatening words to me as the Sentinels marched him from his trial in front of the Assembly *This is not the end, Kyron; I swear we will cross swords again!*"

"Do you think he'll come after you, Kyron?" Lauren asked with fear in her eyes and a slight quiver in her voice.

"Not just after me, but after his father's Company and the Xytrinium reserves." Kyron was absorbed with the thought. He needed to take precautions. "Have they tracked his whereabouts yet?"

Lauren shook her head. "No, the General said the DST Assault ship leaves no heat-sink trail, and the communications housed in the colony's Control Room were destroyed by Jackson as the stolen ship departed. Upsilon has been unable to raise the alarm for two weeks and, if a supply transporter hadn't called there, we'd still be unaware of his escape. So there's no knowing where they are or what they're up to."

"Jackson's very clever and extremely dangerous," said Kyron, obviously concerned about Jackson's capabilities and recklessness.

"Lauren, I want you to contact Terra Iota immediately and let Engineer Grant Thompson know what's happened. Tell him to suspend mining operations and the shipping of Xytrinium until further notice. And have him alert the Sentinels there to increase security levels in case Jackson attempts an attack. I'll deal with the garrison here and contact Captain Dakhar on Tzurac to tell him this megalomaniac is on the loose again."

He paused for a moment, collecting his thoughts. "Can you also arrange a meeting with the Board members for tomorrow? They need to know. And, include your father. Contact the World Assembly for an emergency audience and have my shuttle prepared. Take whatever time the Assembly has available. I'll be addressing them as the CEO of MERIC and as Earth's Tzuracian Ambassador. Assemble the staff in the Main Hall this afternoon. I want to address them personally to keep them in the picture."

Kyron finished with his final thought. "And Lauren, you need to alert Central Reception Control. Inform them Torri and I will be staying in the penthouse suite for an indefinite period of time starting in the next day or two, and without the children. I think that about covers everything. We need to act immediately as we're already two weeks behind Jackson's unknown plans. Okay Lauren, let's move."

"Alright Kyron, I'm onto it." Miss Blake finished punching in the last few directions on her compu-pad, raised herself from the armchair and headed towards the door.

"Thanks, Lauren."

As Lauren left, Kyron hit the direct line on his intercom to his wife, Torri, in her office where she had been promoted to Director of Interactive Communications.

"Hi darling, how's your morning been?" answered Torri, sounding optimistic.

Kyron's reply was more business-like. "Torri, I need to see you straight away. Can you come up to my office now?"

Torri could sense the urgency in his voice. "Yes, of course, I'll be there in five minutes."

"I'll have a hot coffee waiting for you when you arrive. Love you."

Kyron was standing at his office door when Torri arrived and, as she approached, he thought she was as beautiful as ever with her straight, deep-red hair and striking green eyes. He ushered her in, closing the door behind her and motioning her to sit on the couch. On the low-lying marble table were two thermal mugs of steaming coffee. Kyron sat beside her and handed her one of them.

"What's wrong, Kyron? You seem a little anxious."

"I've had some unexpected news this morning, but no need for alarm. Have your coffee and I'll explain."

Torri took a sip or two while Kyron began. She quickly became apprehensive and by the time Kyron had finished, she had stopped drinking, was gripping her mug tightly and was looking pale. "Do you think Jackson would dare come here to seek his revenge? To try to kill you and take control of MERIC again? He'd have to be totally insane knowing he'd be confronting an army of Tzuracian Sentinels now based on Earth, not to mention the force of the Federation."

"I agree Torri; he'd have to be insane. But an insane person can't see reason when they're blinded by hate and power. He's been harbouring these emotions for the last five years, bottling them up, waiting for the chance to release them. He's obsessed and won't rest until he's quenched his obsession."

Kyron put his arm around Torri's shoulder to comfort her. "So, we'll need to stay alert, prepare ourselves for the unexpected and make sure we keep tight security on our home and the MERIC Building. I suggest we take Zuri and Ehrana to my mother's place and you and I stay in the Company's high rise apartments until we know what Jackson has in mind. That way the children will be safe and we'll be close to the action. Jackson's in control of a very powerful battleship which could land on Earth at any time. I'm not trying to frighten you Torri, but we both know what Jackson is capable of."

Torri placed her mug on the table and threw her arms around her husband. "Just hold me Kyron." Several moments passed while they embraced. No words were needed to express what they were feeling.

Then Kyron whispered softly in Torri's ear. "Don't worry my love, we'll be alright. I'll make sure no harm comes to you or the children." Torri released her hold, carefully dabbed small tears from her eyes and regained her composure. "I need you to be strong Torri, and show confidence to your staff that everything's under control. I've seen your inner strength before. That's one of the things I love about you."

Torri chuckled. "You can rely on me Kyron. I'll contact Zelda and ask her to have the children for a while. I'll tell her we have some major deadlines to meet at MERIC and suggest it will give her the chance to spend some quality time with her grandchildren. I'm sure she'll understand and be delighted to have them."

Kyron rose from the couch, nodding in agreement. "Good idea Torri. Let me know when we can drop them over. I'll see you tonight then, darling." They hugged briefly before Torri disappeared out the door.

From the doorway Kyron called out to Lauren. "I need some privacy for the next twenty minutes. Please don't disturb me."

Closing the door, he waved his hand over a small illuminated panel on the wall next to the door frame and the windows darkened. Sitting back down on the couch he pressed a sequence of blue gem studs on the gold Sentinel pledge ring he was wearing, an inheritance from his father. Within seconds, a hazy holograph shot out from the centre of the ring. It cleared to reveal a sharp image of a fair-haired Sentinel soldier with a neatly groomed beard, dressed in a maroon uniform and blue cape.

"You called, my Ambassador friend? It's good to see you." Captain Ehrane Dakhar's deep mellow voice was unmistakable.

"Yes my friend, it's also good to see you and to hear your voice again."

Kyron and Ehrane had become close friends over the last five years, as their Sentinel fathers, Ahrmon Tyros and Rhyk Dakhar, had been in the distant past.

"You sound somewhat relieved to see me. What's troubling you, Kyron?"

"It's my worst fear, Ehrane. I've just been informed that Jackson Jensen and a large number of prisoners escaped two weeks ago from Terra Upsilon in the new Commissioner's battleship. They blew up the communications in the Control Room preventing anyone from sending a distress signal until now. Ehrane, Jackson's on the loose."

Ehrane was shocked by the news. "Are you sure, Kyron? I thought we'd seen the last of this madman after he was sent to prison."

"Yes, I'm sure,' said Kyron nodding his head in confirmation. "I've alerted Terra Iota to be on guard in case Jackson attacks the Colony and I've asked Miss Blake to arrange an audience for me with the World Assembly. If Jackson's managed to orchestrate an escape from a high security prison on Terra Upsilon, there's no telling what he's capable of next."

"You're right. Jackson may attempt to finish what he started five years ago. I fear for Earth's safety as well as for you and your family." Ehrane was quick to formulate a response. "I'll inform the Tzuracian Senate and request my troop of Sentinels be mobilised and ships dispatched to all quadrants of the Universe to hunt for him. I'll return to Earth as soon as I can with a battalion of Sentinels to reinforce the local garrison. We'll be with you soon. Stay alert and in contact. May the Ancients protect you."

Kyron and his Captain exchanged salutes as the holograph vanished.

That evening, Kyron and Torri dined as usual at home with their children, before telling them they would be spending some holiday time with their Grandma, starting tomorrow. The children were excited and couldn't wait to pack, until they learned their mum and dad would not be going with them.

"Why can't you and mum come with us to Grandma's?" said five-year old Zuri in a high-pitched voice. "It won't be any fun if you're not staying with us."

"Yeh Daddy. You and Mummy should come too," echoed Zuri's little sister, Ehrana, who was the image of her mother with red hair and sparkling green eyes. Her sweet three-year old voice was heartfelt with her pleas.

Kyron was soft but firm with his young children. "You know we love you both very much and wish we could be with you, but your mum and I have some important work to finish at MERIC. It won't be for long, and you'll both be home again soon. I want you two to be on your best behaviour for Grandma Zelda. I'm sure it will be fun."

Speaking directly to his son, who was tall for his age with his father's fair hair and steel-blue eyes, Kyron said, "And Zuri Ahrmon, I want you to look after your sister while you're at Grandma's and keep practising your martial arts like we've been doing together each morning." Kyron had recently started training his son in the ways of a Sentinel warrior, just as his own father, Ahrmon Tyros, had trained him.

"Yes Dad," said Zuri, sounding a little disappointed. "I'll look after her and practice every day. But I'll miss you and mum."

"So will I," said Ehrana, giving her mum and dad a big hug in turn.

Torri's eyes were welling with tears as she kissed them on the forehead. "We'll miss you too. Come on, let's pack your bags and work out what you'll need to take to Grandma's."

The following day, while Torri was taking the children to their grandmother's place, Kyron attended the Board meeting as scheduled. Sitting around the large, black onyx, oval table in the diffusely-lit, oak-panelled Board Room, he informed the concerned members of Jackson's escape and the potential danger, not only to MERIC, but also to the World. Lauren's father, General Blake, dressed in his smart, navy-blue airforce blazer, these days showing more silver in his hair, reported he had placed ASPECT under a Code Green, DEFCON 4 alert, and all mining transporter flights were suspended until further notice. The Board members agreed to alert their departments and make security arrangements to prepare for the unexpected.

In the afternoon Kyron addressed the World Assembly, cutting a fine and handsome figure in his maroon Sentinel uniform with blue cape. "Members of the Assembly, I'm here to advise that Jackson Jensen, the man you sentenced to life imprisonment five years ago, has escaped from the prison colony on Terra Upsilon. He has commandeered a DST Assault battleship with stealth capabilities, a ship fully equipped with extremely powerful weapons. We currently have no idea of his whereabouts but suspect he will come to Earth to take back, by force, what he lost. He'll be after his father's Company, MERIC, and control of its mining operations on Terra Iota as well as the stockpiled reserves of Xytrinium here on Earth. If this happens, Jackson will gain control of our planet as he attempted once before."

There were murmurings amongst the Assembly members until Kyron resumed his address, describing the measures he had already put in place. "I suggest you alert your military forces, increase security and remain on high alert until further notice. Report any unusual activities directly to General Blake at ASPECT as well as to the Assembly. Remember, with its stealth capabilities, Jackson's battleship could enter Earth's atmosphere undetected."

As Kyron hastily departed from the dais the Assembly members, now on their feet, began talking loudly amongst themselves, thrashing their arms about and hammering fists on desks to make their points of view heard. Fear and panic had taken hold. They knew Earth was under serious threat.

DESPERATE MEASURES

FOR five years Khaneera Penzark had been incarcerated on Tzurac, doing time for treason and her involvement with Jackson Jensen in an attempt to murder Kyron Shield. Like her father before her, she had been kept in solitary confinement, isolated from the other prisoners with a Sentinel posted outside her cell to guard her day and night. She had limited visiting rights to her high security cell and no contact with the outside world. In the eyes of Tzuracians, a Sentinel who betrays other Sentinels was considered the lowest of the low.

Her only privilege was a two-hour daily exercise period in the gymnasium, an opportunity she seized to maintain her prowess in martial arts and weaponry. Khaneera used this opportunity for a clear purpose, to keep her mind sharp and her body toned. She was determined to escape and settle the score with Kyron Shield.

Over the last two years, one of the sentries guarding her had become infatuated with his prisoner's strength, intelligence, commanding presence and alluring beauty. At first the young Corporal Yarron Blandhar was intimidated by Khaneera's ruthless reputation. He denied any feelings of attraction and maintained his distance. But, in spite of the drab and shapeless prison issue worn by Khaneera, Yarron found her striking Sentinel features appealing. When Khaneera began to confide in him almost as her equal, his feelings grew stronger and he began to let his guard down.

While Khaneera appeared cold-hearted at first and treated the other sentries with complete disdain, she quickly recognised Yarron's growing affection for her and decided to use this to her advantage.

Over time, she encouraged their relationship, knowing she would need the help of an ally if she was ever to escape. And yet, as time passed, she came to enjoy Yarron's company and their momentary conversations. She found herself feeling genuinely attracted to him. After all, he was the epitome of a true Sentinel, handsome, with deep blue eyes and chiselled cheekbones, his thick fair hair neatly groomed into a plaited ponytail which trailed to his broad, muscled shoulder blades.

Determined nothing would distract her from her true passion for revenge, Khaneera resolved to keep her feelings for Yarron in check. She could not afford to let emotional attachment cloud her thinking. Although the attraction between them grew stronger daily, the boundary between guard and prisoner was still intact.

While on sentry duty one night, Yarron initiated a conversation, "Khaneera, may I speak with you?"

Khaneera waved her hand across a wall panel on the inside of her cell, changing the opaque force-field to transparent. "Yes, of course Yarron. It's always good to see you and hear your voice."

"You look radiant tonight, Khaneera." Yarron cleared his throat knowing it was forbidden to talk to prisoners while on sentry duty.

"We're alone Yarron, so speak freely. After all, we have become good friends, haven't we?"

"Yes, we have Khaneera," said Yarron nodding his head in agreement. "There's something I want to tell you even though I know it's breaking the rules. I'm telling you this in strict confidence." He paused, looking in both directions to ensure the passageway was clear before continuing, "The Senate has just received some important news regarding Jackson Jensen."

Khaneera's heart was now beating a little faster and her breathing becoming shallow as she stepped closer to Yarron and the force-field, her speech in short bursts. "What's happened? Is he alright? Has he been hurt? Please tell me."

Yarron knew Khaneera admired Jackson and her response confirmed it. She and Jackson shared the same nemesis, but for different reasons. And, Yarron knew why Khaneera was obsessed with destroying Kyron and the Tyros bloodline. She had shared with him the history behind Zarkwin's revenge.

***

Three hundred years ago, while training in the academy of Sentinels on Tzurac, Khaneera's father, Khane Zarkwin, had his hand severed by Kyron's father, Ahrmon Tyros, during a fencing session. The Tzuracian Senate blamed Khane Zarkwin, determining he had provoked and threatened his opponent and that Ahrmon had acted in self-defence. They decided Zarkwin was not of fit character for the cadetship and expelled him from the elite academy.

For years, Khaneera's disgraced father worked in the lower status position of security officer in the Federation Security Forces. Although eventually becoming Chief of Security, he remained obsessed with the perceived injustice. And his failed attempt to exact revenge on Ahrmon Tyros by framing him for the murder of a fellow Sentinel and friend, Rhyk Dakhar, landed him in prison for life.

Khane Zarkwin's expectant partner, Syrina, was forced to resign her Sentinel position to avoid the shame and stigma of being associated with a criminal. She fled to Urgellan where she raised their child in obscurity, Khaneera never meeting her real father.

As required by her heritage, Khaneera eventually went to Tzurac and trained as a Sentinel, but all the while she secretly resented Sentinel authority and all that the Senate stood for. Then, when Khaneera learned that her father's adversary had a son living on Earth under the name Shield, she too became obsessed with righting the injustice. But her attempt to assassinate Kyron Shield and end the Tyros bloodline had seen her imprisoned on Tzurac for life.

Yarron was disgusted to learn the Senate had destroyed Khaneera's family and filled her with such hatred. And, it was her story of Zarkwin's revenge that led him to question whether the Sentinels were his military family after all.

***

"You know Jackson was imprisoned for life on Terra Upsilon and has been there for the last five years," said Yarron.

Khaneera cut in. "I knew he was in prison but I didn't know where."

"Well," continued Yarron, "just over two weeks ago, Jackson captured the new Commissioner on his arrival at the penal colony, throwing him and his escorts into the prison cells. He commandeered the Commissioner's spacecraft and fled to an unknown destination with fifty other prisoners and guards. The Federation have so far been unable to track his whereabouts."

A subtle smile appeared on Khaneera's face. It was as if she knew Jackson's escape was inevitable. Her mind raced with the thought she too might escape to join forces with Jackson again in a partnership to destroy Kyron Shield and the Tyros name she despised. She realised Jackson would not only be out for Kyron's blood but would also want to take control of MERIC and the mining operations on Terra Iota. And to overthrow the powerful Sentinels, he would want the long-lost, Xytrinium-DNA infusion formula she had told him about.

"Khaneera, are you alright?" Yarron's question brought Khaneera abruptly back to reality.

"Yes, yes Yarron, of course." Khaneera paused for a moment, her expression hardening, before speaking seriously. "Can I trust you with my life and what I ask of you in confidence, Yarron?"

Puzzled by her question, Yarron quickly checked the corridor again for any movement, assuring himself all was clear before responding in hushed tones. "Khaneera, you must know by now how I feel about you. You can trust me with your life. Everything we talk about will always be our secret."

"Thank you, Yarron," Khaneera said gently, "I know you mean what you say now." Then, with an apparent change of attitude she added, rather severely, "But, for your sake, I hope you don't do anything in the future to make me stop trusting you."

Yarron hesitated, taken aback by Khaneera's subtle threat. Sensing his concern, Khaneera spoke again in a soft whisper. "Yarron, you're the only friend I have. You know how fond I am of you. Please forgive me if I spoke harshly, but I've learnt not to trust anyone in my life."

Yarron was reassured. He had fallen for her completely. "I understand how you feel, Khaneera. There is nothing to forgive. I would never deceive you and you have my pledge as a Sentinel and a friend. I'll do anything I can to make you happy."

Khaneera seized the moment. Through many early morning intimate conversations at her cell door she had come to know of Yarron's anguish at being a Sentinel. She knew he was unhappy with the life he'd been living, disillusioned with the military system where complete dedication to the Federation took precedence over the pursuit of any personal life. Here was her opportunity to persuade him to help her.

"If you really do want me to be happy, Yarron, I need your help to free me and leave this planet. If Jackson has managed to escape, it's time I did too. He'll be on a mission to kill Kyron and I have to be part of it."

This time Yarron was astonished. "Are you serious Khaneera? I said I'd do anything, but you're asking me to commit treason and risk a death sentence if captured. And you want to work with Jackson again?"

"I know I'm asking a lot, but the one thing I need to do before I can rest is kill Kyron Shield and avenge my father and my best chance of doing so is with Jackson. You would be coming with me Yarron as my companion and, once my mission is over, we would be together without any distractions. Do you always want to stay a sentry with no excitement, no adventure, and no recognition of your real potential? You don't have a family of your own and how old are you now? This is an opportunity to leave the daily regimented routine, to depart from a life in which you have limited choice, to make your own future and be with others who prefer their freedom; to choose the life *you* want and not what *others* want for you. Come on Yarron; let me seal our bond with a kiss. You can shut down the force-field and I promise I won't attempt to escape … just yet."

Yarron was tempted by the prospect of a better, more exciting life, at the possibility of casting off his military shackles of routine and tasting real freedom. His heart was beating strong with excitement and danger. He felt he loved Khaneera, wanting to be with her and the life she offered. But he knew he'd be a hunted fugitive; always on the run, looking over his shoulder, hiding from the Federation. Was it possible he and Khaneera might find a safe refuge somewhere to live out the rest of their lives happily together, in freedom? Or would his life always be at stake?

His thoughts were interrupted by Khaneera's soft voice calling him. "Yarron, what do you say? Do you want to help me?"

Yarron stared into Khaneera's hypnotic, wanting eyes, standing motionless for some time before making a move. Then, with a decisive action, he waved his hand across the panel on the wall outside Khaneera's cell, shutting down the force-field. With a warm inviting smile, and her eyes still focussing on his, Khaneera walked slowly out of the cell towards him, arms outstretched. Yarron welcomed her in his arms and they held each other tightly, kissing passionately. Yarron's dreams of romance with Khaneera had finally come true and the feeling was overwhelming. His whole body tingled with electricity.

When they finally drew breath, Khaneera whispered to Yarron, "I take it you're with me in my quest?"

"Yes, Khaneera, I am," he said, devotedly.

"Thank you Yarron, you won't regret your decision."

While Yarron was still buzzing with excitement, emotionally and sexually, Khaneera suppressed any feelings she had to focus on her objectives. Having persuaded Yarron to assist in her escape, she needed another favour from him. Looking into his eyes, she whispered again in her soft, mesmerising voice, "Yarron, there's something else I need to ask of you, something that will help ensure our safety once we leave this planet."

Yarron calmed himself to concentrate on Khaneera's words as she continued, "I need to have the Xytrinium infusion formula and the method used to introduce it into the Sentinel DNA. I know the original formula was lost when Kharmar was destroyed centuries ago, but I've heard rumours the Alchemists have developed a new formula. Is it true? And, is it possible for you to get hold of it?"

Yarron was surprised by Khaneera's request and by her knowledge of work on the formula. He dropped his arms from around her body, stepped back and replied with curiosity, "Why do you need this, Khaneera? Once we have our freedom, and you have completed your mission, we can go anywhere in the Universe. Why complicate things by stealing the precious formula?"

Her response was cautious. "Because, Yarron, there are marauding Bladers out there and if we encounter them, we can use the formula as bargaining power to save our lives."

Yarron took a moment to think. Khaneera was asking him not only to help her escape, but also to steal Tzurac's most heavily guarded secret. But he could see her reasoning. "Yes, you're right Khaneera, if stealing the formula will help save our lives, I guess we should consider it. I'll tell you what I know.

"I don't know what you've heard, or how, but the Tzuracians were unable to locate the city of Kharmar or the formula buried with it. They believe explosions during the Grekadian Wars opened up a deep cavern beneath the city, swallowing all traces of it and burying it under tons of soil. There's no hope of finding the formula there.

"But for some time the Senate has known the Sentinels were not producing enough offspring to replenish their armies. Each time a fully-infused Sentinel mated with a non-Sentinel, the offspring would either have no Xytrinium in their DNA or its effects on the DNA would be partially diluted. Over generations the effects were further diluted, weakening the enhancements. Experiments have shown that Sentinels of the tenth generation will have average powers and life spans. At some point in the not too distant future our army will not be strong enough to protect Tzurac or the rest of the Universe from our enemies. We'd be totally vulnerable.

"So five years ago, the Senate, in secret, agreed to start a project to rediscover the formula for Xytrinium DNA infusion. The alchemists at the Science Academy have just commenced the last phase of testing on non-Sentinel army personnel and are confident it will work, having eliminated any side-effects on Tzuracians."

Khaneera was intrigued but curious as to how Yarron knew so much detail. "How do you know all this if it's secret and confidential?"

"Trust me, Khaneera. I know because my mother is one of the alchemists working on the project. She told me, in confidence, about her work."

Khaneera was finding it hard to contain her excitement. The news was getting better all the time. She sensed a real opportunity. "Well then, there might be a chance to get hold of the new formula?"

Yarron hesitated. "Perhaps, but the project is classified as high security and is so well guarded that everyone who enters the Science Academy is under close scrutiny. I don't want to implicate my mother. It's going to take some serious planning and I need time to work on it."

"Yarron, I have faith in you. I know you'll be able to solve this quickly."

"Why the urgency, Khaneera? If we take more time to plan this, we have a better chance of getting away clean."

"Because the longer I wait, the less chance I have of catching up with Jackson and I need his help to find and kill Kyron Shield."

Yarron hesitated with the enormity of the task. "Well Khaneera, even if I'm able to secure the formula for you, and it's going to be difficult, we'll need to leave the planet immediately. Federation Security will be down on us in full force once they find out I've stolen their most valuable asset."

Khaneera stood listening to Yarron while he began to think aloud, planning a strategy. "Hopefully, most of the Sentinels and the Federation Security Forces will be out hunting Jackson, but I'll need to do some reconnaissance to find out what ships are available and determine what security is like at the Air Base. And, if there's a ship we can commandeer, you'll need to be dressed in your Sentinel uniform to be less conspicuous when we make our way to the Base."

Khaneera interrupted Yarron by placing a hand on his lips. "My uniform. The last time I saw it was when Captain Dakhar removed it five years ago and placed it, together with my blade staff and pledge ring, in a black leather satchel."

Yarron nodded, knowingly. "He most likely stored the satchel in the Supply Depot. I'll look into it Khaneera. My shift finishes in half an hour, so I best secure you in your cell. I'm back on duty again in three night's time and if I can organise things by then, be ready to go. We'll only have one chance. May I have one last kiss before I bid you goodnight?"

Without a word, Khaneera placed her hands gently each side of Yarron's face and drew him to her lips for a long passionate kiss. When they separated, Yarron stood momentarily stunned, enjoying the electricity that ran throughout his whole body.

"Thank you Yarron, I'll be forever grateful to you for giving me back my freedom. You won't regret this, I promise."

"Thank *you* Khaneera for awakening me," Yarron replied. "I pray the Ancient spirits will be with us to protect and guide us in our journey."

The distant, hollow sound of heeled boots marching down the passageway hastened Yarron and Khaneera to return to their respective places. By the time the sentry arrived for change of guard, Yarron was standing at attention and the opaque force-field was operational on Khaneera's cell.

"Everything alright, Corporal Blandhar?" inquired the incoming soldier in a gruff voice as Yarron exchanged salutes.

"Yes Sergeant, nothing out of the ordinary."

"Good, I'm here to relieve you of your shift."

Sergeant Qhondez sensed something unusual in the atmosphere but was unable to work out what it was. He was unsure whether it emanated from the Corporal or from Khaneera's cell, but as a highly-attuned Sentinel he sensed something was different.

"Good night Sergeant," said Yarron in a formal voice. Another salute and Yarron headed off briskly down the dimly-lit corridor. His mind was racing with anticipation and mixed emotions.

RISK AND RECONNAISSANCE

RETURNING to the barracks in the early hours of the morning, Yarron fleshed out his plans. He would need his mother's bracelet and her thumb print to gain access to the Science Academy and its computers. Like all alchemists working there his mother had a wrist bracelet made of carbon fibre bearing her identity information and access code. He knew staff could enter the Academy day and night to oversee their science projects and, as long as he could remain unseen, his entry would go unquestioned using his mother's personal access.

The DNA infusion formula and the schematics of the infusion instruments would be on the alchemists' computers in the laboratory. Once he gained access to the Academy, he would need to interrogate the computers and download the relevant information. And, he would need to procure these data on the night of their escape so by the time the authorities realised the breach of the missing data, he would be long gone.

He would visit his mother for dinner on the night of the escape, using this opportunity to steal her bracelet and obtain her thumbprint while paying a private farewell to her before departing Tzurac for his unknown future. Although he was fond of his mother and felt both guilty about betraying her trust and sad about leaving her, the closeness they had once shared had diminished. Following the death of his father, Yarron's mother had hardened her emotions and committed herself single-mindedly to her work. Separation from his mother would be less painful now than it might otherwise have been.

His thoughts turned to locating Khaneera's belongings. Small storage containers were located in the Supply Depot within the Citadel. Personal items not claimed by the families of Sentinels who had fallen in battle, passed away or, on occasion been imprisoned, were stored there. Being a traitor to the Sentinels, Khaneera's belongings would most certainly be kept in one of these storage containers. An idea sprang to mind that just might work to procure her belongings. He needed to follow up on details of a former friend of his who had not returned from battle. And he would have to secure Khaneera's belongings on the night of their escape. Everything depended on the right timing.

Finally, he planned to visit the Air Base the following afternoon on his reconnaissance, under the pretext of his flight training.

Satisfied with these plans, Yarron tried to get some sleep, although his rest was interrupted by thoughts drifting in and out of his head. Yarron was an only child. Born late in his parents' lives, his father passed away with old age soon after Yarron graduated to the Regiment. With only his ageing mother left, he considered the Sentinels his family. Yarron lived a military life of rules and regulations, commitment and loyalty forcing him to channel his feelings into being the best at what he was – a soldier. He achieved high grades during his cadetship, topping the class in most subjects. His classmates and peers respected him for this, although his success had prevented him from fitting in socially.

Khaneera showed him something different. She accepted him and admired his successes, encouraging him to express his emotions to someone who seemed to understand his needs. And, he began to question his loyalty to the Sentinels under her influence, Khaneera's deep-seated animosity towards her fellow Sentinels rubbing off on him.

He woke at mid-day reflecting on the decision he'd made to desert the Sentinels and his mother for a life of freedom. Yarron pushed aside any second thoughts. Now he was ready to abandon Tzurac and the Sentinels for a new life of freedom and adventure with Khaneera.

***

The following afternoon, Yarron arrived at the Air Base hangars on his reconnaissance and was confronted by one of the senior flight instructors, Flight Lieutenant Hadran. He was tall and wiry with short-cropped hair and a trimmed moustache. Yarron summed him up immediately as scrupulous and meticulous.

Towering over Yarron, Hadran addressed him sternly. "What brings you to my Division without authorisation young soldier? Where's your ID and what's your name, rank and unit?"

Saluting the Lieutenant and bracing himself at attention, Yarron blurted out, "Yes, Sir, sorry Sir, I didn't know permission was required to visit the premises, Sir." The Lieutenant returned the salute, staring hard at Yarron, while waiting for an explanation.

"I'm Sentinel Corporal Yarron Blandhar of the 77th Infantry Unit, Sir! Here is my ID tag." Yarron pointed to the ID card clipped to his belt. "I've come to ask about the spacecraft I may be piloting once I pass my exams for promotion to the next level, Sir."

The Lieutenant's manner softened noticeably. "So, you have ambitions do you? Well soldier, stand easy. I'm apprehensive about unknowns on this base, especially when we're on Red Alert following Jackson Jensen's escape from Terra Upsilon. I'm surprised you made it this far without being stopped and questioned. I'll have to see about tightening security. But now that you *are* here, I'll answer your questions."

Yarron was relieved. "Thank you Sir, I appreciate it."

"If you're promoted to Flight Sergeant, the ships you'll be allowed to fly are heavy transporters and warships which require two pilots at the helm. Of course, you won't be hopping in these birds of prey until you've been thoroughly trained using the simulators and battle strategies." The Lieutenant continued with a tone of authority. He was proud of his fleet and keen to ensure that those who piloted his crafts were more than competent.

While listening to the Lieutenant and appearing very interested in what he had to say, Yarron spotted four Class 10 Advance Destroyers standing isolated outside the hangar. He needed to know whether these might be accessible. "Excuse me Sir, but why are those craft stationed outside the hangar if the Base is on Red Alert? Isn't that a risk?"

"Well in fact that's the reason, Corporal. They're fuelled and ready to take off at a moment's notice to combat any incoming enemy spacecraft. It's part of the Red Alert protocol."

Perfect, thought Yarron as he responded in a casual manner. "Oh, yes, of course Sir, that's logical."

"Well, Corporal, I'd like to give you a tour of the ships you'll be flying but this is an inconvenient time while the Red Alert is active. Besides, all the warships are out on patrol."

"Yes, Sir, I understand. But thank you, Sir, for your time and help. I'll leave with your permission, Sir, but I'd like to return at a later date to take you up on your offer of a tour." Yarron saluted, and as the salute was reciprocated by the Flight Lieutenant, Yarron strode off towards the Base exit. He was satisfied that, unless there was an enemy attack on Tzurac, he and Khaneera would have a craft at their disposal.

***

It was dusk on the day of his planned escape, when Yarron headed off to his mother's quarters for their pre-arranged dinner. His mother, a rather plain-looking woman whose greying hair revealed her autumn years, welcomed him, offering him a glass of fermented fruit wine and asking him to sit down.

"You're looking a little edgy Yarron," she said with some concern. "Are you okay?"

Yarron nodded, "I'm fine thank you Mother, there's just a lot happening at work."

She returned to the adjoining kitchen to prepare their meal and, still within hearing distance, asked Yarron what he had on at work and what he'd been up to since they last met. As only a mother knows, she sensed her son was uneasy and she was keen to find out what might be upsetting him.

While responding casually to the conversation, Yarron carefully scanned the room, looking for where his mother might have left her identity bracelet. He spotted it sitting on a white marble side cabinet, next to the framed holograph photos of his father and himself in their younger days. Both were presented proudly in their Sentinel uniforms at Yarron's graduation. Walking quickly to the cabinet, Yarron picked up the slim wristlet, conscious of breaching his mother's trust. It was something he had never done before.

He was still clutching the bracelet in his hand when his mother entered the room with her glass of wine. She hesitated seeing Yarron at the cabinet with his back to her, realising she had left her bracelet there exposed to inquisitive eyes. "What are you doing my son?" she asked with a hint of suspicion in her voice.

Caught off guard, Yarron reached for the holograph photo of his father, cleverly replacing the bracelet on the cabinet in the same motion. He turned to his mother and answered affectionately, "I was just remembering how proud dad was of me on my graduation day. I really miss him, mum."

Relieved by his response, Yarron's mother took the photo from his hand saying fondly, "I also miss him very much, my son." She rested her glass of wine on the cabinet and carefully replaced the precious photo in its original position. She turned towards her bedroom. "I'm just going to change for dinner Yarron. Take a seat at the table and I'll be back in a minute."

When his mother disappeared from sight, Yarron moved swiftly. He picked up her crystal wine glass, holding it towards the light, studying it for any visible finger prints. He could see the translucent residue of her thumb print on one surface of the glass. Setting the glass down on the cabinet, Yarron placed the top of his pledge ring close to the image and pressed one of the tiny blue gemstones on the side of the ring. A thin beam of pale blue light shot out from the ring's surface and silently scanned the imprint. Releasing the pressure on the gem, the beam shut off instantly. Yarron couldn't help but feel guilty as he took his place at the table and checked his timepiece, calculating that he had only another hour to spend with his mother before leaving to complete the next stage of his plan.

Over dinner, Yarron turned the conversation to focus on his mother's work. "How's your project going mum? Still enjoying it?"

"Yes I'm happy it's coming to an end after all our efforts, but I could do without the current heightened security. Sentries are now on twenty-four hour shifts outside all entrances to the building and, even as a scientist, I'm under scrutiny. I'm looking forward to retirement very soon, Yarron."

Yarron was alarmed at hearing about the unexpected additional security at the Science Academy, and while maintaining his composure, began to rethink his plan. *I'll need a diversion to gain entry unseen.*

An hour later, Yarron left his mother's place for the Citadel, his mother unaware he had said his last farewell. He carried a heavy heart and was tense, hoping it would not be until the following morning that she discovered the missing bracelet he had pocketed while she was distracted clearing the dishes. He was now under extreme time pressure to coordinate the remaining parts of his escape plan.

***

Back at the barracks, Yarron prepared to leave his Sentinel life behind. He gathered what he needed, set his pistol on stun, took a cursory glance around the room that had been his military home for most of his adult life, then made for the Supply Depot to confront the Keeper.

As Yarron stepped through the thick, automatic entry doors to the Supply Depot, he was caught unawares by a low, gravelly voice saying, "Can I help you Soldier?"

As the doors snapped shut behind him and Yarron turned towards the sound of the voice, he saw a burly-looking Sentinel seated behind a metal-grilled counter just inside the room. The Sentinel, Sergeant Brazhart, who had been Keeper of Supplies for the last twenty years, still maintained a military appearance. He was neatly groomed with a full beard, matching fair hair swept back tightly in the distinctive, long, plaited ponytail and piercing blue eyes. A large sign on the wall behind him warned, 'No admittance beyond this point'.

"Ah yes, I think you can, Sergeant," replied Yarron in a slightly parched voice. Yarron could feel his heart thumping and his jugular pulsating, his breathing now short and shallow. Knowing he was there on false pretences, the young corporal was almost unable to utter his words. He cleared his dry throat and continued, "I'm Corporal Yarron Blandhar of the 77th Infantry Unit and I have a favour to ask, rather than a formal request."

The Sergeant glared at Yarron. "A favour, eh? I don't do favours. I'm in the habit of taking orders from senior officers, not doing favours for lower ranks."

"Look sir," responded Yarron, timidly, "I know you keep in storage the personal items of soldiers who have passed away and I want to see the belongings of a friend of mine who died in battle."

The Sergeant was sceptical. "Why do you want to see them Corporal? Only families of the deceased have permission to view stored items."

Yarron was prepared for this. "My friend had no family or relatives and I'd like to apply to have one of his items for a keepsake, as a reminder of our friendship. It would mean a lot to me."

The Sergeant was unmoved by Yarron's personal plea. "This is not the usual protocol Corporal."

Yarron tried to appeal to the Sergeant's emotions. "I know Sergeant, but even though my friend has been gone for four years I still miss him so much. I've been thinking recently how sad it is that nobody has come to collect any of his things. It would be nice to have something of his to feel closer to his spirit. Besides, they're only gathering dust and what harm would it do to anyone?"

"Alright soldier, no more bleeding heart. So tell me your friend's name?"

"Private Mhantar Peldoz, 77th Infantry Unit," said Yarron, gently. "We were like brothers."

The Sergeant shifted his attention to the computer on the desk in front of him and, within seconds, lifted his head to face Yarron. "Okay, I've found the record. Now, if you were so close to him, tell me how did your friend die? And where?"

The Sergeant quizzed Yarron on the details of Private Peldoz and decided from the answers he received, Yarron was genuine. "Okay, since Peldoz had no family to collect his things, this time I'll make an exception. I can't see that it will cause any harm. The container is located in one of the storage bays at the far end of the depot. Give me a moment to lock up and I'll escort you there."

"Thank you Sergeant," said Yarron with apparent gratitude.

The two were soon walking briskly, in military step, into the bowels of the building, past possessions donated by deceased souls of ages past. The dimly-lit passageway exaggerated the eerie feeling and Yarron felt as if he were trespassing on hallowed ground. He kept looking apprehensively behind him as they travelled past rows and rows of storage containers on either side of the passageway. The containers were stored alphabetically showing the name, rank and unit of the deceased stencilled on the front of them.

Ten paces further the Sergeant stopped in his tracks; his head swivelled to the left, his eyes fixated on one of the containers. "Here it is Corporal Blandhar, your friend's locker."

As Sergeant Brazhart reached with his left hand to deactivate the lock code, Yarron quickly unholstered his pistol and aimed it directly at the Sergeant's head. "Don't move Sergeant!" he threatened. "Sorry about this, but I need you to open Khaneera Penzark's container instead."

The Sergeant froze on hearing Yarron's threat but replied calmly. He had been in life-threatening situations before and knew not to make any sudden movements. "And if I refuse?" he asked, testing Yarron's mettle.

"I really don't want to harm you, Sergeant, but I will if I have to. I hate to think what damage this weapon can do at point-blank range." Only Yarron knew the weapon was set on stun.

The Sergeant knew better than to argue with someone serious who was pointing a pistol at his head. "Okay Corporal, follow me."

Walking a couple of paces behind with the pistol still pointing at the Sergeant, Yarron followed his lead for another few yards, before the Sergeant stopped. The beam of the Sergeant's torch was now shining on one of the cabinets to the right side of the passageway. "Khaneera Penzark's locker as requested, Corporal."

"Alright Sergeant, open it," Yarron ordered, menacing the Sergeant by pointing the firearm nearer to his head. As the Sergeant pressed a code on the keypad at the side of the locker, the small front panel shot upward revealing a sealed, black-leather case inside the now-illuminated locker. "Take the case out slowly Sergeant, and open it. I want to see the contents."

Removing the black satchel carefully from the locker and avoiding any sudden movements, the Sergeant knelt down on his haunches and placed the case on the floor in front of him. He peeled back the flap and proceeded to lift out the contents, the fixed light overhead revealing each item as it was removed. There was a midnight blue robe, a maroon Sentinel uniform, a pair of black-leather, knee-high boots, a blade-staff and a sheathed dagger.

"Where's her Sentinel gold ring?" asked Yarron.

"The Senate destroys the rings of dishonoured Sentinels who have brought shame to their families and to the Regiment," the Sergeant responded. He had instantly recognised Khaneera's name as a well-known traitor. "They are considered unworthy of passing on their rings to their offspring."

"Alright Sergeant, don't push your luck. You can put her things back in the case and seal it," demanded Yarron. "And hurry up!"

As the Sergeant closed and sealed the case, Yarron fired his pistol and the Sergeant slumped to the ground, stunned by a blast to his rib cage. "Sorry Sarge, nothing personal." Yarron felt somewhat guilty about using his weapon on his brother-in-arms, but he had to prevent an alarm being raised.

Yarron dragged the deadweight Sergeant to a gap in between the cabinets and leant him against the wall. He scooped the satchel from the floor, flung it over his shoulder and made his way back towards the entrance, detouring through the armoury. There, Yarron grabbed a handgun with its belted holster, a small incendiary grenade and two wrist communicators, burying them under the uniform in the satchel without stopping.

Nightfall had arrived by the time Yarron left the Supply Depot. He was thankful the three moons were veiled by cloud and, in semi-darkness, he moved silently to the Science Academy, hugging the shadows of the tall surrounding structures to avoid being seen. He was hoping all the Academy staff would have vacated the premises by this hour but he was expecting the building to be guarded.

Stopping two hundred yards from the structure, Yarron could see two sentries standing rigid under the floodlights guarding the entrance. He took a small incendiary device from the satchel, armed it, and set the timer to ignite in three minutes. Casting it into the garden immediately in front of the building, he waited for the device to explode into flames. As soon as the sentries raced from their posts to investigate the explosion, Yarron put the floodlights out of commission by firing two laser blasts. The sentries were too distracted by the fire to notice.

Yarron moved quickly in the moon shadows to the entrance. Removing his mother's bracelet from his pocket he hastily pressed it into the indented shape in the access panel and projected her thumbprint image from his ring onto the small screen beside it. As the wristlet glowed with a fluorescent yellow, he heard a soft electronic click and the dark-tinted, armour-plate, glass doors silently slid open. Snatching the bracelet from the access panel he entered the building and, once inside, repeated the procedure to disable the alarm. The doors shut tightly behind him. A quick blast from his pistol disabled the internal security cameras. Now he had little time to act.

As he strode forward, his heeled boots echoed in the silence on the smooth, stone-cobbled floor, the sound resonating loudly with each step as if in an amphitheatre. Dimmed lights in the spacious, open foyer partially illuminated the internal structure. Huge, colourful tapestries depicting scenes of battles adorned the white marble walls. Models of flying craft from days of old hung like giant mobiles from the ceiling, suspended by long, super-fine wire cables. On the floor in the centre of the room was an enormous, clear cube precariously balanced on one corner. The sculpture, much like a prism, captured a swirling, rainbow-coloured laser light that repeatedly changed shape and direction without light escaping from the cube.

At the far end of the long foyer, several passageways veered off in various directions, large printed signs indicating the area to which they led. The signs hadn't changed since the last time Yarron had visited his mother at work and Yarron well knew the passageway which led to the experimental laboratories. Satisfied there were no sentries or workers inside the building, he hurried down the dark corridor to the main laboratory using the blue illuminator from his blade-staff to light the way.

On reaching the opaque doors, Yarron again pressed his mother's bracelet on the panel and projected her thumbprint, allowing him easy access. As he entered, the pneumatic, frosted-glass doors closed automatically behind him. A cold sweat came upon him and his pulse quickened. The thumping sound of his fast-beating heart was noticeable in the room's stillness. With fear and apprehension at the thought of being discovered in a highly restricted area, perspiration began seeping through the raised hairs on the back of his neck. *I need to focus.*

In the dark room mauve lights emanated from three softly-lit, horizontal screens embedded in the surface of a long marble bench, stretching almost twenty feet in length. He waved his hand over the nearest screen. A bluish luminescent holograph, three feet high, sprang from the surface. It was a quad helix diagram of Tzuracian DNA and slowly rotated clockwise. As it rotated a thin, fluorescent, azure-blue thread slowly weaved its way from the base through one of the pairs in the helix, snaking its way to the top of the image. At the same time, a complex equation of several lines flashed in white on the left side of the holograph with cryptic notes containing chemical symbols written underneath. Instantaneously, the holograph began to pulse with a humming sound whilst emitting intermittent bursts of rainbow light which switched intensity from dullness to brilliance. It was the blueprint file for the infusion method. Yarron opened another file to reveal schematics of intricately designed instruments and probes highlighting complex calibrations.

Yarron hurriedly withdrew the memory rod which he had packed into his breast pocket and slid the crystal device into a slot on the benchtop computer, pressing one of the imprints to transfer copies of the files. Within seconds he had successfully captured the necessary data, removed the crystal rod, and tucked it back into his pocket. He quickly shut down the computer before further computer activity alerted his presence in the building.

Suddenly, without warning, the building alarms screamed out with high-pitched sirens. Above the ear-piercing noise Yarron could hear the sound of footsteps on the hard floor surface racing along the passageways and becoming increasingly louder as they approached the laboratory. He heard a muffled order being shouted and then more footsteps. Through the frosted-glass doors, he could discern shadowy figures and flashes of light from search beams. Yarron's heart started to beat faster. *I've been sprung.*

Diving under the computer bench, Yarron unholstered his pistol and set it on stun in anticipation. He heard the pneumatic doors of the laboratory slide open and, from his confined position, he watched a bright, narrow search beam track slowly across the room. He controlled his breathing to make it shallow and quiet, listening for any sounds of movement other than the pounding of the pulse in his jugular. Seconds seemed like minutes. He was tensed like a coiled snake ready to strike.

"No sign of anyone in here," yelled the intruder in a powerful deep voice. "Try the other labs!"

The search beam snapped off and Yarron heard the lab doors draw shut. But he remained still and hidden for some time, not willing to move in case the intruder was waiting to strike in the dark. Straining his acute hearing, Yarron waited patiently until he was sure he could not detect any sounds of breathing or movement other than his own. Then, he carefully unfolded himself from his position and, still kneeling on the floor, raised his head hesitantly above the bench. His eyes rapidly scanned the room confirming the intruder had left. Breathing a sigh of relief, he reholstered his weapon and waited long enough to satisfy himself the security detail had vacated the building.

When the incessant screaming alarm ceased, Yarron decided it was safe to make his move. Shouldering the satchel, he stalked out of the laboratory and made his way apprehensively to the front entrance, all the while prepared for Federation security officers to come rushing down the other passageways towards him.

At the entrance, he inserted the bracelet and scanned in his mother's thumbprint, then pulled the pistol from his holster. As the doors drew apart, he saw the two sentries had returned to their posts and stunned them immediately with two blasts from his pistol before they had any chance to react. Re-holstering his weapon, he dragged their limp, unconscious bodies back into the building and resealed the entry doors from the outside.

Then, just when he thought he had completed this important part of his mission, a Red Alert warning signal began to echo loudly throughout the Citadel. It sent several Sentinel patrols jogging at double time in different directions. The sentries had obviously put everyone on alert. He had to get to the prison quickly, without being caught out.

Yarron quickly distanced himself from the Science Academy and then composed himself, making his way towards the prison as unobtrusively as he could. He was almost there when he was stopped by one of the patrols.

"Hey you! What are you up to?"

Yarron's heart stood still. *Am I to fail this close to the moment of escape? And without seeing Khaneera?* It took all his composure to convince the patrol he was simply reporting for guard duty with a spare uniform in his satchel.

BREAKOUT

INSIDE the Citadel prison, Yarron was apprehensive as he approached Khaneera's cell. Although he appeared calm on the surface, his heart and mind were racing. The thought of leaving Tzurac and the Sentinels had not occurred to him until a few nights ago, and now it had become reality. Tonight, he and Khaneera were going to escape, Khaneera fleeing her condemned life of imprisonment while he broke free from a traditional life of loyalty and service to the Regiment.

The robe he wore concealed the satchel he was carrying under his left arm. He hugged the satchel close to his body to avoid being detected as he neared the Corporal standing guard outside Khaneera's cell. The Corporal gave a formal salute which Yarron returned, and then started to question Yarron about the Red Alert siren still sounding in the Citadel.

"Corporal Blandhar, do you know what's happening and why the siren has been activated?"

"No," replied Yarron, shrugging his shoulders innocently. "But I saw plenty of units on the move out there and I suppose we'll be told soon enough."

"Yes, I suppose we will. Well you're now on watch, Blandhar. Stay alert. I'll check in with headquarters." After exchanging routine salutes, the Corporal marched away without looking back.

Once the Corporal was out of sight, Yarron focused his thoughts. Time and speed were of the essence. "Khaneera," he called firmly, "are you ready?"

The opaque cell door became transparent. Standing before him was Khaneera, smiling gently, her deep blue eyes fixed on his. "I've been ready for a long time, Yarron."

"You look good, even in your prison uniform," Yarron said in admiration. He waved his hand across the illuminated control at the side of the cell, turning off the force-field. "Here, take this satchel, Khaneera, and change into your Sentinel uniform as fast as you can."

As she reached for the satchel, Khaneera leaned closer and kissed her accomplice passionately. When their lips parted Khaneera sighed, whispering, "Thank you my hero but what's going on? Why the sirens? Is everything under control?"

"Don't thank me yet, Khaneera, we have more obstacles to tackle," Yarron explained. "The Red Alert siren has been triggered because the Security Forces know someone's broken into the Science Academy. It won't take them long to find out that the culprit gained access using my mother's identity bracelet. Things didn't go exactly according to plan."

"Did you get the formula and the instruments for the DNA infusion?" Khaneera asked anxiously as she opened the satchel.

"Yes it's all on the memory rod," replied Yarron, pulling the small, crystal object from inside the breast pocket of his uniform to show her.

Khaneera looked concerned. "But, what about the instruments? It won't work without them."

"Stop worrying Khaneera. The blueprint to make the instruments is also on the memory rod. Now hurry, we don't have much time!"

With a sigh of relief, Khaneera disappeared into the cell to change while Yarron nervously checked up and down the passageway to make sure they were still alone. When he peered into Khaneera's cell to see if she was ready, he inadvertently spied a mirrored reflection of her undressing. His heart quickened and he stood with fixed gaze, knowing it was wrong to intrude on her privacy. He couldn't resist the temptation to savour the moment and admire her naked, athletic body with smooth, silky skin, firm breasts, tight buttocks and long shapely legs. *Khaneera is perfection.*

When Khaneera caught sight of Yarron's reflection looking at her in the mirror, she stopped momentarily, smiled, and caught his eye. Yarron's face flushed red with embarrassment and he quickly turned to look away.

When Khaneera reappeared dressed in her Sentinel uniform, she asked with a grin, "Did you like what you saw?"

Feeling embarrassed and still blushing, Yarron's voice quivered as he spoke, "I apologise for intruding on your privacy but you're beautiful, Khaneera."

Khaneera placed a finger on his lips. "I knew you were looking and I wanted to show you all that I am. Sorry we don't have time to discover each other now, but I'm sure we'll make up for lost time as soon as we leave this place."

"I hope so Khaneera, I truly hope so."

Yarron was stunned by Khaneera's new look. Her maroon Sentinel outfit fitted her perfectly, emphasizing her sculptured contours. It was obvious she had maintained her strength and fitness while in prison. With her blonde hair pulled back tightly into a ponytail and her weapons fixed at her side, she looked a formidable opponent for anyone willing to confront her.

"What do you think Yarron? Do I look the part?" Khaneera said, confidently.

"Fabulous, just fabulous."

"Thank you for the compliment, Yarron. But, where's my ring?"

Yarron had anticipated this question. "It wasn't with your uniform. I was told pledge rings of dishonoured Sentinels are destroyed. Sorry Khaneera."

Khaneera was infuriated by the answer. Her pledge ring was the connection to her family and represented the very reason she was avenging her father's downfall at the hands of the Federation. The destruction of this symbol fuelled her vengeance even more and her mood suddenly changed, her face now showing stone coldness. "Let's go Yarron, the sooner the better."

"Listen Khaneera," cautioned Yarron, gripping her right arm firmly as she was about to stride off, "there are numerous Sentinel units patrolling the grounds of the Citadel. So, keep your head down to avoid the security monitors sighting your face, and walk slowly. Hopefully you won't be recognised dressed in your uniform. You've been in solitary confinement for five years and there's only a handful of Sentinels that could identify you. If we meet any patrols on the way to the hangars, just salute and let me do the talking. Set your pistol on stun just in case but stay calm and don't do anything that might draw attention to us."

Khaneera unholstered her pistol, reluctantly setting it to stun and returned it to its pouch. "Okay, Yarron, I'll follow your lead."

They left the prison complex cautiously, to see Sentinel troops still jogging at double time in different directions and to hear orders being shouted above the sirens. The atmosphere was tense as heavily-armed soldiers continued searching frantically for the suspected intruders, ready to shoot on sight.

Khaneera and Yarron made their way carefully and inconspicuously through the grounds, lucky to avoid unwanted encounters. And, within ten minutes, they were crouched behind the meshed wire fence close to the front gates of the Air Base.

"So far, so good," said Yarron, relieved this part of their escape had gone unnoticed.

The grounds were in semi light from the reflection of the three moons now in clear view. Several flood lights illuminated the hangars and the four spacecraft stationed beside them. There was no movement near the ships.

"Are they the vessels we intend stealing?" whispered Khaneera, drawing her weapon.

"Yes," whispered Yarron, "that's them. But we only need one to get us out of here."

Yarron's pulse was beating faster than usual, anticipating their next move. He checked his timepiece. "It's 02.00 hours, Khaneera. That gives us five hours head start before my shift finishes and they realize a high risk prisoner has escaped and I'm part of it. Let's go."

Moving from their crouched position but remaining hunched low, they crept silently towards the hangar, with pistols at the ready. Suddenly, two sentries stepped into the light at the front of the hangar spotting the two silhouettes approaching them. Before the sentries could raise their firearms, they were stunned unconscious from two blasts fired in quick succession by Khaneera.

Yarron was amazed at his partner's speed and accuracy. "I see you've kept up your target practice, Khaneera."

"Thought it might come in handy someday," she replied, flashing a confident smile.

Surveying the surrounds to ensure there were no other sentries, Khaneera and Yarron ran over to the two limp bodies, each grabbing one by the arms and dragging them quickly out of sight, some distance behind the hangar. Then Yarron led Khaneera with urgency to the rear of the closest spacecraft and tapped a code into the control panel at the base of the hatch.

At first there was no movement. Khaneera turned to Yarron and raised an eyebrow in doubt. Then, without warning, the door unhinged itself and sprang forward, lowering a set of metal stairs to the ground. The stairs shone in the reflection of the floodlights. Yarron winked at Khaneera and climbed to the entry hatch, Khaneera following close behind.

Once inside with the hatch door locked shut, Yarron headed for the pilot console, Khaneera shadowing him. Just as the Flight Lieutenant had explained, the craft was prepared for immediate departure.

"You take the co-pilot's seat on the left Khaneera, and please don't touch anything on the console." Khaneera nodded in agreement, climbed in and quickly made herself comfortable while Yarron manoeuvred himself into the Pilot's seat.

Before Yarron activated any of the controls, he used his thumb to depress a tiny red button on a black box mounted in the console above his head. Khaneera watched with keen interest as a lid slowly slid open from the black box. Yarron reached inside and carefully retrieved a shiny, flat disc, about half an inch in thickness and two inches in diameter.

"What's that?" asked Khaneera.

Yarron was a trained pilot and answered confidently. "It's a powerful homing transmitter that monitors the location of the craft no matter where it's located in the known Federation galaxies. It needs to be de-activated into sleep mode. You can't just switch it off with the 'kill' switch or it will automatically start transmitting. There's a specific code sequence used for sleep mode. All spacecraft have these devices installed with the code dedicated to the Class of ship."

Yarron flipped the disc over to show the underside. On the base was a matrix of twelve evenly-marked segments, each segment having a different symbol etched into it. Khaneera watched with intrigue as

Yarron tapped six different symbols. As he touched the last one the disc emitted a faint indigo glow, and Yarron breathed a sigh of relief.

"I didn't say anything to you Khaneera until I had completed the sequence just in case you panicked."

"Why would I panic?" Khaneera asked, again raising an eyebrow.

"Because one press out of sequence on these symbols and we would have been blown into microns."

Khaneera raised her voice in anger. "You could have killed both of us Yarron. Weren't you thinking?" she snapped. "Next time you're trying something dangerous, warn me so I have a say in how we do things."

Her response was unexpected, but this was the second time Khaneera had changed suddenly, questioning Yarron's loyalty or intentions. He realised she was a strong woman who commanded respect and complete allegiance. "Sorry Khaneera, you're right. We're in this together."

Yarron placed his left hand on a flat round dish in the centre of the console and waved his other hand over a bank of small flat panels on the right. The console illuminated with panels of coloured lights that started to pulse. Khaneera watched as he deftly pressed the illuminated panels in sequence to bring the craft to life. As the craft began to hum, she turned to him with a look of anticipation.

"I've set the craft on stealth mode. Are you ready to leave your home?" Yarron asked, knowingly.

"What do you think, Yarron?" Khaneera grinned. "But, before we go," she said, suddenly looking deadly serious, "I want you to obliterate the remaining ships."

"What?" He hadn't expected this. Yarron turned to face Khaneera. "If I do that, the noise will raise the alarm to the Citadel that the Air Base is under attack and the Security Forces will be on us in no time at all. It will leave Khazor without air defence for some time while they call in the other ships from the quadrants."

Khaneera was quick and definite in her response. "They might be onto us sooner than planned, but they won't be able to follow us until they regroup their warships. As for their transporters, they're far too slow to chase a battleship. Our heat trail will have long gone cold. Besides, I'd like the Sentinels to experience what it's like to feel vulnerable and helpless. Wouldn't you? But, if it eases your conscience, Yarron, you won't be killing any Sentinels or innocent citizens. And keep in mind, if they catch us, you'll be thrown into solitary confinement or worse, whether you destroy their ships or not. But we *will* have a better chance of escape if they are unable to fly those Destroyers."

Khaneera was being assertive and somewhat callous, but he knew she was right. He moved his left hand over the circular dish on the console and the ship started to lift and hover. As it rose to the height of two hundred feet, he manoeuvred the craft in position, pointed the laser cannons towards the grounded Destroyers and gave the computer the order to fire.

"Computer, discharge four rounds at the three ships stationed at the front of the hangar."

'Yes Corporal Blandhar, as you command.'

On the Pilot's screen Yarron and Khaneera watched the computer lock onto the target within seconds and instantly discharge four laser blasts. The ships as well as the hangar exploded violently in a huge ball of fire.

For Yarron there was no going back. He turned to Khaneera, "So where are we headed?"

Khaneera was sure of herself. "We're bound for Terra Iota. I suspect that's where Jackson's going."

Yarron hesitated. "But there's a unit of Sentinels there protecting the place."

"We'll deal with that, Yarron. Just make it Terra Iota."

Yarron complied. "Computer, set coordinates for Terra Iota."

The speaker on the console responded in a simulated monotone voice, *'Terra Iota, also known as Nebularis: Located in the Sideros-Hudor System: Colonised for mining by Terranians: Small unit of Sentinels on guard.'*

"How long to reach Nebularis?" ordered Khaneera, abruptly. There was no response.

She was about to ask the question again when Yarron intervened. "It won't respond to unrecognized voices, Khaneera. Computer, what's the estimated time of arrival at Terra Iota?"

'Ten Tzuracian days at maximum hyperspeed.'

"Computer, take us to Terra Iota."

The ship turned in a north-westerly direction and started to pick up speed. Within seconds, the thrusters ignited and the ship disappeared into the night sky.

Freedom at last, Khaneera thought to herself.

Khaneera slipped out of her co-pilot seat and without a word, leant over to kiss Yarron. Yarron put his arms around her and drew her closer. They held each other for some time until Khaneera pulled away, saying, "Thank you Yarron for helping me escape and for joining me in this mission."

"The pleasure's all mine, Khaneera." There were broad smiles on both their faces knowing they had made a clean getaway and were safe from pursuit, at least for some time.

Although Khaneera's real passion still lay in revenge, her sexual feelings towards her young, handsome partner were aroused. "Yarron, can you put this craft on auto pilot and show me the rest of this ship, as well as our sleeping quarters?" she asked, invitingly.

"Yes of course, I'd be delighted," responded Yarron, encouraged by the suggestion of intimacy after some tense moments between them. "Computer, place craft on auto and alert me if there are any changes. Maintain shields at sixty percent. If Federation contacts us, ignore any requests. Do not respond to their communications. This craft is on a secret mission and we don't want them to know our whereabouts. Oh, and assimilate my passenger's voice for command recognition."

'*Yes Corporal Blandhar, as you command. What is your passenger's rank and name?*'

"Corporal Areenahk."

'*Affirmative.*'

As Khaneera and Yarron departed the Bridge heading along the wide passageway, Khaneera asked, "Why Areenahk?"

"There would be a block on the name Corporal Penzark in the computer's database."

"Good thinking, Yarron. Corporal Areenahk, it is."

They were relaxed as they headed for the sleeping quarters in anticipation.

CLOSE ENCOUNTERS

DURING the first week of their voyage, Flight Lieutenant Dawson gave Jackson intensive instructions on the operations of the high-tech battleship and read the Captain's Flight Manual with him to help him learn the protocols. The time spent together gave them the opportunity to find out more about each other, and the more they discovered, the closer their relationship became.

Jackson was the first to ask questions about his pilot, trying initially to gain confirmation of her loyalty to his cause. He needed to know how serious she was about opposing her employer.

"Is that why you joined up with ASPECT, Pam? Because your father was on their payroll?"

"No!" replied Dawson defiantly. "My father wasn't always with ASPECT. He used to be a fighter pilot in the Middle East Wars and only joined ASPECT after I did. My childhood was very different from that of most children. I didn't stay in one place and at one school like my friends, hanging out on week-ends with the gang. No, I was dragged from country to country, military base to military base, my father taking his family with him whenever and wherever he was ordered to go. I continually had to make new friends and leave old ones behind. And we were often stationed close to war zones, not knowing if and when the airforce bases would be bombed. That's what killed my mother."

"When the airforce base was bombed?" Jackson asked, trying to empathize with Dawson's situation.

"No, Jackson, that's not what killed her," said Dawson shaking her head. "Are you following my drift?"

"I'm trying. Go on."

Dawson explained. "The medics said my mother had a heart attack due to natural causes, but the emotional stress was simply too much for her to bear. We lived anxiously, hoping my father would make it back safely after each mission. Then, without my mother and with my father away constantly on missions, I was left largely on my own. So, to cope, I occupied myself learning mechanics and aerodynamics from the engineers on the base and mastering how to fly. By the time I was sixteen, I was more qualified than most of the other pilots. Then, my father agreed to send me to the Space Academy, to be trained as an officer and qualify to fly spacecrafts."

"So you joined ASPECT when you completed your cadetship?" said Jackson, trying to show more understanding.

"I joined ASPECT when they took over control of the Space Academy. I had no choice. And my father eventually joined ASPECT too when the wars came to an end. Leading into his retirement he wanted an easier and safer job, transporting ores from planet to planet. And perhaps he also wanted to make up for lost time with me."

"Oh, I get it now. So why would you want to ditch ASPECT Pam, and disappoint your father by joining us? As a Flight Lieutenant, you're obviously on track for promotion."

"Promotion!" Pam said, bitterly. "If they can't recognise a pilot who outstrips any other in her class and instead promote a snotty-nosed kid like Newman, who I taught to fly, then ASPECT doesn't cut it with me. Being an Air-Marshall, Newman's father pulled rank to promote him Captain over me. It makes me sick. People should earn their stripes by their own efforts and not have 'daddy' leaning on others to get what they want."

Jackson had clearly struck a raw nerve.

"Okay, Pam, I know exactly how you feel. I've been through something similar. My mother died when I was seven so my father, who was more interested in his company, MERIC, than in me, sent me away to boarding school. He didn't consider how emotionally upset I was by my mother's death and he wasn't there to help me through my grieving. He channelled his emotions into his work and left me to fend for myself."

"Well that would've been an easy ride," cut in Dawson, "being in boarding school with all the other wimps, being waited on hand and foot, not having to struggle for everything."

Jackson took offence. "You think? Not coming from a very rich family like the other kids at the private boarding school, I was looked down upon as inferior by the others, even by the tutors. The other kids' parents donated huge amounts of money and the school favoured them as a consequence. Being bullied by the others made me realise that if I was to succeed and be respected, I would have to harden up and give them a taste of their own medicine."

"So, Jackson, how did you manage that?" Dawson was keenly interested in what was hidden behind the façade of this man who projected strength and a hardened heart. Jackson had deeper emotions than met the eye.

Jackson confided in her. "I pushed myself harder with everything I did, to reach further and further, beyond my limits. While the other students went home to their parents every holiday break to be pampered, I stayed behind at the school, studying over and over our assignments and homework. And, in the gym, which I practically had to myself for weeks at a time, I trained in boxing and fencing. I forced myself to bury my emotions and channel my energy into winning at all costs. I realised very early, emotions make you vulnerable. To be vulnerable is to show weakness, which leads to others taking advantage and having control. To win at anything, at everything, and to win in life, one has to be determined and fearless, not weak and fearful.

"The school wasn't recognised for its sporting achievements until I raised the level of its competitive prowess by winning medals and cups. It was only then the other students and tutors acknowledged me as equal and began to show me respect. Many of the students feared my ruthlessness, but there were many who admired my strength and determination to achieve."

Hearing about his past life, Dawson admired what Jackson had done in order to establish himself independently, first as a success at school and then in the corporate world of power and wealth. But she was curious to find out how he ended up in his current situation.

"So, Jackson, with your intelligence and ability, and not being remotely like the rest of the rabble on board the *Jolly Roger*, how did you land yourself in a penal colony for those not fit to be in society?"

Jackson disclosed more. "Yes, I guess it does seem a little odd that a person of my calibre, with my upbringing and breeding, would end up associating with psychopaths. But life often has strange twists of fate and you never know what awaits you around the corner. When my father heard of my academic and sporting achievements at school, he finally started to show more interest in me. I thought he would welcome me more as his son and we could rekindle the love lost from the past. But eventually I realised it was mainly for him and for his Company's benefit that he encouraged me to join MERIC. He just wanted to gloat to his peers and parade me like a prize show dog, keeping the Company in the family name.

"I tried to show my father I was ready to manage the Company by demonstrating my initiative to start mining Xytrinium and stockpiling the resource on Earth. But instead of embracing me and my initiatives, he scolded me like a headmaster punishing a school boy, telling me how successful the Company had been by maintaining rules and moral standards. He didn't praise me for thinking smart. Instead, he told me he was very disappointed in me. He showed more affection for a farmboy-cum-engineer, Kyron Shield. Shield had studied at the same College of Royal Engineers as my father and followed my father's papers with keen interest.

"In no uncertain terms, I told my father to change his old-fashioned protocols and keep up with the modern times. I said he was a stupid old fool clinging onto old-fashioned traditions. He was going to let the World Assembly decide what to do with the Xytrinium and lose the advantage of MERIC having control and that naïve farmboy Shield, supported him."

Jackson grew angrier as he relived these events. "So, I took matters into my own hands and arranged for an 'accident' to stop my father so I could take control of the company. And then I learned my father had bequeathed MERIC to the farmboy. He'd handed over *my inheritance* to someone who wasn't even family. You can understand how I felt Pam, can't you? I was hurt, pissed off and publicly humiliated." He paused in thought before continuing, "So to answer your question, Pam, sometimes you need to break the rules to achieve your objectives. But I guess … I went too far."

For a moment Dawson saw Jackson show some remorse at his wrong doing, but quickly he snapped out of it, determined not to show any weakness of emotion.

"This time, my determination had serious consequences. The authorities agreed I couldn't be rehabilitated, my animosity being too deep. So they thought the best way to deal with me was to send me to some place where I wouldn't be a threat to anyone on Earth again – Terra Upsilon. So now you know."

Dawson seemed sympathetic. She could see how the tough exterior Jackson portrayed was protecting a soft heart, hardened by years of rejection by others, including his own father. "I can understand how you felt Jackson and why you did what you felt you had to. I guess desperate situations call for desperate measures."

Jackson was impressed. "Precisely, Pam! My sentiments exactly. You know, Dawson, you're the only person I've confided in about my past and the only one who seems to understand why I'm so determined to regain control of MERIC. You're starting to grow on me."

"The feeling's mutual, Jackson," said Dawson, warmly.

"But it's time to toughen up on the emotions, Pam, before we become too vulnerable."

The conversation ended with both of them unable to contain a warm satisfied smile.

***

The *Jolly Roger* was now halfway to its destination of Terra Iota and the voyage had been without incident, save for a few minor skirmishes amongst some of the motley crew. Although they were now on the same side, past differences were hard to forget and there was still residual resentment between the convicts and guards. Jackson had appointed the experienced, burly Sergeant Stoltz to deal with the culprits, giving him a free hand in reprimands to keep the peace. Jackson needed every one of his troops in peak condition for the battles that lay ahead.

On Jackson's instruction CT had been broadcasting messages in Treldarian dialect, hoping to make contact with the Bladers, but there had been no response. Then, without warning, three alien spacecraft suddenly appeared on the main screen. They were travelling at the same speed as the *Jolly Roger*, but keeping their distance.

Flight Lieutenant Dawson identified the dreaded black-scorpion warships spread out in a half-circle formation, their position five clicks away. Frantically, she raised the alarm to Jackson, who was in his quarters. "Captain, we have three Blader ships accompanying us and they're within striking distance."

Jackson sensed the panic in Dawson's voice and sprang into action. "Raise the shields to full capacity and sound the 'battle stations' alarm. We're on Red Alert! I'm on my way."

"Aye, aye Captain," replied Dawson.

Jackson donned his Captain's cap, placing it squarely on his head with the peak sitting low over his eyes. He grabbed the belt with his pistols and charged down the passageway to the Bridge.

Within seconds a heavy metallic alarm resonated over the intercom and the lighting throughout the craft changed to a red hue as the crew scrambled hastily to the call. A loud simulated voice was heard over the PA system, *'This is not a drill. Mount battle stations. This is not a drill.'*

There was ordered chaos aboard the craft as the troops scurried in all directions like ants on the warpath. They had undertaken several practice drills over the last five days and were prepared despite the apparent confusion under pressure.

On the Bridge and seated in the Captain's chair, Jackson took control. "Lieutenant Dawson, cut the Alert tone but maintain the Red Alert protocol."

"Aye, Captain."

"Stoltz, open the intercom. I want to address the crew."

"Go ahead Captain."

"Attention troops, this is your Captain. We have three Blader ships surrounding the *Jolly Roger*, all within striking distance. Hopefully they have responded to my invitation to join forces with us. But they outnumber and outgun us. Hold your positions and *do not* attempt to fire on them unless I give the word. Otherwise we could be annihilated. Over and out for now."

All the crew on board the *Jolly Roger* were apprehensive because the ruthless reputation of the Bladers was well known. The inhabitants of the planet Treldar were traditionally a race of warmongers and barbarians, who preyed on other planets for food and armaments, commandeering their spacecraft, enslaving alien males and mating forcibly with alien females. They were heartless marauders having no regard for others' lives. The two-hundred-year Grekadian War had divided the Treldarians into two factions, both factions fighting against the Tzuracians. There was an organised army of disciplined Treldarian soldiers and a lawless militia of freedom fighters who used guerrilla warfare tactics.

The Treldarian armed forces were eventually defeated by the Sentinels' unique strength and agility and the tribes who remained on Treldar were forced to change their ways and carve out a meagre living from farming and bartering their produce and handicrafts among the scattered nomadic tribes. Reluctantly, they accepted life under Tzuracian protection.

But the lawless Treldarian rebels, who swore never to accept Tzuracian rule, deserted their planet and continued with their savage ways, finding sanctuary on uninhabited or uncharted planets and shifting their base camps regularly to avoid capture. They became ruthless pirates known as 'Bladers', their deadly reputation with the short sword and dagger spreading fear throughout the galaxies.

They made their livelihood from selling stolen cargo plundered from unsuspecting traders who travelled unescorted through space. The Bladers' main objective was to procure supplies of Xytrinium to power their crafts and laser weapons or sell to the highest bidder. Black-market business clients who harboured the Bladers paid handsomely for their Xytrinium caches and their slaves.

Over the decades the Bladers had tried unsuccessfully to mate with captured female Sentinels in an effort to gain the unique qualities for their own offspring. They had also continued searching, in vain, for the lost formula which could alter their DNA to match that of the Sentinels. The frustrated Bladers continued to menace the Federation hoping that one day they would be in a position to overpower them.

The crew of the *Jolly Roger*, including Jackson, realised they were now facing a life and death situation. Stoltz shut off the intercom and turned to Jackson for further orders. Jackson was staring at the main screen, his eyes fixed on the three menacing Blader ships which were well camouflaged against the dark space void.

"Lieutenant Dawson, reduce speed and bring us to a standstill. Sergeant Stoltz, switch on the Interpreter and let me speak to them."

"Okay, JB you're live on all Treldarian frequencies."

Jackson spoke calmly. "Welcome Bladers. This is Captain Jackson Jensen of the *Jolly Roger*. Thank you for responding to my invitation. I'd like to speak with your Commander to discuss a treaty of alliance."

The main screen flickered and a close-up of an alien face replaced the visuals of the Blader ships. The face was like nothing Jackson had encountered before; pitted, copper-coloured skin, sunken almond eyes, flat nose and oily, jet-black hair pulled tightly into a short ponytail. The alien's full black beard was neatly trimmed around the jaw exposing three lined scars etched deeply into each cheek.

"No need for the interpreter device, I understand your primitive language." The gravelly voice sounded loud and threatening. "I am General Dranz, Commander of the Fifth Legion of Bladers. What do you want before I decide your fate?"

Jackson was both fearful of, and fascinated by, the strange alien image that spoke with such authority and superiority. He was momentarily speechless.

"JB, he wants an answer *now*!" Stoltz called out frantically to Jackson to act immediately before the aliens fired on their vessel.

Jackson suddenly snapped into focus, projecting a calm façade which camouflaged his anxiety. Realizing his life and the lives of his crew were at stake he responded in a slow, controlled voice. "I believe you and I have the same objectives and we could both benefit immensely by joining forces. But, I would rather discuss this in a more personal setting than exchange words by screen. You never know who might be listening out there."

Commander Dranz raised a hand to his chin and ran his fingers slowly through his thick black beard. His suspicious eyes were fixed on Jackson, contemplating whether to accept Jackson's invitation or obliterate the *Jolly Roger*. Dranz knew the name Jensen and the MERIC mining company that drilled for the valuable resource Xytrinium. *Perhaps this alliance might work to our advantage?* Dranz thought to himself. Without flinching, he spoke again. "I will send a small craft to bring you and another of your choosing to my ship for further discussion."

The screen flickered momentarily before returning to the scene showing the three surrounding Blader ships. Then a small illuminated object, the Bladers' shuttle, could be seen leaving the lead ship.

"Lieutenant Dawson, make preparations for their craft to land in the Launch Bay and then take command of the Bridge. Lower the shields only while the Bladers' shuttle is berthing and departing. Stoltz, you come with me."

"Aye, aye Captain."

As Jackson and Stoltz strapped on their pistols, Jackson turned to CT. "CT, I need two wrist communicators."

"Here you go JB," said CT, handing him the items. "But, you know you're taking a huge risk going there unescorted into a den of murdering cutthroats."

"Thanks CT, I appreciate your concern, but I have something they need, and besides, it adds a little excitement to the journey, don't you think?" Jackson, was trying to be light-hearted. "CT, tell Evans to send down an armed escort of half-a-dozen soldiers to greet our guests in the Launch Bay. Remind them to behave themselves and not to fire under any circumstances. This is a delicate situation so we need to tread very carefully. Our lives hang in the balance."

"Understood, JB."

Dawson called to Jackson, "Captain, the Bladers' shuttle is entering the Launch Bay."

"Come on Stoltz, we don't want to antagonize them by keeping them waiting."

"Aye, Captain."

Arriving at the Launch Bay, Jackson saw his seven men lined up at attention in front of the compact alien shuttle but there were no Bladers in sight. Evans saluted as Jackson passed by on his way to mount the steps that had been lowered from the opened hatch and Jackson returned the salute. As soon as Jackson and Stoltz entered the unmanned craft, the hatch door closed behind them and the craft sped off on remote, returning to the Bladers' mother ship.

As the hatch door of the shuttle opened in the landing bay of the alien craft, Jackson and Stoltz were confronted by ten fearsome Bladers aiming guns in their direction. The Bladers all looked alike. They averaged more than six feet in height with a solid muscular build and were clothed in well-worn, leather battle-jackets and tight-fitting, leather pants tucked into knee-high boots. Underneath their jackets they wore blood-red shirts with round collars embossed with strange metallic symbols. All were armed with two short swords strapped in an X-formation across their back, a long dagger sheathed on one side of their waist and a laser pistol hanging from the other.

With raised hands in a surrender position, Jackson and Stoltz stepped slowly down the stair-cased gangplank towards them. As they reached the base of the stairs, one of the Bladers, who wore a yellow sash around his waist, blurted out something in his native tongue. Two of his soldiers responded by breaking rank and charging at Jackson and Stoltz, brutally wrenching at the visitors' belt straps and confiscating their holstered weapons.

"Yes, greetings and welcome to you also," remarked Jackson sarcastically, turning his head to Stoltz and raising an eyebrow. Stoltz nodded in silent agreement, disgusted by the uncivilized reception. *Ugly barbarians,* he thought.

Gesturing with his raised arm the alien with the yellow sash commanded in guttural broken English, "You follow; I take to General Dranz!"

The two visitors were marched off in formation through a dimly-lit passageway flanked by the armed welcoming party who exuded a pungent, alien body odour. They were escorted through a dull, metal-grey, skeletal hull, devoid of colour and fixtures. The noise of their heavy footsteps reverberated through the empty, uninviting structure until they were halted by the raised arm of the yellow-sashed Blader.

"You wait," he ordered as he strode through the doorway where they had stopped. The other members of the escort surrounded Jackson and Stoltz with their laser pistols still targeted on the two guests.

The Blader leader soon reappeared. "Go!" He gestured with his pointed arm for the Terranians to enter the room.

The large room appeared to be an 'Operations Command' facility. The walls were covered in glowing holographic images of star systems, maps with trajectory lines, and strange symbols similar to patterns of mathematical equations used on Earth. Embedded into the round table in the centre of the room were fluorescent holographic pictures of unknown planets pinpointed with small white lights over their surfaces.

"Greetings, Captain Jackson Jensen." It was the guttural voice of an imposing Blader seated on one of the chairs at the table. "I am General Dranz. You say you have something of mutual interest to discuss? I hope you're not wasting my time. Sit down and tell me what it is you think may interest me."

As he took a seat, Jackson could not help but notice that the General had an even larger and more solid physique than the other Bladers. He wore similar uniformed leathers, the exception being that the sleeves of his battle jacket had dark red bands on the cuffs with matching braiding on each of his epaulettes. He also wore a wide, dark-red sash around his waist. These distinctive features obviously identified his superior rank.

Dranz turned to the yellow-sashed Blader and gave an order, "Ramlok! Bring a jug of fermented fruit wine for our Terranian guests."

"Yes General." The Blader saluted by raising a clenched fist across his chest and beating it down hard on his heart. He snapped his heels to attention and briskly marched off.

"Greetings, General Dranz," Jackson responded. "This is Sergeant Stoltz, my second in command." Stoltz nodded in respect. "Thank you for inviting us aboard your ship. Yes, I *do* have some things of great interest to you and to me which would work to benefit both our races."

Jackson was interrupted by the return of Ramlok carrying a tray holding several brass goblets and a black, glazed, ceramic jug, which he placed on the table within reach of both leaders. After pouring the liquid into three goblets and returning the jug to the tray, Ramlok retreated silently behind the General.

Dranz leaned back in his chair taking a sip from the goblet while staring intently into Jackson's eyes with a look of arrogance. "Go on Captain, enlighten me," he prompted.

"I know you want to get your hands on as much Xytrinium as you can. When I reclaim my company MERIC back on Earth, I can supply this resource to you without you having to use unnecessary force or risk damage to your ships or casualties to your army. But to do this, I need your alliance to fight off the Sentinels and eradicate them permanently. Something we both want."

Dranz was indignant. "You think your small band of misfits is going to make a difference to what we Bladers have been trying to do for centuries?" Jackson was offended by the reference to his crew as a band of misfits. But before he could retaliate, the General continued. "Yes, Jackson we know all about your daring prison escape with your fifty inmates from Terra Upsilon as you call it. But I was curious to know what you had to trade. Now I know you have very little, I think I'll dispose of you and your prisoners and take that ship of yours."

Stoltz was not one to give up without a fight. He rose to his feet with clenched teeth and fists, ready for action, his adrenalin running high. At the same time, Ramlok drew his laser pistol and pointed it directly at Stoltz's head.

"Sit down Stoltz!" ordered Jackson with a raised voice, quickly intervening before any shots were fired. The Sergeant reluctantly obeyed.

"There's one other thing you may be interested in before you decide our fate General."

The General gave a sceptical response, "Surprise me Earthling."

Jackson drew a deep breath. "Would you be willing to join forces if I could give you the means to equal the odds against the Sentinels' strength and enhanced powers, as well as their longevity?"

The General's eyes lit up with renewed interest. "And how do you propose to do that Captain when *we* have been trying for centuries to achieve this?"

"I know where the lost formula is located and the type of equipment needed to infuse the Xytrinium into DNA," said Jackson confidently.

"You can't know this," sneered the General. "The formula was destroyed during the Grekadian wars, along with the only Tzuracian alchemists who knew the secret. You're stalling for time to save your worthless lives."

"No, General Dranz," said Jackson, trying to maintain credibility. "I have a Sentinel ally who told me *exactly* where it's hidden on Tzurac and how to find the place."

Stoltz was totally astounded by Jackson's response, also assuming it was a lie. Like the Blader General, he too believed Jackson was delaying the inevitable.

"Besides," said Jackson feeling more confident, "what have you got to lose if you think this is all fiction? But, think of what you and your soldiers have to gain if I'm right?"

Now Dranz was inquisitive. "Alright Jackson, suppose you *are* telling the truth. How do you propose to obtain this formula when Tzurac is so heavily guarded?"

"By stealth and cunning and *not* by the brute force on which *you* Bladers pride yourself. My crew are not a bunch of misfits as you would foolishly believe, but selected specialists experienced in combat, explosives, communications and war tactics; a match for any of *your* soldiers. With our combined efforts, I propose to work out a more detailed plan using the most up-to-date geological maps of Tzurac, Tzuracian flight paths and time schedules, the type of security they have and the current locations of their troops. To do this we need a safe retreat. Hanging here in space is not my idea of a sanctuary. Once we have the formula, we'll need laboratory facilities to process the Xytrinium." Jackson reclined confidently in his chair, waiting patiently for the General's response.

Dranz paused for a moment before replying. "I'll say one thing in your favour, Jackson Jensen, you have a bold attitude under threat of death and I like that in a leader. You have a deal."

Jackson offered an outstretched hand to shake on the deal, "Thank you General. What's your next move?"

"Put your hand away, Captain, we don't use primitive Terranian gestures in our culture. Our word is our bond, even amongst rebels, and we celebrate a treaty with a drink." He raised his goblet and Jackson and Stoltz did the same, sealing the agreement by taking a gulp of the strange, bitter-tasting, dark liquid.

One mouthful and the General slammed his goblet back down on the table. "You return to your vessel and I'll send you the coordinates to our sanctuary. Ramlok! Escort our new friends to the shuttle. See you and the *Jolly Roger* at our base camp, Captain Jackson Jensen."

Ramlok saluted the General, turned to face the two guests and gave a short sharp order, "You follow, Terranians!"

As they left the room, Jackson and Stoltz were again surrounded by the escort of beastly Bladers and marched off. And it was only when they were safely back on board the *Jolly Roger* that Stoltz burst out in a heavy Austrian accent, "What have you got us into Jackson? Tell me your plan and it had better be convincing. Ya?"

TREASURE HUNTING

TRAVELLING at hyperspeed for several days, the *Jolly Roger* reached a small star cluster known as the Erémos System. According to the ship's log the star system comprised a number of planets surrounded by asteroid belts and constant electrical storms. It was mapped as wasteland twenty light years from Earth and considered off-limits to all vessels following reports of spacecrafts being destroyed after entering the zone.

Adhering to the navigation instructions transmitted by General Dranz and weaving carefully through the debris of asteroids at cruise speed, the *Jolly Roger* arrived in orbit of the planet Steiros, the Bladers' hideout. The visuals on the data screens said it all. Before them was a dustbowl landscape of ochre, desert sand dunes dotted with windswept sculptured pillars of rust-coloured rock. In the hazy distance, and barely visible, were outcrops of lofty, rugged mountain ranges. The dust in the atmosphere painted the sky with a pale burnt-orange hue. Computer readings showed the surface temperature as fifty degrees centigrade, no signs of vegetation and moisture density only thirty percent. The planet was barely habitable even with breathing apparatus.

While Jackson was gazing at the main screen wondering what other surprises were to come, a voice on the Comms snapped him back.

"Captain! Flight Lieutenant Dawson here. We've just been snared by a traction beam. I have no control of the ship's steering and we're being pulled towards the entrance of a large cave ahead of us."

"Thank you Dawson. Reduce power and let them beam us in."

"Aye, aye Captain."

Jackson leaned back in his Captain's chair and waved his hand over the intercom panel on one of the arm rests. "This is your Captain speaking. We are now guests of our alien allies. Do *not* do anything to provoke them. Bladers have very short tempers: It takes little to upset them and they react violently. Treat them with respect and be tolerant of their abruptness. We need their help to achieve our mission and you may even learn something from them. I repeat, do not anger them or you'll suffer the consequences. Captain, out."

Within minutes the traction beam had pulled the *Jolly Roger* into the depths of the huge cavern, landing the craft amongst other ships housed in the structure resembling a giant hangar. Behind them, two large sliding metal doors slid noisily across the entrance, sealing all within and cutting off the poisonous atmosphere outside.

"This is your Captain, again," said Jackson's broadcast to the crew before disembarking. "I want you all to leave your weapons on board for the time being to show we're friendly. We'll be here for a few weeks while organising a plan of attack on the planet Tzurac to extract the Xytrinium formula from the ruins where it's buried. So learn what you can about this race, their weaponry, their fighting skills and language, and perhaps about their other safe havens. Keep alert but stay on good terms. Remember, you were chosen from all the other prisoners on Terra Upsilon to be with me in this vital mission. I have confidence and faith in you and I expect your loyalty to me as your leader. Now, let's go."

As they filed through the vessel's hatch, Jackson and his crew were met by a small group of Bladers led by Ramlok, wearing his yellow sash.

"I Ramlok. Earthlings follow," he ordered, motioning with a raised hand the direction in which they were to move.

Entering through another set of metal doors which closed behind them, Jackson and his crew were herded through a gently-sloping, dark tunnel, the walls sealed with molten rock and lit by faint-blue, incandescent lights, evenly spaced at intervals above head height. The tunnel soon opened up into a well-lit, formally-structured, round hall. The high ceiling was criss-crossed with thick wooden rafters from which hung a variety of different armaments. The hall was filled with about twenty solid, rough-hewn, wooden tables each surrounded by a collection of crudely-fashioned wooden chairs. Wooden cabinets with shelving containing an assortment of metal canisters, clay pots and bowls lined the walls.

"Halt!" shouted Ramlok raising his arm and pointing at the tables. "Sit. Wait."

Jackson and his men took their places around the tables, each inspecting their rudimentary surroundings, wondering what to expect next. Ramlok's troops stood at the ready while Ramlok disappeared through another doorway into a tunnel at the far end of the hall. Shortly, he reappeared in the doorway behind General Dranz who was taking slow, broad strides towards Jackson. Reaching the table, Dranz wrenched back one of the wooden chairs. Eyeing Jackson intensely, he sat himself down, his weight causing the chair to protest with a loud, painful creak.

"I see you can follow a map," Dranz said bluntly in his deep, gruff voice.

"Of course," replied Jackson with a parched throat. He didn't know whether it was from the dry, dusty environment in the room or fear of the unknown. He was sitting with his unarmed men face to face with a cutthroat marauder and surrounded by armed Bladers. Without weapons, they were vulnerable and at the mercy of their host.

Without warning, the General slammed his tightly clenched fist down on the table. Those seated jumped with fright, the silence hanging in the atmosphere. "Bring the fermented brew Ramlok!" he yelled with a smile. "We need to seal our union again and have everyone celebrate our allegiance to destroy the Federation."

As Ramlok ordered two of the Bladers to fetch drinking goblets and jugs of brew, Jackson breathed a quiet sigh of relief while forcing a smile of friendliness. His men did likewise. While waiting for their wine, General Dranz began to explain things, waving his arms about to demonstrate as he spoke.

"This primitive sanctuary you see before you wasn't built by us. It belonged to the barbaric tribe who inhabit this planet underground. We found this place by accident when one of our ships crash-landed here and, because the savages rejected our offer to join us, we enslaved them. My soldiers now use this hall as a meal room or mess hall in your language."

Typical, thought Jackson. *The Bladers haven't changed their brutal habits. They would just as much kill you as shake your hand. But we have no choice. Right now, the Bladers have what we need; a safe haven, shelter, food, military strength and armaments, a place to formulate plans and work on the infusion method for Xytrinium.*

The refreshments arrived by way of two Bladers and a team of petite female servants, obviously from the indigenous tribe. They all had a primitive, natural beauty, their face devoid of any emotion, with dark, bewildering eyes, a pale, anaemic complexion, and long, coarse, dark-brown hair cascading past their shoulders. They walked timidly around the tables with bowed heads, quietly filling everyone's goblets. And, after placing a jug on each table, they silently slipped away.

While toasting to their alliance and draining their goblets of wine, Dranz told Jackson his troops of Bladers had constructed laboratories on Steiros. The laboratories were used for processing Xytrinium fuel to power their vessels and recharge their weapons' power-packs.

"Captain Jackson, once we secure the DNA infusion formula my alchemists can assist you to build the instruments with which to administer this precious elixir biologically into our soldiers. We have ample supplies of Xytrinium here and, if we run out, I know where to get more."

"Thank you General; this is *just* what I need," said Jackson. "But we need to work out a plan on the best way to extract the buried treasure from Tzurac, preferably undetected. Can you retrieve the information about Tzuracian security we spoke of earlier?"

"Yes Captain, I can readily supply you with this. We've been studying our enemies for a very long time. But first, I need to show you and your men where your sleeping quarters are. You need to prepare yourselves for tonight's celebration feast and then we'll get down to business."

Jackson looked curious, prompting the General to ask, "You have a problem with this Captain Jackson?"

"Not a problem, more of a question. I'm curious to know not only how you can throw a feast, but also how you survive on a desert planet like this with only thirty percent moisture content in the atmosphere and the dust pollution so thick nothing would grow."

"The planet is very deceptive on the surface, Captain. But underground reservoirs are continuously replenished by slow water-seepage through the sandstone rock. It supplies fresh, filtered drinking water and irrigation to crops harvested by the savages. An ideal retreat wouldn't you say?"

Jackson was impressed. "Perfect to harbour an army and keep them satisfied."

"Precisely. Now let's get all of you bunked in. Ramlok!" yelled Dranz. "See my guests to their quarters and tell them when to return for the festivities."

"Yes General," responded Ramlok, standing briskly to attention with another salute. "Terranians, you follow!"

Jackson and his troops were led deeper into a maze of dank, moss-covered tunnels. On each side of the tunnel were small cavities or rooms marginally bigger than the prison cells back on Terra Upsilon. The rooms had been carved out of the sandstone and the cavity walls sealed with clay and painted roughly with red ochre in an attempt to prevent the growth of mould and lichen. This did not inhibit the stale smell of stagnation.

The rooms had Spartan furnishings: a wooden-framed slatted bed, a small side table with clay wash bowl and water jug and a bench fixed on the opposite wall to store items such as satchels and clothes. After years in small cells, Jackson's soldiers were faced again with basic confined quarters, barely sufficient in which to sleep. They hoped the rest of their time would be spent in more congenial areas of this underground maze.

Jackson's men had been allocated two to a room and, as the only female member of the crew, Flight-Lieutenant Dawson readily volunteered to bunk in with Jackson, a suggestion he was quick to accept.

***

Judging by some of the clever constructions they found over the following days, Jackson and his men realized that the native inhabitants showed signs of reasonable intelligence. To capture the sunlight they had installed large, thick, glass windows on the surface which acted as skylights, channelling light and heat through shafts strategically placed around the complex. Large mirrors were installed to redirect this sunlight into the living and sleeping quarters. In their crop growing areas, huge glass plates created an ideal 'hothouse' and sealed clay aqueducts from the reservoirs channelled water for irrigation. In other areas, hot water was also delivered by this method with the thermo-ducts containing water placed just underneath the surface of the glass plates. Large communal thermal baths had also been constructed and these brought welcome relief to Jackson's crew who often bathed in the company of the petite slave women.

While Jackson worked steadily on his plan, his crew were kept occupied training with the Bladers in readiness for battle and both sides began to learn each other's styles of martial arts and combat techniques. His men were introduced to the Treldarian dialect as well as the Bladers' strange cuisine. The food was peculiar in looks, colour and taste but an improvement on the prison slop they had endured whilst incarcerated. Jackson's soldiers also began to enjoy 'closer' relationships with some of the enslaved women.

Jackson and General Dranz acknowledged the alliance had been successful for both races, but the General was growing impatient with Jackson's progress. He was not one to sit around.

"I have given you everything you asked for Captain Jackson. When will you be finished with this plan of yours?"

"I've almost finished General, but there's some discrepancy between your topographical maps and the information I have about where the ancient city of Kharmar is buried. We need to be certain of the exact location so we can be in and out of there swiftly. We also need more detailed and more current information about the security surrounding Tzurac. I worry that some of what you already have isn't up-to-date. I need to know where fortified garrisons are located, weapons installations are placed and airfields established. Otherwise we'll be going in blind and we won't be coming out."

Dranz sat silently with his face buried in his hands, thinking deeply. After several moments he raised his head, focusing his glazed eyes into Jackson's. His speech was slow and serious. "I thought you had everything you needed Jackson. I suspect you're stalling for time."

Jackson shook his head, defensively, "No General, I want this as much as you."

There was a moment of stony silence before Dranz responded, "Well, the only way to get this information is to capture another Tzuracian vessel and interrogate its computers. Are you and your men courageous enough to join a war party?" He was testing Jackson's motives.

Jackson's answer surprised him. "Lead the way, General. My men will enjoy the adventure and relish the break from this giant mud hut."

Dranz was not only relieved, but also keen for action. "Then it's settled Captain Jackson. I'll have my soldiers locate the closest Tzuracian vessel. Inform your troops to prepare for the hunt."

As the General rose to his feet, Jackson headed out the door to find his crew. Reaching the Mess Hall, he sighted CT thumbing through some schematics of a Bladers' spacecraft manual.

"Hey JB, what's happening?" said CT, looking up from his research.

"Round up the men, CT. We've been invited to go with a Blader hunting party to capture a Tzuracian vessel. Tell the men to meet here immediately."

"What about Kharmar?"

"There's been a change of plan, CT. We need more up-to-date information on Tzurac security and there's only one way to get it."

"Okay JB, I'm on it."

By the time CT rounded up the crew, the Mess Hall was filled with Bladers and the General was about to address the gathering. Dranz cleared his throat and commenced broadcasting in his native tongue.

"Troops, we're going hunting to capture a Tzuracian vessel so we can gain access to their computers. Do not attempt to destroy the vessel. We'll be bringing it back with us." A Blader standing next to Dranz interpreted the words, relaying Dranz's message to Jackson and his crew above the noise of the cheering and jeering Bladers.

The General continued his speech. "I want you to capture the on-board crew alive. Interrogate them and then, once we're finished with them, you can have your fun." There were raucous cheers amongst the marauders as they repeatedly clashed their sword blades together and thrust their hand-held weapons towards the ceiling with outstretched arms. "We'll be navigating towards the Sideros-Hudor System where we have identified a sole Tzuracian vessel ten light years from here. Take three ships as we may encounter other Tzuracian vessels on the way. Right!" Finally, Dranz shouted, "The Battle cry, Death to the Federation!"

His followers repeatedly echoed the loud cry, "Death to the Federation! Death to the Federation!"

"Captain Jackson, you and your soldiers come with me in my vessel. Bladers, board your ships!" Dranz ordered.

There was a mad dash to the hangar in the mouth of the cave, leaving Jackson unnerved by the exhilaration shown by the Bladers. *They're just after blood,* he thought. *Is this alliance with the Treldarians going to work?*

NEGOTIATION

KHANEERA and Yarron had been travelling for just over a week to their destination of Terra Iota and Khaneera was now familiar with the flight controls of the Destroyer, routinely sitting alongside Yarron at the console. Their relationship had become more intimate and Yarron wished they could just keep on travelling to somewhere safe, away from Tzurac and the Security Forces. But Khaneera was on a mission and nothing would interfere with her plans, no matter how strongly she felt about her new-found love. Khaneera's determination was stronger than her devotion, her hate greater than her love. Until her thirst for deep-seated revenge had been quenched, her emotions would remain divided.

While seated in their pilot seats on the Bridge with Yarron instructing Khaneera in weapons operations, they were suddenly alerted by a signal from the Comms. *'Warning, warning, three unknown vessels have entered the Sideros-Hudor System, bearing north-west at a distance of one thousand miles on a trajectory towards this craft.'*

Without hesitation Yarron gave the first command. He wasn't taking any chances in being unprepared. "Computer, raise shields to one hundred percent and fix laser cannons on target."

Adrenalin rushed through Khaneera's veins. "Do you think they're Federation ships which have located our trail?"

"Unlikely, Khaneera." Yarron seemed confident about this. "They couldn't have caught up so fast given our vessel's hyperspeed. This is the fastest Destroyer battleship in the fleet and it's operating at full capacity. It would be impossible unless these ships were already scouting in the area and the Federation alerted them to our escape. But our computer didn't detect any alien vessels in this quadrant when we entered it."

"So, what do we do now?"

"Wait to see who they are, and what they want. At the speed they're moving, outrunning them is not an option. We might have to negotiate with them or fight our way out of this."

Another computer alert came over the Comms. *'Corporal Blandhar, the three vessels are Treldarian, travelling at hyperspeed and will be within striking range in five minutes.'*

Yarron and Khaneera exchanged glances. They shared the same frightening thought, *Was this better or worse than pursuit by the Federation?*

"Hold steady computer," Yarron instructed, "and switch on the Interpreter."

On the main screen Yarron and Khaneera watched the vessels rapidly approaching. The screen flickered. Then, a full-screen image of a Blader's face appeared and the alien began to speak Treldarian in a deep guttural tone.

"Ahoy crew of the Tzuracian spacecraft. I am General Dranz, Commander of the Fifth Legion of Bladers. If you want to live, I suggest you surrender. You are outnumbered and outgunned and you cannot outrun our ships. What is your answer?"

Khaneera looked at Yarron and smiled. She had been prepared for this, knowing the stolen Xytrinium formula and instrument blue prints would be their salvation. "Patch me into their frequency Yarron and let me talk to them. We have bargaining power."

Yarron waved his hand across the controls. "Okay Khaneera, go ahead."

On board the Bladers' vessel, Khaneera's face flashed onto the screen in full view of Jackson. Jackson's heart raced and he had to restrain himself from speaking out. It was obvious to Dranz that Jackson recognised this Sentinel.

"General Dranz, this is Sentinel Khaneera Penzark, daughter of Khane Zarkwin, a fugitive from Tzurac. We accept your offer to surrender our ship on the condition you let us live and do not go back on your word. I have something you'll find extremely beneficial in your cause against the Federation as well as inside knowledge of the Sentinels and their movements. Are you interested, General?"

Dranz raised his eyebrows in acknowledgement before muting the sound and turning to Jackson, who was out of screen vision. "Well, Captain Jackson, can we trust her?"

Jackson spoke in a rush. "What an amazing coincidence, General. This is the Sentinel I was telling you about earlier; the one who informed me about the location of the Xytrinium formula on Tzurac. I would trust her with my life. With her knowledge and experience she would be a great asset to have on our side. She has proven to me on several occasions she wants to eradicate the Sentinels and destroy the Federation. Why don't you invite her on board and interrogate her yourself to see what she has to offer?"

Dranz swung back to the screen and unmuted the sound. "Alright, Sentinel Penzark, you have my attention and a truce to discuss what you're offering. Cut your thrusters. We'll send a small craft to collect you and bring you aboard my ship. But, be warned, if you are lying, your lives will be at risk."

"I'll be waiting," said Khaneera defiantly. "Penzark, out."

Khaneera shut down the screen and turned to Yarron. "I want you to stay here in readiness, just in case they decide to double-cross us and take me hostage. I won't give them the blueprints of the formula just yet, not while they have the advantage and I still have the bargaining power. Hide the crystal memory rod in case they storm our vessel."

"As you command, Khaneera," said Yarron, leaning over and kissing her farewell. They embraced the moment and, as their lips parted, Yarron whispered, "Be very careful and don't trust anyone, Khaneera. Just come back to me safely."

She nodded. "I will Yarron, but you stay vigilant."

The Bladers' unmanned shuttle arrived within minutes and Khaneera calmly boarded the vessel. She felt quietly confident as she travelled alone to meet the General. Despite his intimidating appearance, she showed no fear.

When the hatch door on Dranz's ship opened Khaneera was greeted by an escort party of six burly Bladers led by Ramlok.

"Surrender weapons, Sentinel!" demanded the Blader with the yellow sash.

Khaneera placed her hand on the blade-staff tucked into her belt before responding to the order with a tone of authority and a stony look. "You may have my pistol Blader, but not my staff. Any attempt to remove it and none of you will live to tell the tale. I don't think your General would be too pleased if any harm came to me."

"Alright. Give me pistol!" Ramlok demanded.

Khaneera slowly unholstered her pistol and held it out in front of her, dangling it loosely by the handle. Snatching the pistol from Khaneera's hand, Ramlok waved his arm, commanding her to join the escort. Surrounded by Bladers she was marched off to where the General was now seated in a small conference room.

As she entered the room and saw Jackson standing next to the General, Khaneera's severe expression turned immediately to a broad smile. *Things are getting better by the minute!*

"Jackson, what a pleasant surprise!" she said, ignoring the General and addressing her ex-accomplice. "I can't believe I've found you so easily. It was your escape from Terra Upsilon that instigated *my* escape from Tzurac. I hoped to join up with you and finish what we started five years ago. I was on my way to Terra Iota thinking you would most likely be heading there with your crew."

Jackson's pleasure was obvious too. "Khaneera, I'm glad you made it. And you're right; I was heading to Terra Iota until I encountered the Bladers. It was my intention to break you out of your imprisonment after my soldiers and the Bladers joined forces to infiltrate Tzurac."

Jackson turned to Dranz and Stoltz to introduce his former ally. "General Dranz, I would like you to meet Khaneera Penzark, and Khaneera, this is Sergeant Stoltz, my Second-in-Command."

Stoltz nodded politely while the General slammed his fist hard on the table, speaking loudly in his raucous voice. "Well, now the niceties are over and you've joined our tea party, what do you have to offer, Sentinel Khaneera Penzark, daughter of Khane Zarkwin? Your father's name is well known among our people and respected for his conspiracy against the Federation. But why should I trust you?"

Khaneera was both surprised and honoured to hear her father's name and reputation spoken of positively. It was something she was unaccustomed to on Tzurac and, in the company of those who admired her father, she was proud to be following in his footsteps. "I have the key to destroy the Sentinels of Tzurac and the Federation by using their own biological protection against them."

Dranz didn't seem surprised at what she'd said. "And how do you propose to do that, Sentinel Khaneera?" he enquired somewhat sarcastically, his steely eyes still fixed on hers.

Khaneera played her trump card. "By infusing Xytrinium into the DNA of Bladers and making Bladers just as powerful as Sentinels, with a four-hundred-year lifespan."

Dranz was still unmoved. "Sorry to disappoint you Sentinel, but Captain Jackson has already devised a plan to visit the city of Kharmar under cover, find the buried city and recover the secret formula. All we need is to interrogate your ship's computer to determine Tzurac's security and the exact location of the buried city. In fact, this is why your vessel came under attack." He stared at Khaneera, menacingly. "So what *else* do you have to offer that may save your life and convince me of your loyalty?"

"That plan will never work," said Khaneera defensively. "Don't you think we Tzuracians haven't already tried to do this over the centuries with all the modern technology and equipment we have at our disposal. You would take another century to try to find the buried treasure and, even then, there are no guarantees."

Dranz turned to Jackson, tilting his head slightly to question him. "I thought you said she'd be able to help us with our plans?"

Embarrassed and exposed, Jackson stammered. "Well, ah, the last thing she told me was that she knew where it was."

Visibly peeved by all this, the General shrugged his shoulders and raised his outstretched arms in an open gesture. "Well, what *now* Captain Jackson?"

"Wait," interjected Khaneera, playing the wildcard. "No need to interrogate my computer and go treasure hunting. The thing is, I already have the Xytrinium infusion formula and the blueprints needed to build the equipment for infusion. It's a long story, but let's say our Tzuracian scientists have been working on it."

Jackson's jaw dropped in surprise and relief and the General's demeanour changed immediately to a glimmer of eagerness. He leaned towards Khaneera. "You have? Well, where are they?" he demanded.

"They are with my partner, Sentinel Corporal Blandhar, on board my vessel," Khaneera said, laying all her cards on the table. "But he has instructions from me to destroy the craft and everything in it if I don't return safely." She realised Jackson had joined forces with the Bladers and this was her way forward. "I want to team up with you General. We both have the same goals as my father; to destroy the Federation and anyone who stands in our way. If we work together we can do this."

As the General paused to consider her proposal, the large screen on the wall suddenly activated and Yarron's distressed face appeared.

"Yarron, what is it?" Khaneera called out, surprised by the unexpected intrusion.

There was urgency in Yarron's voice. "Khaneera, I have just intercepted a transmission from Tzurac Command. Six Destroyer battle ships have been sent to hunt for us. They know we have the stolen formula. Two of the ships from Terra Major are heading deeper into the Sideros-Hudor system and will be here soon. We need to move fast if we intend losing them."

"I'll return to the ship now, Yarron. Out." Khaneera immediately turned on her heel to address Dranz. "Well General, are you with me?"

Dranz chuckled at Khaneera's brashness. "I admire your courage Sentinel. Together, we'll certainly be a power to reckon with. Return to your ship. I will transmit the co-ordinates of our sanctuary. We'll meet you there. It's a dangerous trek through asteroid belts so adhere closely to the charted path and use your manual controls."

Dranz turned to Jackson. "Jackson, you can catch up with your Sentinel friend back at base." Slamming his tightly-clenched fist on the table, he called out, "Let's move it!" and Jackson and his men were quick to fall into line.

***

Khaneera returned to the Destroyer keen to tell Yarron what had happened. "The Bladers have agreed to work with us, Yarron, and are sending us the coordinates for their sanctuary. As soon as the coordinates come through, we're out of here."

Yarron was surprised by Khaneera's quick decision to join forces with the cutthroat Bladers. He had never envisaged working with these rebels who were despised by all in the Universe. And Yarron was more unsettled when he learned that Jackson Jensen was on-board the Bladers' ship and in league with them too.

With the Federation Destroyer battleships bearing down hard upon them, Yarron had no choice but to lock in the coordinates and follow Khaneera's lead – they had to make their escape. But things were happening all too quickly and, with no control of the situation that had been forced upon him, for an instant Yarron thought, *What have I got myself into?*

***

Having successfully evaded the Tzuracian battleships, Khaneera and Yarron arrived a week later at the Erémos System and carefully navigated their way through the treacherous, rocky obstacle course to Planet Steiros. The large console screen presented a stark picture of desolation. The space around their ship was spattered with asteroids and a graveyard of mangled spacecrafts that had collided with these huge fragments of scattered rock. The General had warned them about the danger of being hit by shifting debris. *'Keep your shields up and steer through the maze using manual controls'* were the last words from Dranz that echoed in Yarron's mind.

Yarron was relieved when a traction beam began to draw their ship into a huge cavernous hangar to land them safely at the Bladers' sanctuary. After disembarking, Yarron and Khaneera were guided by Ramlok and his band of burly Bladers down dimly-lit passageways to their temporary Spartan accommodation.

Yarron was pleased they had escaped the Federation Security Forces and the Bladers hadn't taken their lives. But he was surprised at how willingly Khaneera handed over the valuable crystal memory rod to their former arch enemies. He had taken such risks with his life to steal the information and now Khaneera was sharing it freely. *But was there a choice?*

The Bladers' alchemists immediately began processing Xytrinium while their technicians busied themselves making the instruments needed to infuse the powerful crystalline substance. Jackson and

Dranz were impatient for completion of both projects but they had other pressing issues to keep them occupied. In Dranz's makeshift office the General, together with Jackson and Khaneera, were hatching a plan of attack.

Yarron found himself excluded from these talks and largely ignored by all those he met on Steiros, leaving him unnoticed as the silent partner of Khaneera. Khaneera was the main attraction and Yarron was both disgusted and jealous when Jackson's men turned their attention from the petite female servants to the alluring Khaneera and began lusting after her. His protective instincts were ignited.

When five of Jackson's sex-starved soldiers ganged up on Khaneera in one of the isolated tunnels leading to the science laboratories, Yarron realised Khaneera didn't really need his protection. Her assailants came off second best. They were no match for the elite Sentinel, two of them ending up in comas and the other three sustaining serious injuries. It was a lesson not only for Jackson's soldiers, but also for Yarron. Khaneera was as deadly and self-sufficient as she was beautiful.

COUNTER MEASURES

IT had been almost three weeks since Kyron first informed Ehrane Dakhar about Jackson's escape and his Captain had now arrived on Terra Major, Earth, bringing with him from Tzurac five hundred Sentinel reinforcements. In the ASPECT hangar where the warship docked, Kyron greeted his visitor with the traditional Sentinel salute and a warm hug of friendship.

"Ehrane my friend," said Kyron, "it's good to see you again, even under these circumstances. Let me escort you and the troops to the Citadel where we can catch up on what's been happening."

Dakhar shook his head to decline the offer. There was urgency in his manner. "No Kyron, thank you for your kind invitation, but plans have just changed and I can't spare the time. You already know of Jackson's escape from Terra Upsilon but I have just heard more bad news. Khaneera Penzark has escaped from Tzurac and I have been ordered to Terra Iota."

Kyron showed disbelief. "Khaneera? Surely that's not possible. I thought she was being held in high security and guarded day and night?"

"Yes, she was Kyron," said Dakhar apologetically, "but she escaped with the help of the Sentinel who had been guarding her for the last two years. The young, naïve Sentinel must have fallen under her spell. And that's only half the bad news. She also persuaded this young Sentinel to steal the new formula and blueprints for Xytrinium infusion, something our scientists had been working on in top secret for the last five years."

Kyron could not believe what he was hearing. "What, a new formula? Are you serious? So now we have to defend ourselves against *two* extremely dangerous forces; the madman Jackson who has the means to destroy Earth and the cold-hearted Khaneera who has the formula to destroy the Sentinels and the Federation. How did this happen, Captain?"

Dakhar shook his head as if to say 'who knows'. "It doesn't matter how it happened Kyron. The thing is they've been gone for more than a week. The Senators fear that if enemies of the Federation get hold of the formula, another war might erupt, with Tzurac as well as Earth, fighting for survival against armies of super-soldiers."

Dakhar could see Kyron realised the gravity of the situation. "They've been ordered to stop Khaneera and her accomplice at all costs and we have dispatched four more warships from Tzurac and two from Earth. Those in the quadrants already searching for Jackson have been alerted to Khaneera's escape, and their directive changed to 'search and destroy'. I must leave immediately."

"I'll come with you Ehrane," Kyron offered.

Again Dakhar shook his head to decline the offer. "I appreciate your loyalty my friend, but you must remain here in case Jackson or Khaneera make it to Earth. You need to be here to protect your planet, the reserves of Xytrinium and your family. I'll ask for more reinforcements from Tzurac and the Senate will be requesting military support from other planets in the Federation. I'll stay in close communication, but I must go. May the spirits of the Ancients protect you and your family."

Dakhar reached out his arm to Kyron in the Sentinels' seal of friendship, "To the Regiment!"

"To the Regiment!" mimicked Kyron, with the Sentinel salute.

Kyron stood downhearted as Dakhar about-turned and marched back towards his vessel. He didn't move as the ship departed, waiting until the small, bright light disappeared in the sky. His mind was racing with the thought of both Khaneera and Jackson coming back for their revenge. At the same time, he was devising a plan of action.

***

Back in his penthouse at the MERIC Building Kyron called to Miss Blake to join him in his office with her compu-pad. "Lauren, please sit down and make yourself comfortable."

"Thank you Kyron. You look somewhat perplexed. Is there something wrong?"

"Yes, unfortunately there is."

Kyron quickly relayed the latest news to Lauren who reacted by cradling her face in the palms of her hands muttering, "This *is* serious, Kyron."

"Exactly, Lauren. That's why we need to act urgently. Here's what I want you to do."

Lauren re-focused and readied herself to take notes.

"Contact your father at ASPECT under 'Highly Confidential'. Although he's already increased security following the previous warning about Jackson, the General needs to re-assess the DEFCON level. We could be dealing not only with an almost indestructible warship with stealth capabilities piloted by Jackson, but also with a rebel Tzuracian battleship. He needs to be alert to any UFOs entering our space zone. Ask him if he needs assistance from the Sentinels.

"Organise a staff meeting in the Main Hall for this afternoon. MERIC will be suspending all operations and vacating the building until further notice. The staff will be put on leave with full pay. Also, organise to double the Security in the MERIC Building as well as the warehouse where the reserves of Xytrinium are stored. We can use Sentinels from the Battalion to double reinforcements. I'll be contacting the Barracks myself to arrange the security there. And arrange a flight for me to the Assembly."

After taking notes in quick succession, Lauren nodded confirmation to Kyron, before adding, "Have you told Torri yet?"

"I'll do that as soon as we're finished, Lauren. And thank you for your concern, it's much appreciated."

As Lauren left the room, closing the door behind her, Kyron pressed the intercom to Torri's office.

"Are you calling me to have lunch?" responded Torri, enthusiastically.

"Not exactly Torri. But if you meet me in my office, I'll order room service."

Torri was excited by the idea. They had never had an intimate lunch together in Samuel Jackson's penthouse office.

"What a splendid idea. When would you like me to be there?"

"Right now would be a good time," Kyron insisted.

"But it's only eleven-thirty, darling?"

"Yeah, I know, but I thought I would allow some extra time for us."

"I'll blank out my diary for the next two hours and I'll see you very soon. Bye my love."

Five minutes later Torri strolled into Kyron's office flashing a broad smile.

"Sweetheart, what took you so long?" said Kyron, moving from his office chair to the leather couch. "Come on in."

"Those internal transporters are so slow," Torri replied instantly. They both laughed, knowing Torri's office was now on the same floor, just down the passageway. They hadn't joked like that since everything had been put on high alert in response to Jackson's escape and it provided temporary relief from the tension in the MERIC Building. "So, my love, what would you like me to do first?"

Kyron spoke in a soft seductive voice while patting the leather cushion on the couch beside him. "Well, you could start by gently closing the door and changing the windows to a darker shade, then coming over here and sitting close to me."

"Ooh, this is getting rather interesting." Torri started to tingle all over as she strolled seductively towards Kyron, slowly peeling off her corporate blazer. For a mother of two, she still had a slender, shapely figure. Sitting down close to Kyron on the couch, she leaned across and gave him a lingering kiss. For the moment, they were immersed in their romantic intimacy.

As their lips finally parted, Kyron whispered into Torri's ear, "I have something very important to tell you which I couldn't say over the intercom."

Just as he finished, the intercom suddenly sprang to life, jolting the two bolt-upright and, instantly killing the mood.

"Kyron, is everything alright?" It was Miss Blake's amplified voice.

"Yes, Lauren," said Kyron, speaking loudly, out of shock. "I was just having a quiet conversation with my wife."

"Sorry for the disturbance, Kyron. I just wanted to let you know the meeting in the Main Hall is scheduled for 14:00 hours this afternoon."

"That's alright Lauren, thank you for the update. But while I have you, could you please send in some gourmet club sandwiches and a pot of herbal tea for two?"

"Yes Kyron, right away."

Kyron turned to resume his conversation with Torri. "Sorry my love, I should have told Lauren not to disturb us. And I was *so* much enjoying the moment. Oh yes, where were we?"

"You were about to tell me something important," said Torri still sitting up straight and using her hands to tidy her shiny, dark red hair which she still kept long. She looked very smart in her corporate, charcoal-grey trousers and black blouse, secured at the neckline with the transcorder star brooch Captain Dakhar had given her. Sitting together on the couch in their corporate attire, Kyron and Torri almost looked like matching book-ends.

"Yes, I was." But before Kyron could continue, he was interrupted again by a timid knock on the office door.

"Come in," Kyron called out abruptly.

The door opened and in walked Miss Blake with a sterling silver tray carrying an antique teapot and two Royal Doulton china cups. "Sorry to disturb you Kyron, your sandwiches are on the way. But here's your herbal tea," she said, setting the tray down gently in the middle of the large marble coffee table and making a discreet exit.

"Thank you Lauren," said Kyron as Miss Blake walked to the door. She turned her head with a smile of acknowledgement as she closed the door, the faint scent of her jasmine perfume lingering in the room.

"Well darling, you sure know how to show a girl a good time," Torri said, tongue-in-cheek, in her very British accent.

"Would you like me to treat you to a nice cup of tea?" Kyron teased.

Torri nodded while Kyron poured the brew into the two china cups from Samuel Jensen's personal collection. Samuel Jensen had been a man of taste who appreciated quality and refinement, features Kyron admired. Setting down the cup and saucer in front of Torri, he leant back on the comfortable leather couch sipping his tea and began telling Torri the serious news he had just received.

"I've been speaking with Ehrane this morning after he arrived from Tzurac. He didn't have time to see you and the children as plans have suddenly changed and he had to leave immediately for Terra Iota. Torri I need to tell you his mission was not only to find Jackson, but also to find and stop Khaneera Penzark who escaped from prison just over a week ago."

Torri almost choked on her mouthful of tea. "Khaneera has escaped?" she spluttered. "The bitch that almost killed you?"

Kyron had expected Torri to be concerned, but he was thrown by her uncharacteristic language. "Yes Torri, and to make matters worse, and this is highly confidential, she has escaped in a Tzuracian warship and has the formula for Xytrinium infusion. Apparently, the Tzuracian scientists had it almost ready for use."

Torri tried to come to terms with Kyron's shocking news, taking several quick sips of her tea. She was clearly agitated. "Khaneera has a warship? And she has a formula for infusion as well? This just keeps getting better. Do you think she'll be coming here to get her revenge? Will she be coming for you?"

Now Kyron showed grave concern. "I'm not taking *any* chances this time, Torri. I want you to stay at my mother's place with the children until this is all over, no matter how long it takes. The last time Jackson kidnapped you, I feared for your life. I won't endanger your life again or the children's with these two maniacs on the loose."

Kyron reached over and touched Torri's shoulder, gently. "Ehrane has ordered me to stay here and protect you and the children as well as guard the Company and its Xytrinium reserves. He's brought reinforcements from Tzurac. All projects are to be suspended until further notice. I'll be addressing the staff later this afternoon to let them know they are being sent home for their own safety and I'll be flying to Washington tomorrow to address the Assembly."

Torri nodded understandingly, acknowledging her husband's responsibilities not only as CEO and Tzuracian Ambassador, but also as a concerned father. "I hate the thought of leaving you alone to face the music, Kyron, but I guess it has to be done. I'll leave tonight and will wait for your calls to keep me up-to-date."

"Alright darling, but we'll use our encrypted communicators. I don't want either Jackson or Khaneera to know the whereabouts of you or the children."

"I understand. I'll miss you so much." Torri leant over to Kyron and they locked in a long embrace. No words were needed to express their deep feelings for each other.

***

After a restless night's sleep in the Company's penthouse apartment, Kyron took his flight in the Company transporter to Washington. By 10.00 hours he was standing on the podium in his maroon Sentinel uniform addressing members of the Assembly.

"Senators and distinguished members of the Assembly, thank you for attending this meeting at such short notice. You won't have heard the latest and most serious news. Khaneera Penzark, the treacherous Sentinel who conspired with Jackson Jensen, has escaped from her prison on Tzurac and we don't know her whereabouts or her intentions. The Tzuracian Senate has requested additional vessels to scour the universe for both fugitives."

There were gasps of surprise around the room.

"Here on Earth I have alerted General Blake at ASPECT and advised him to increase security, suggesting the ore transporters cease operations until further notice. Sentinel security at the MERIC Building has been increased and the regular staff sent home. Now we face threats from two ruthless enemies."

The now-agitated members started to talk loudly amongst themselves. One of the Senators called out, "And what is the Federation of Planets doing about protecting Earth, seeing they're the ones who offered their protection when Earth signed the treaty?"

This provoked other members to call out. A second member protested, "Yes, where are *they* when we need them. Where is *their* army of Sentinels?"

Yet another raised his voice, "We wouldn't have had this problem if we hadn't joined the Federation!"

The room became loud, filled with mixed emotions of fear and anger, until the Senior Senator slammed his hammer down several times calling for order. The noise died down as Kyron, disgusted by the members' ungratefulness, continued with professional diplomacy.

"Members of the Assembly, Captain Dakhar arrived yesterday

morning with a battalion of Sentinel reinforcements. He had to leave immediately for Terra Iota but is mobilising his ships to assist us. I would like to remind you if it wasn't for the help of the Sentinels, and their invitation to join their Federation of Planets, Earth would have been in the control of Jackson Jensen already, and Jackson would have made an evil dictator. The world would have been in chaos with wars everywhere, famine and hunger in most countries, toxic pollution and none of the advanced technology we have today. We owe a deep debt of gratitude to the Tzuracians for saving our planet and improving our quality of life."

Silence reigned over the crowded room, the members reluctantly nodding their heads in agreement. Kyron was right. The benefits of being allies with the friendly Tzuracians far outweighed the alternative. Terranians had gained much for what the extra-terrestrials had requested in return.

Kyron continued. "I suggest you call out your military forces, place them on high alert, and mobilise them in strategic positions in case either Jackson or Khaneera attempt to attack Earth. I'll keep you informed of any developments but communications between myself, as the Tzuracian Ambassador, the Assembly, and your military leaders should be through encrypted dialogue only. Are there any questions?"

The Members of the Assembly were shocked by the magnitude of the threat to Earth and began chattering feverishly amongst themselves, discussing strategies and making hurried arrangements with their government leaders via their communicators. When the Senior Senator slammed his hammer down several times to announce adjournment of the meeting, it went largely unnoticed. The meeting had already dissolved.

BATTLE PREPARATIONS

KHANEERA and Yarron had been in the Bladers' sanctuary on Planet Steiros for a few weeks. After a short delay caused by a minor explosion in one of the laboratories, the processing of Xytrinium for a serum was almost complete. The instruments for administering the infusion were also almost ready, the Bladers' technicians having improvised in the manufacture of some of the complex parts. These modifications to the instruments meant the infusion process would take longer than originally planned, using manual injections rather than automation.

CT had been asked to assist in helping speed up the process and had found himself in his element. While working in the laboratory he had become very fond of one of the female Blader technicians, spending more time in the laboratory than warranted. Despite their physical differences, their shared interest in technology fuelled their attraction. Other members of Jackson's crew had satisfied their lust with the female slaves, keeping them preoccupied save for a couple of isolated jealous altercations with Bladers over the attention of particular women.

Yarron had noticed Khaneera spending more and more time with Jackson since their arrival. He had known all along she admired Jackson, assuming their relationship was based solely on their mutual desire to dispose of Kyron Shield. But now Yarron sensed – even when he was making love to Khaneera – her thoughts were elsewhere. It was clear Khaneera secretly had very strong feelings for Jackson.

***

As the project neared completion, the three leaders, Dranz, Jackson and Khaneera, gathered in the Command Room to finalise strategies for their assault on Terra Iota and Earth. Khaneera had discarded her Sentinel uniform and was wearing a black outfit similar to Jackson's, a leather combat uniform with matching jacket and pants which she found on board the Terranian warship, the *Jolly Roger*. The uniform fitted like a glove and accentuated her shapely figure. Over this she wore her Sentinel shield-cape in reverse with the maroon side displayed on the outside and dark blue on the inside. With her hair cut short and dyed jet black, the new look Khaneera was not only more stunning and intimidating but also less recognisable as a Sentinel.

"I need to tell you something," said Dranz, addressing Jackson and Khaneera. "As we need the numbers, I've taken the liberty to send out invitations to the tribes on some of the other planets in the Grekadian Domain who are sympathetic to our cause. I've informed them we possess the formula for Xytrinium infusion. I've guaranteed those who join our rebellion will be infused with it, giving them the attributes of a Sentinel, thereby equalising the odds."

Khaneera was quick to air her disapproval. "You did what?" She hadn't anticipated the infusion process would be spread so widely. "How can we trust them? You realise, General, you may have opened old wounds which could start another two hundred year war or worse."

The General turned to Khaneera with an evil glint in his eye. Chuckling loudly, he began wringing his hands with enthusiasm. "They hate the Federation and the Sentinels as much as we do. So, they're with us. And if a war follows, which may well happen, my dear, I'll rejoice to see other races having to defend themselves against these new super soldiers. For wars create havoc, chaos and panic, which causes confusion; confusion creates opportunity; and opportunity leads to power for those who are victorious. And *we* will be the victors this time."

While Khaneera considered Dranz's strategy, Jackson focused on how it might impact his own ambitions. He didn't mind if Dranz invoked a full-scale war between other races, but he wanted Earth and the Xytrinium reserves for himself. Now he had not only the Bladers, but also other tribes to try and bargain with. *I'll have to convince them Tzurac is the planet to conquer, leaving planet Earth to me.*

Raising a clenched fist, the General spoke again, this time with anger and hate. "And maybe it's not such a bad thing. For nearly a thousand years the Tzuracians have lorded over the other planets with their Federation rules, inhabiting our planets with their Sentinel patrols, living off our produce and giving us little of their Xytrinium to support our advancement. The races on these planets have had to serve two masters, their own governments and the Tzuracians. The Federation even prohibited us from using Xytrinium in our weapons. The time has come to take back our freedom and independence, to reclaim what rightfully belongs to us. And the more numbers we have, the better chance we stand of successfully defeating the Federation. Chaos is needed to restore the balance."

Khaneera was persuaded and nodded her support, while Jackson stepped in with a plan of his own. "General, may I express my thoughts on a plan of attack?"

"By all means Captain, we're all open to ideas," said Dranz.

"Well, I propose a two-pronged attack. I suggest the Bladers, with your armada of rebels from the other planets, attack Terra Iota and take control of the mines. This will draw fortifications away from Earth and leave Earth vulnerable. While this is happening, I'll take Khaneera and my soldiers to Earth and, by stealth, kill off Kyron Shield and take over the MERIC Building with its Xytrinium reserves. I can hold Earth to ransom, threatening to destroy the planet or have it invaded by your Blader armada. Then, together, we will have control of both planets and the supply of Xytrinium."

Dranz looked somewhat sceptical and after some thought responded, "And what about the Tzuracian fleet? How do you intend warding them off?"

Jackson had already considered this and replied quickly. "While *en route* here we eavesdropped on the communications being sent from Tzurac to Earth. The Tzuracians have dispersed six of their warships—four from Tzurac and two from Earth—into the other quadrants of the Universe, looking for us. They already have the rest of their fleet scattered in other galaxies. By the time they receive word of the attack on Terra Iota and redirect their forces there, you will have taken the colony and have your rebel warships in place surrounding the planet in readiness for their arrival. You can ambush them as they arrive, wiping out their fleet. This will leave the planet Tzurac vulnerable to attack from us in a second phase."

Khaneera joined in. "Jackson's right. Yarron and I also heard on our ship the communications directing Tzuracian warships to the outer regions in the hunt for us. I'm confident Jackson's plan will work. There'll be too much at stake for the Tzuracians to defend their planet at full strength, at least not while your rebel army has complete control of Terra Iota and Earth is under threat."

Dranz listened intently, silently working through the moves as if playing out a game of chess in his head. He rubbed his bearded chin with his right hand while combing the fingers of his left hand through his head of thick, coarse, black hair. After a lengthy pause, he grabbed the goblet of fruit wine from the table and, raising it, gave his confirmation. "I'll toast to that battle plan, Jackson."

With that, the other two did likewise and all three skulled a mouthful in unison. Jackson was relieved the General had accepted his plan so readily.

Khaneera continued. "General, you said you had sent out invitations to other Grekadian planets to join us. How do you know those communications have not been intercepted by the Tzuracians or Terranians? Could our enemies know about this and be planning to intercept and strike at the other rebels travelling to your base camp?"

"Good to see how alert you are, Khaneera," replied Dranz. "You needn't worry though. The message was only directed to Kyronis and Diunon and only in the old cryptic code used by our allies during the Two Hundred Year War. Even if the Tzuracians intercepted the transmissions, they'd be unable to decipher them. I've instructed the Kyroni and Diunons to rendezvous in ten days' time in the Northern Quadrant of the Hiera Domain on the deserted Planet Agorra. I didn't want them to know my sanctuary was here on Planet Steiros.

"Our enemies won't venture there to look for us as Agorra is an unstable volcanic planet with constant eruptions and molten lava spewing from its mountains. The atmosphere is unbreathable, containing poisonous sulphur gases. It's ideal to hide our spacecrafts.

In some areas where the volcanic activity has died down, large caverns now lead to underground labyrinths formed by the hardening of the molten lava. The structures are strong enough to withstand thermal ground movements and the underground environment hasn't been contaminated by sulphur gases. Breathing apparatus isn't needed while underground. This place is where the rebels gathered in the Grekadian wars and this is where our allies will be infused in preparation for our assault. History has a way of repeating itself, but not always with the same outcome."

General Dranz grinned with evil anticipation.

***

That night when Khaneera told Yarron of the plan of attack and explained that a cryptic-coded invitation to join the Bladers had been sent to other planets in the Grekadian Domain, Yarron was immediately ill at ease. As Khaneera explained these allies too would be infused with Xytrinium, Yarron became more uncomfortable. He hid his thoughts from Khaneera as she continued, but secretly he was wracked by feelings of anxiety and guilt, his mind pressured with myriad thoughts. By the time she had finished, he was confronted with a horrible realization which caused a sick feeling in his stomach.

What have I done? What have I unleashed? Khaneera has deceived me. Her intentions all along have been to join forces with Jackson and the rebels and destroy the Federation. The spirits of the Ancients will never forgive me. I have betrayed my own people and jeopardized their lives for my own selfish wants.

Yarron had naively believed that once Khaneera's revenge was satisfied by the elimination of Kyron Shield, he and Khaneera would be free to enjoy each other's company. He now realised, too late, that in the simple act of stealing the infusion formula as Khaneera's bargaining chip, he had potentially destroyed peace within the entire Universe, torn apart the fabric of stability and shifted the balance of power into the wrong hands. If the formula worked on races other than Sentinels, thousands of innocent lives would be killed in a new inter-planetary war and the blood of innocents would stain his hands for the rest of his life. He would be the instigator of history repeating itself.

Yarron was now in a complete quandary. He thought he loved Khaneera, but his emotions conflicted with his guilt-ridden conscience. When Khaneera suggested rather bluntly it was high time Yarron too discarded his Sentinel uniform and dressed in black like Jackson, he couldn't tell whether she wanted him to be disguised for his own protection or whether she had forsaken the Sentinel identity and him completely. Reluctantly, and with much regret, he cut off his long fair plait, dyed his hair dark and donned the colour black.

***

Soon after this meeting, the infusion commenced. The first to undergo the process were the Bladers, five hundred of them, including Dranz. Jackson cunningly let the Bladers be the guinea pigs, while he and his men offered to join the queue in a couple of days. He was keen to observe whether there were any unanticipated ill-effects on the Bladers, before subjecting himself and his army to the process.

In fact the only reactions following infusion seemed positive. The Bladers' energy levels increased. They appeared even more confident, walking with gusto. To test their strength they started to have playful fights amongst themselves, easily lifting their opponents with two arms above their heads and throwing them some distance, only to have them land on the ground without injury, as if immune to harm. Arm wrestling and running races continued for two days. When pitted against Jackson's hardened criminals, the Bladers were easy winners, having acquired four times the strength and agility. Jackson's men couldn't wait to be infused and were eager with anticipation. And, Jackson realised if they didn't follow suit quickly, his own army were vulnerable to turncoat Bladers.

The morning of the first day after his own infusion, Jackson woke feeling different, if not strange. His head felt clearer and more focused and he seemed to have an abundance of energy. He rolled over in bed to face the sleeping Lieutenant Dawson, who was now his companion.

Sensing Jackson was staring at her, Dawson opened her eyes. "Good morning lover," she said seductively. "How are you feeling this morning?"

"I'm feeling great," he replied, "slightly unbalanced, but I feel terrific. How are *you* feeling Pam?"

"Same as normal," she said. "But *you're* looking younger JB. You're eyes are sparkling."

"Yeh, this Xytrinium certainly packs a punch," Jackson replied with a grin.

Jackson rose from the bed and sauntered over to the small, shabby, circular mirror hanging on the wall above the rudimentary basin. Although the reflected sunlight wasn't the best, he could see his image in the dusty mirror. He wiped a thin film from the surface with the side of his hand and, looking back at him, was a man at least ten years younger.

"You should've tried this stuff, Pam," he said enthusiastically. "It makes one feel, ah…" – he was searching for the appropriate words – "invincible, young, fresh, alive. It's like discovering the fountain of youth."

Pam was more cautious. "I'll see if you look and feel this way in a month's time, Jackson, and then I'll reconsider."

Jackson laughed. "Okay, but you *really* don't know what you're missing."

The benefits of the infusion continued to emerge over the next few days. At first, Jackson could feel the strength surging through his veins to every muscle in his anatomy. He likened it to the description given by body builders and gym jockeys on steroids. The sensation of the power pulsating through his entire body was indescribable.

The effects were more exciting when Jackson's hearing became so sensitive that even the rustling of the sheets on his bed sounded like a fire crackling or the tyres of a vehicle slowly rolling over a gravel road. The normal volume of talking was amplified threefold and his eyesight was sharper, allowing him to see better in the dark than if wearing infra-red lenses. And Jackson's crew of motley misfits all enjoyed the same positive effects of the infusion. All was going to plan.

The next stage of their battle strategy was to meet up with their rebel allies, the Kyroni and Diunons, and share with them the benefits of Xytrinium infusion. Four days later General Dranz decided it was time to leave Steiros for Agorra in the Hiera Domain. It would take a week, travelling at hyperspeed, to reach the planned rendezvous.

There was a flurry of activity as Dranz ordered everyone to prepare their vessels, check their weapons and stock up on supplies of food and ammunition. In a final briefing Dranz gave instructions to communicate only in cryptic code, to be alert for Federation patrols and not engage them.

The doors to the cavernous hangar opened and, one by one, the craft – three Blader ships, the *Jolly Roger* and the battleship piloted by Yarron and Khaneera – accelerated into space.

WARRING TRIBES

AS the Tzuracian convict and Sentinel deserter sped towards the Hiera Domain star system, following the Bladers' warships at hyperspeed, Yarron was anxious about what was to unfold. The voyage to Planet Agorra allowed him time to think seriously about the dilemma he was in. His conscience played on him continually, and he wondered if what he had done could ever be undone.

He struggled to understand Khaneera's true feelings and motives. It looked increasingly as if she would toss aside their plans for a future together and, disregarding Dawson, take up with Jackson. He had been prepared for Khaneera to take her revenge on Kyron Shield, but he hadn't planned to be involved in a full-scale war which would destroy thousands of innocent lives.

After struggling with his thoughts and feelings, he made his decision. He must contact Captain Dakhar before it was too late, forewarning him of the planned attacks by an enhanced army. But he had to find the right opportunity to make his move—betraying the rebels, and Khaneera, would put his life in immediate danger. While on the ship with Khaneera, he would bide his time, blocking his thought patterns from her probing mind. Then, on Agorra, he would take a chance and risk sending a secret holographic message.

***

Soon after the three Blader ships, the *Jolly Roger* and the battleship piloted by Yarron and Khaneera entered Agorra's orbit, the tribes from

Diunon and Kyronis also rendezvoused. There was tension on all sides as the different armies assembled on the isolated volcanic planet. They were apprehensive not only about meeting each other for the first time since the Grekadian Wars, but also about what they were intending to embark on together.

As the Kyroni stepped from their shuttles onto the planet Agorra, they looked as fierce as ever – bare-chested, tattooed warriors, with brown, leathery skin, armed with deadly weapons. Their heads were shaved smooth revealing pointed ears, leaving only a long plaited ponytail of thick hair stemming from the back of their crown. The only other visible facial hair was their thick eyebrows which shaded slanted, dark eyes. Their trousers made of dark-brown leather tucked into their above-knee leather boots. A broad leather sash worn diagonally across their bare chests sheathed a wide-bladed scimitar on one hip and, strapped to their other hip, was a long-barrelled pistol. Some Kyroni carried whips tied to their belts, while others had small two-bladed tomahawks strapped to their backs.

A warlike race, the Kyroni had fought fiercely against the Tzuracians in the Grekadian Wars, and remained strongly opposed to the Federation Peace Treaty. But they had decided to bide their time and use for their survival the Xytrinium rationed out to them by the Federation in exchange for Kyronis' metal ores. At the same time, they maintained a military presence and secretly made weapons and warships with some of the Xytrinium to increase the strength of their military might.

The Kyroni military had needed no persuasion to join forces with the Bladers, particularly when offered Xytrinium DNA infusion and the chance to fight on equal terms with the Sentinels. They seized the opportunity for their planet to break free from the Federation and share equally in the bounty of Xytrinium, as well as to test what their new physical enhancements would give them. The Kyroni had feasted and celebrated for two days before flying three ships with two thousand soldiers to the Hiera Domain.

When the Diunons emerged from their crafts, they looked distinctly different in appearance. They were strange creatures, much smaller in build, with reddish scaly skin, red beady eyes and rusty-coloured hair, reflecting their ferrous (iron) molecular structure. Their round ears were pinned tightly against their heads and their noses wide and flattened. When two massive, mechanical monsters emerged behind them, escorting the devilish Diunons onto Agorran soil, Dranz and the others were stunned and amazed. The Diunons had brought not only themselves, but also an army of robots.

Like the Kyroni, the Diunon armies too had welcomed the opportunity to join forces with the Bladers against the Federation. They had been waiting for this for a very long time. In the Grekadian Wars they had suffered losses and humiliation due to their limited technology and firepower. Although Diunon soldiers were proficient in hand-to-hand combat, their weapons and warships were inferior to those of the Tzuracians and other races. They had reluctantly signed the agreement with Tzurac to receive Xytrinium in exchange for iron ore and zinc, which their planet had in abundance, tolerating the rule of the Federation. But they vowed to seek revenge when the time was right.

Undertaking never again to be beaten in battle because of inferior weapons, they had embarked on a mission to develop advanced equipment and machines, using Xytrinium illegally to build and power them. They built a large army of mechanical soldiers known as 'Diutrons' based on cybernetic blueprints stolen from the Tzuracians. Standing eight feet tall and constructed of Xytrinium and iron with built-in pulse cannons, Diutrons were controlled by radio-wave remote from an orbiting ship or a soldier on the ground. War crafts had also been built from stolen schematics. Although their legions of super robots had yet to be tested in battle, the Diunons now considered themselves to be a mean force and the time had come for them to show their superiority and might. They too had been keen to join the Rebellion and be infused with Xytrinium, sending three warships to Planet Agorra with a thousand soldiers and three thousand Diutrons.

As the masses assembled in one of the huge caverns in the underground volcanic labyrinth, Dranz, Khaneera and Jackson were impressed with what they saw. To communicate in their different tongues, the tribes had inserted interpreter transceivers into their ears and Dranz chose his words carefully as he introduced them. Emphasising their mutual goal of destroying the Sentinels and the

Federation and then sharing in the Xytrinium bounty, General Dranz wasted no time, ordering the infusion process to commence immediately.

***

On the second day, while Khaneera and the others were preoccupied overseeing the infusions, Yarron discreetly slipped away to search for a safe place to send his vital holographic transmission to Captain Dakhar. Checking nervously to avoid detection at every turn in the maze of passages leading deeper into the bowels of the planet, Yarron finally found an isolated, unlit tunnel. He was uncomfortable from the sweat being secreted under his tight-fitting clothing, not knowing whether it was caused by the heat generated from being trapped in the claustrophobic volcanic rock cavities or the fear of being caught for treason. He knew what the bloodthirsty rebels would do to him if they caught him.

Aware that time was limited, Yarron illuminated the small space with his staff light, then activated his pledge ring. Within minutes of the broadcast Captain Dakhar, who was on his way to Terra Iota, received the unexpected holographic transmission. The hazed image he received showed a figure dressed in black with short-cropped, dark hair who spoke in a hushed and hurried voice.

"Captain Dakhar, you won't recognize me, but I'm Corporal Yarron Blandhar, the fugitive you've been hunting. I have my mother's Science Academy security bracelet to prove it."

As soon as Yarron revealed the bracelet he stopped abruptly and peered around cautiously, checking the dark space around him before proceeding. When he spoke again, it was almost in a whisper, and Dakhar had to strain to hear the words.

"I don't have much time to talk, so you need to listen and pay close attention. Khaneera Penzark and I are with Jackson Jensen and the rebel Bladers on Planet Agorra in the Hiera Domain. The Bladers, as well as Jackson and his men, along with Kyroni and Diunon allies have all been infused with Xytrinium and the Diunons have amassed an army of three thousand cyber-robots called Diutrons. They're planning a two-pronged attack in a week's time; Jackson and his escapees will be coming to Earth with Khaneera, a day after the other rebels attack Planet Terra Iota. They hope their attack on the outpost at Terra Iota will attract all the Tzuracian forces there, leaving Earth and Tzurac vulnerable."

Yarron paused for a moment before finishing, "I've made a huge mistake Captain Dakhar – I'm with an army of ruthless rebels who plan to bring the Federation down. This message to you is the only way I can hope to make amends. But there's no time – I must go before I'm exposed. Out."

Dakhar was astonished. But before he could question Yarron, the image quickly faded and Dakhar was left in a quandary. His thoughts raced. Was this really the fugitive Yarron Blandhar? If so, was the Corporal telling the truth? Or was this part of a deceptive plan to divert resources away from Tzurac? After all, Corporal Blandhar had deserted, taking with him a highly dangerous prisoner and Tzurac's top-level secret. How could he be trusted? Was it possible that so many races had been infused with the new formula in such a short space of time? And that Jackson had amassed such an army of rebels?

Although Dakhar hesitated momentarily, his gut feeling said to trust the informant. Dakhar couldn't afford to ignore the possibility of an attack on Iota and Earth and there was no time to lose. He had to put counter plans in place and use this inside information to his strategic advantage. *Our enemies must continue to believe they are primed for a surprise attack on the Federation, if they are to be thwarted by a surprise defence not only on Terra Iota but also on Earth. And, from now on, the Sentinels must use one-to-one communication using their pledge rings and encrypt all open communications.*

First Dakhar contacted Lieutenant Montark, recently promoted from Sergeant on the basis of his length of service and his experience as a leader in field battles. Montark was now in charge of Strategic Operations in the Citadel at Khazor. Dakhar's image appeared without warning from Montark's pledge ring while Montark was seated at his console in the Operations Room.

"Lieutenant Montark, I've just received a holographic transmission from the fugitive Corporal Yarron Blandhar." Montark's eyes lit up in surprise as Dakhar described the planned two-pronged attack. But Dakhar gave Montark no opportunity to question or to comment. He had a series of orders to give and time was of the essence.

"Montark, I need you to approach the Senate on my behalf. The situation is critical as the Diunons and Kyroni have joined forces with the Bladers. The rebels have strength not only in numbers, but also in physical powers. They've all been infused with Xytrinium. Reckless as it might be, if the infusion works, we need urgent assistance.

"Have the Senate recall all our vessels in the field and direct them towards Planet Terra Iota and Earth, assuming there will be attacks on both. But maintain several vessels and battalions on Tzurac, just in case it's a trap. Activate Tzurac's force-field immediately.

"Request they send an emissary to the planet Urgellan to ask Queen Zamira Tarune for help. We have less than a week to increase our armies in readiness for a rebel attack by super soldiers. Ask that each of the two hundred Urgellan clans sends volunteers. We'd like at least five thousand warriors. And, to battle the rebels on equal terms, we're going to have to take a risk and request the warriors of the clans of the Urgellans are also infused with Xytrinium. Among our allies, they are the closest genetically and if the infusion is to work effectively, they are our best bet. Remind them, if the Federation falls, the Bladers will most certainly invade other unprotected planets, including Urgellan.

"Ask the Senate also to authorize an emissary to the planet Armonus. We won't ask the peace-loving Armonusians to fight the enemy, but they may be able to support us with their superior psychic powers and medical technology. We need them ready.

"Let the Senate know of the restrictions on communication. It is imperative that we keep knowledge of the rebels' planned attack a secret, so the rebels don't change their strategy. This is the only way we will have the advantage of surprising them with an enhanced defence if and when they attack Terra Iota and Terra Major, Earth. Keep everything confidential and speak only to those who need to know. Do I make myself clear Lieutenant?"

"Yes Sir, perfectly clear, Sir."

"I'll holograph Cadet Shield on Terra Major so he can prepare for a surprise visit by Jackson and Khaneera while I return with one of our warships to Earth to strengthen our battalion there. Inform the Senate I'll also contact Lieutenant Kal Zawkon, who is in charge of the

Planet Iota battalion, to arrange their defences. That's all. But, keep me informed by holograph of the outcomes of the negotiations with Urgellan and Armonus. Over and out." Dakhar saluted as his image started to fade.

Dakhar immediately contacted Lieutenant Zawkon on his sister warship heading to Planet Iota, charging him with the responsibility of arranging the defences there. "I'm heading back to Terra Major to assist Ambassador Kyron Shield in preparing a defence there. But I've arranged for other warships to be deployed to support you on Terra Iota. I hope they reach you before the rebel armada arrives. When you get to Iota, have Engineer Grant Thompson work with you on your battle strategy. Do not use the normal Comms. If you need to contact me, use your ring. Are we all clear Lieutenant?"

"Yes, Captain, all clear Sir."

Closing their communication with salutes, the holographic images faded and while Zawkon's craft continued at hyperspeed for Terra Iota, Dakhar's craft veered in a south-westerly direction towards Terra Major, Earth.

***

Kyron was in his office when he received an incoming holograph.

"Hello Kyron my friend," said Ehrane. "I have vital information which needs to be acted upon immediately."

Kyron sat upright in his chair. "You have my full attention Ehrane."

"I've alerted the Senate on Tzurac and all the other Sentinels in the field. Arrangements are being made as I speak to combat a possible imminent attack."

Kyron listened intently as Dakhar explained. His eyes widened and his heart beat faster when told that Jackson and Khaneera had joined forces and intended to return to Earth, Jackson and his soldiers now infused with Xytrinium. Kyron's mind churned at the thought of defending himself and Earth against the two adversaries he'd previously fought and put behind bars, supposedly for life. Now, attacking together with a super army, they potentially had the ability to defeat him and take over Earth.

His thoughts were interrupted by Dakhar's sharp tone. "Don't worry Kyron; I'll be with you before this dynamic duo arrives. My ship had only travelled halfway to Planet Terra Iota when I received the information and we've already changed course. Lieutenant Zawkon has been contacted to organise defences on Terra Iota. You need to instruct General Blake to have his warships readied and alert the Assembly in person. No Comms. Only inform those who need to know and have them maintain discretion. Can you do this Kyron?"

Kyron saluted. "Yes, Ehrane, I'll attend to it immediately."

"Very good, and keep Torri and the children safe. Out." Dakhar's image faded within seconds.

Kyron's mind was still racing as he leaned forward to speak into the intercom. "Lauren? I need you to arrange a flight for me to attend the World Assembly this afternoon. And contact your father. I need to speak with him urgently, in person. In the meantime ask the Head of Security and the Sentinels' Sergeant-in-Arms to see me in my office, straight away."

"Yes Kyron, I'm on it." Lauren knew something very serious had happened.

Within fifteen minutes the Head of Security, Chief Richard Hammond, and the Sergeant-in-Arms, Dharma Hazhan, were seated on the couch in Kyron's office, the door closed, the windows shaded. Both men drew breath as Kyron informed them of the rebels' plans and their use of Xytrinium infusion.

Shocked, Chief Hammond interrupted, "You mean they'll possess the same increased abilities as the Sentinels?"

"If it works, I'm afraid so Richard," said Kyron, shaking his head.

Hammond was quick thinking. "So, if the formula's ready for use, why can't our MERIC security officers be infused with Xytrinium to give us an equal chance?"

But Kyron was unenthusiastic. "Because Richard, we don't yet know whether the new formula works on humans or what side-effects it might have. The old formula, destroyed on Tzurac in the Two Hundred Year War, was not compatible with human DNA. So the risk is too great.

"More Sentinel reinforcements, commanded by Captain Dakhar, are on their way here in another warship and will be arriving within the week to help us. In the meantime our best option is to pair a Sentinel with each MERIC security officer. Last time the Building was infiltrated, the roof was the most vulnerable entry. So I want Security to increase battlements on top of the building and patrol it day and night. The basement was another vulnerable access point. So again, reinforce security there and have the men wear oxygen masks. In the last attack, the Sentinels threw concentrated tear gas bombs into the corridors.

"I'll be away tomorrow briefing the World Assembly but I'll be back the following day. If you have any issues before then, contact Miss Blake. Use only the Sentinel Comms system and at this stage, do *not* tell your troops about the infusion enhancement. It may cause panic and we don't want any deserters."

As Kyron finished his briefing and ushered the two guests out of his office, the intercom buzzed.

"General Blake is here to see you Kyron." It was the sweet voice of Miss Blake on the line. Kyron stood up to greet his visitor, pointing him in the direction of the leather couch while closing the door behind him.

Both comfortably seated, the General spoke impatiently. "What did you want to see me about in person that you couldn't tell me over the phone?"

Kyron explained the urgent need for enhanced security on the ASPECT complex. "Can you have enough security in place General to defend against two battleships and protect the stock-piled reserves of Xytrinium?"

General Blake nodded confidently. "Yes Kyron. The reserves have been moved from the ASPECT warehouses to a secret underground storage silo located fifty kilometres away. The silo is lead-lined with two-foot-thick, reinforced, concrete walls to avoid heat detection and dampen any vibrations that could trigger an explosion. Even if someone broke into the silo, they would need very sophisticated equipment to get through the time-locked, Xytrinium-titanium door."

"As for the ASPECT building," Blake continued, "I've had laser cannons mounted on the roof and two warships are under cover ready to launch and strike at any foreign spacecraft entering our orbit without clearance. All security personnel have been issued gas masks and armed with laser rifles."

Kyron was impressed. "Well General, I think you've covered every contingency and you've helped to put my mind at ease. Captain Dakhar will be arriving within the week and will dock at the ASPECT building. Thank you, General and good luck."

The General rose from his seat, shook hands with Kyron and spoke in a friendlier manner. "Please, call me Malcolm. Samuel Jensen would be proud of all you've done."

"Alright, thank you Malcolm," said Kyron with a smile, "and he'd be proud of you too."

After General Blake departed, Kyron contacted Torri to keep her informed of what had happened and tell her how much he missed her and the children. "Don't call me, I'll call you. I love you Torri. Give the children a big hug and kiss for me."

That afternoon Kyron was again on a flight to the World Assembly, this time to warn them that Earth was on alert to a possible attack not by Jackson or Khaneera alone, but by the two of them together, along with fifty mercenaries who had been infused with Xytrinium. They were facing old foes with new powers.

ATTACK AND DEFENCE

WITHIN two days the infusion process was completed on the Kyroni and Diunon allies. The Diunons took immediate refuge in their warships which were still hovering above the planet with the other spacecrafts. Conscious of their unique appearance, they were intimidated by the aggressive Kyroni and wanted to avoid being the target of ridicule and abuse. Jackson and Dranz had to wait for reports on the effects of the Xytrinium infusion on the Diunons.

But changes in the Kyroni were noticeable almost immediately. They quickly became more aggressive, squabbling among themselves, their killer instincts amplified by their reckless consumption of alcohol. Soon, they were not only becoming dangerous to themselves, but also endangering everyone else, provoking fights. It took little provocation for the Kyroni to draw their scimitars and issue death threats to anyone who crossed them. General Dranz was increasingly worried that the Kyroni would be unable to follow orders when the time came for the assault on Terra Iota. He ordered their leaders to take more control and restrict the wine intake of their soldiers. For the time, at least, control was restored, but Dranz realized he had to act quickly to channel the aggression of the Kyroni towards the real enemy.

As soon as Dranz was satisfied the infusion process had also enhanced the powers of the devilish Diunons, he called a strategy meeting. Captain Jackson and Khaneera and the heads of the tribes, the Diunon leader, General Tarrel Grammik, and the Kyroni leader, General Hordaq Marzon, met him in his temporary command post.

"We'll be leaving tomorrow for our attack. Have your troops prepare for war. The Kyroni and the Diunons will accompany my fleet to Terra Iota, a journey of ten days. Captain Jackson, together with his crew, and Khaneera with Yarron, aboard their two warships, will continue to Terra Major, a journey that will take an extra day. Jackson has more knowledge of the Terranians' operations and is best placed to lead the attack there.

"We should be able to take the planet Terra Iota by stealth, fighting the enemy on the ground. With our surprise attack on the small garrison of Sentinels stationed there the battle should be over in a day but this time we *will* be taking prisoners to use in the mines. And I insist all of you refrain from using your laser weapons to avoid any possibility of causing the Xytrinium to ignite. Remember, it's an extremely volatile substance.

"Once we've taken Iota we'll wait for the Tzuracian fleet to show up and blast them out of the sky. They won't know what hit them. After we dispose of them, we'll leave the Terra Iota colony workers mining the Xytrinium under our rule and we'll move onto Tzurac to annihilate the Federation. Jackson and Khaneera, we'll leave Earth and its stock-piled Xytrinium to you. All going to plan, between us, we should soon have control of the whole Xytrinium operation. Any questions?"

All nodded in agreement, raising their goblets as a toast to their rebel pact. "Well, let's get moving," said Dranz, hungry for action. "Return to your ships and keep the communications to a minimum using the old codes."

Jackson spoke to Dranz. "General, you need to give me and Khaneera the old codes before we leave tomorrow."

"Yes, yes of course, Captain. I'll send them to you first thing."

Jackson saluted the General as they all departed, Khaneera turning and tipping her head before disappearing from sight. The plot was set.

***

When the burly and battle-scarred Lieutenant Zawkon arrived on Terra Iota with his battalion of one thousand Sentinels, he was met by Engineer Thompson, the man whose life he had saved on this very planet many years ago.

"Hello Sergeant," called out a smiling Thompson in his thick Irish accent as he greeted Zawkon at the landing pad. "It's been five years since I last saw ya and ya haven't aged a bit laddy."

Zawkon saluted Thompson, speaking in his strong raspy voice, "It's been a while Grant. I see your beard's grown longer, and I'm now a Lieutenant."

"What, they haven't made you a General yet? They must be daft." They both chuckled.

After Zawkon assembled his troops on the landing pad, Thompson led him into his site office. There, Zawkon explained the events which had taken place over the last several weeks and the plans he had in mind for the protection and security of the planet and its inhabitants.

Thompson was stunned by the news. "Holy Mother of Mary! This is total madness. It's like a bad dream." He shook his head in disbelief. Then, holding his fists in a boxing pose he said with a raised voice through clenched teeth, "They want a fight, we'll *give 'em one*. What can I do to help, Lieutenant? Just ask and I'll have me men follow your instructions. Anythin' to beat these buggers from takin' what don't belong to 'em."

"Last time I was here Grant, Jackson's security officers planted land mines around the mining complex which we detected and diffused without incident. I suggest we apply the same strategy. But our land mines will be buried together with Electro Surge Mines, ESMs. That way, whether a rebel or a cyber Diutron steps on them, they'll be annihilated."

"Diutrons? What the bloody hell are those?" questioned Thompson, scratching his rust-coloured beard.

"You'll know them when you see them Grant. There'll be three thousand of them."

"T'ree t'ousand of the buggers!" exclaimed Thompson. "B' Jesus man! How do we kill them?"

"The ESMs will help. I want you and your engineers to place the land mines in a one-mile radius around the mining complex and living quarters. You'll need to work quickly as we only have a few days to get prepared. I'll have some of my Sentinels accompany your men to help you do this. Next, I'll have my soldiers install laser and pulse cannons in the eight towers on the walls surrounding the mine."

Thompson interjected, protesting, "B' Jesus man, won't that cause a serious problem? If the laser fire comes into contact with the Xytrinium, we'll all be blown to kingdom come!"

"Normally you'd be right, Grant, but I'll be setting up a force-field, much like a dome, covering the entire mine. Trust me Grant, nothing will penetrate this shield. The battlements need to remain outside this force-field but I'll have four Sentinels on each tower, two manning the cannons and two sharp shooters. I'm expecting three or four more warships within the next few days carrying another two thousand Sentinels. We'll be using guerrilla warfare tactics as a counter-measure. I'll station groups of Sentinels on the eight major compass points in a half-mile radius around the complex. This will ensure no matter what direction the rebels approach, we'll be ready for them. The troops will be armed with laser pistols and pulse pistols, or pulsars as we call them, as well as miniature magnetic ESMs.

"They'll wait, in silence for the enemy, like a predator stalking its prey. Surprise and stealth are our best weapons. We'll kill quickly and silently, and then retreat into the woods without alerting the other rebels, ready to strike again. Communications between the strike groups will be kept to a minimum.

"When our other Tzuracian warships arrive, they'll be strategically located around the planet in stealth mode and cloaked in readiness for the arrival of the rebel ships. Grant, I need you to gather the miners and their families and secure them in a safe place. Are there any underground facilities in this complex?"

"Yes, Sergeant … I mean, Lieutenant. Since you were last here we've constructed emergency rooms twenty feet below the main building. These can accommodate up to five hundred people with food supplies for at least a month."

"Good man, although I'm hoping the battle won't last *that* long. Alright, Grant, let's get moving as we *are* pressed for time."

"Aye, Lieutenant, I'm on me way."

Within a day of preparing the defence preparations, a Tzuracian Warship from the Western Quadrant search-and-destroy mission, arrived at Iota. On board were another five hundred Sentinels under the command of Lieutenant Sark Tazhanna. Zawkon briefed the new arrivals on his strategic plan and the Lieutenant rapidly deployed his battalion into the woods.

When Zawkon sent a holographic transmission to Captain Dakhar, now back on Earth, Dakhar complimented Zawkon on his progress.

"Very good, Lieutenant. A sound strategy. Carry on. The emissary has arrived safely on Urgellan and I'll keep you posted of the outcome. Another three warships have already left Tzurac and should be with you within a couple of days. Instruct the commanders of these warships to maintain cloaking while stationed around Iota. It's imperative we maintain our invisibility and communication silence."

Dakhar saluted as the holographic image faded.

SEEKING ALLIES

AFTER voyaging for three days, Senator Volhardtz, the emissary sent from Tzurac, docked his Destroyer at the landing site of Asram, the capital city of Urgellan. He was met by the colourful Royal Guard and escorted with his Company of fifty Sentinels to the Royal Court of Queen Tarune.

Volhardtz was impressed with the bright, gaudy colours and flamboyant design of the Royal Guards' uniforms. Their high-collared, dark-blue-velvet tunics had puffed sleeves of red and blue horizontal stripes edged in gold braiding. The long, knee-length jackets were teamed with highly-polished, black, knee-high boots. Their broad-brimmed, black felt hats were pinned with a large matching red feather. All the guards brandished a fancy, gold-handled rapier sword at their left side and all but their leader carried a wooden lance or pike with a gold-pointed metal head, held upright tight against the right side of their body.

As the visitors were marched into the huge hall, the Senator couldn't help noticing the rich surroundings. The black-marble floor supported sculptured, white-marble columns reaching up to white high-arched domes. The domes were embedded with coloured leadlight windows bathing the sunlit hall in faint rainbow hues. The surrounding walls were decorated with huge, richly woven tapestries, in dark reds and golds, capturing stories of past battles and interspersed with shields of royal coats-of-arms. Long silk drapes of golden thread were tied back at either side of the huge expansive windows with gold tasselled cords, providing a view of the perfectly pruned, palace rose gardens which were in full bloom. The perfumed gardens were surrounded by lush manicured lawns with several large ponds adorned by sculptured marble statues and shapely bronze fountains. Compared to the Spartan Tzuracian citadel in the city of Khazor, Volhardtz thought the Urgellan palace at Asram was a picture of indulgence and extravagance.

Courtesans dressed in bright, colourful costumes wandering aimlessly about chatting and laughing frivolously amongst themselves, stopped abruptly as soon as the Royal Guard with their visitors entered the hall. The guard in charge gave an order to halt and paced towards the Queen who was seated on her elevated throne. Stopping ten feet away and holding the hilt of the sword at his side, he took a deep bow whilst removing his wide-brimmed hat with his other hand, sweeping it low in front of him. Then he rose to speak.

"My Queen, I wish to announce the arrival of Senator Volhardtz, the emissary from Tzurac."

All was now silent in the Royal Court and everyone's eyes were on Queen Tarune. For some time the Queen stared coldly at the newcomers with her piercing, dark, emerald-green eyes, before responding with a friendly, dignified voice, in fluent Tzuracian.

"Senator Volhardtz, welcome to Urgellan. We were not expecting you."

Volhardtz was impressed with his first glimpse of this regal figure. She was reasonably young with a striking beauty. A sparkling, diamond-emerald-encrusted, gold tiara was neatly secured atop her long, thick auburn hair which trailed ringlets down to her shoulders. Dressed in a long, emerald-green, satin dress with a high collar and long flared sleeves, she portrayed all the fineries and characteristics of royalty. Following protocol, Volhardtz bowed slowly, returned to his upright stance and replied in a humble, yet confident voice.

"Your Majesty, thank you for allowing an audience with me at such short notice. I apologise for not sending a formal request for an invitation, but the matter I have to discuss is of a very serious nature and we have little time to act. We Tzuracians could not risk sending any communications for fear of interception by rogue elements. This is the reason we broke formal protocol and came uninvited to meet you in person."

"Well Senator, you are forgiven," said the Queen, speaking in a more serious tone and then waving her hand in a gesture for him to speak, "and you best quickly explain yourself if this matter is *so* urgent."

"Before explaining my presence, Your Majesty, I have another humble request to ask of you," said Volhardtz. "As this matter should only be discussed in private, would Your Majesty please clear the Court?"

Eyeing him inquisitively, Queen Tarune raised her right arm and swept it over her head, calling out sternly in her native tongue, "Everyone leave!" Within two minutes the large hall was emptied of scurrying courtesans and the Royal Guard. "You may speak now Senator Volhardtz," commanded the Queen. "We are quite alone."

"Thank you Your Majesty." Volhardtz lowered his voice just above a whisper. "What I have to tell you should remain confidential. There have been many incidents of late involving treachery and conspiracy and one cannot assume everyone is loyal to the cause."

"Come closer, Senator. I agree with you entirely. No-one can be trusted. But do go on."

The Senator moved a few paces closer. "Thank you, Your Majesty. You may not have heard about the recent escape from prison by one of our most dangerous Sentinels, Khaneera Penzark. She stole a top-secret, new formula for Xytrinium infusion that our Tzuracian scientists had been developing and has joined forces with the Bladers, the Diunons and Kyroni. They have formed a powerful alliance and are planning to invade Terra Iota. We have learned from a rogue Sentinel who helped Khaneera escape and is now travelling with her, that the rebels are all being infused with Xytrinium to enhance their powers."

The Queen appeared interested. "But, what does this have to do with we Urgellans, Senator?"

"I have been sent here by the Senate to ask for your support in fighting this rebellion. We believe our enemies now outnumber our armies and have the same enhanced abilities as our Sentinels. The Tzuracian Sentinels could once defeat the rebels, but now we will be struggling against a force of super-soldiers. If Terra Iota falls, the savages will plunder the rest of the planets, including Tzurac and Urgellan, enslave their hostages to mine the Xytrinium, rape our women and feed their armies on our produce. For over five hundred years the Tzuracians have asked for nothing more of the Urgellans other than to supply produce in exchange for our Xytrinium resource and Federation protection. We are now humbly asking for the support of your soldiers."

By the time the Senator had finished speaking, the expression on Queen Tarune's face had changed dramatically from a placid look to one of fear and concern. The Bladers' plans to overthrow the Federation and the threat of another war were unexpected and she needed time to think. She sat in silence, while Volhardtz waited respectfully for her response.

The planet Urgellan was inhabited by two hundred clans, each comprising about one thousand members. Averaging six feet in height with red hair and green eyes, the clan members were strong and hard-working farmers and traders. They were a peace-loving people with a happy temperament, unless provoked to protect their families and homes.

At the head of each clan was an elected chieftain and the chieftains all swore allegiance to their benevolent sovereign, Queen Tarune, respecting the Tarune lineage that had ruled the planet in peace for many generations. Major decisions affecting the welfare of the country were made via a gathering of the chieftains and voting on issues in consultation with the Queen. Over the years, Urgellan had maintained a small army including the Royal Guards to protect the clans and the Royals respectively, recruiting youths when they were of age, to serve in the ranks for two years before returning to their families.

During the Two Hundred Year War the Urgellans had supported the Tzuracians and in return, the Sentinels had protected Urgellan. And, as part of the Peace Treaty, Urgellan agreed to supply farm produce annually to Tzurac in return for a portion of Xytrinium. The agreement had worked well for the Urgellans, leaving them to manage their own affairs without intervention.

After several moments of gathering her thoughts, the Queen spoke. "We cannot afford to have another two hundred year war. It would devastate out planet and our peaceful way of life. Although we are a non-violent nation, we need to defend our people and our planet. But what help could we give Tzurac against a massive army of super beings? Our farmers, although trained to be soldiers in the event of a threat, would not stand a chance."

"I agree, Your Majesty, but I have a suggestion which may help us all."

The Queen leaned forward in her chair intently, waiting to hear a possible solution.

"What if the Tzuracians infused your soldiers with Xytrinium to give them an equal chance? If we could do this, how many soldiers would need to be treated?"

The Queen replied without hesitation. "Given there are two hundred clans with approximately half of each having been trained as soldiers, there would be almost ten thousand soldiers available. However, I would need to keep half of them here to guard the planet against any unexpected invasion. We couldn't leave ourselves vulnerable. Would five thousand soldiers suffice, Senator?"

"Yes, Your Majesty. It would help immensely and we would be forever grateful."

"But would this Xytrinium have negative side effects on my subjects?" she asked.

"I understand your concerns, Your Majesty. But we would not have suggested the infusion if we weren't confident there would be no harmful effects. The DNA structure and physiology of the Urgellans is similar to that of the Tzuracians and we anticipate only positive effects, those that enhance natural abilities. Your soldiers would be as strong as our Sentinels."

The Queen appeared to be reassured with the explanation but, as the Head of State, she had learnt never to give complete trust to foreign diplomats without having the upper hand. "I will allow my soldiers to be infused with this powerful resource and join in the fight against the warmongers. But, be warned Senator Volhardtz, if this Xytrinium has detrimental effects on my soldiers, there will be dire consequences for the Tzuracians and your planet."

"I understand your Majesty. We would not ask this of you if the situation were not so serious. And I implore you to use discretion when informing your Chieftains of our plans. We intend to use the element of surprise and the less they know the better. How soon can your soldiers be available?"

"I understand, Senator. I can have them here within two days. They will gladly obey my command to defend their homes. But how will you be able to transport them to Tzurac in time to be infused and join the battle?"

"I hope you'll forgive me Your Majesty, but I took the liberty of anticipating your agreement and have on board my ship a scientific team experienced in Xytrinium infusion. While your soldiers are being prepared, I will send word to Tzurac, via a Sentinel holograph, requesting another four war ships to rendezvous at Urgellan. They will be here within two days and will then travel at hyperspeed to Terra Iota. Our plan is that your soldiers will be deployed there before the rebels arrive."

"You make a very wise emissary, Senator. I can see why they sent you to Urgellan. I will make haste. I'll have my Royal Guards escort you and your entourage to your quarters as my guests."

As the Queen signalled for the Royal Guards to re-enter the Court, Volhardtz bowed respectfully and offered his humble gratitude. "Thank you, Your Majesty, we are most grateful."

After their departure Queen Tarune remained seated on her throne, mulling over the idea of her subjects being enhanced with Xytrinium. *The infusion process will protect my soldiers in battle, matching them with our enemies. And, when the Federation defeats the rebels, my young subjects will return. In due course they will produce offspring carrying the Xytrinium DNA like the Sentinels have done for centuries. And, in the future, Urgellan will no longer be reliant on the Federation for protection.*

As the courtesans slowly filtered back into the Royal Court, they noticed a smile had replaced the concerned look on the Queen's face.

***

On the planet Armonus, another emissary was making his appeal for help, consulting with the high priests of Armonus, and asking them to reaffirm their allegiance to the Federation.

The Armonusians were a race with superior intellect and advanced medical technology, devoted to healing, meditation and spiritual enlightenment. Living on a simple diet of grains and vegetables and harmonizing with nature, they had mastered the powers of telekinesis, out-of-body travel, shape-shifting and super-healing, the secrets to which they guarded closely. Peaceful people, they had avoided fighting during the Grekadian Wars, while secretly helping to heal injured Tzuracian soldiers. Being self-sufficient the Armonusians needed nothing from the other Federation planets, except for Xytrinium from Tzurac to use in their medical treatments.

Senator Pyrham Morzhan and his company of Sentinels landed in the grounds of a huge monastery carved into granite rock on one of the planet's highest mountains. It was home to six high priests and their young trainee monks. Senator Morzhan had been to this small planet previously and was familiar with its pleasant natural environment, its customs and the culture of its inhabitants. He was also fluent in the Armonusian dialect.

After being greeted by one of the monks, Senator Morzhan and his Sentinel escorts were led through a long, semi-dark tunnel to a large temple. A subtle scent of sweet orange-blossom complemented the quiet atmosphere in this holy place. The source was a whispery, white smoke trail rising from a slim-necked, beige ceramic vase at the far end of the room. Behind the vase was a larger-than-life bronze statue of a long-haired woman in a monk's robe. She stood erect, her hands clasped at the front of her chest in prayer, her eyes closed and her face serene. The atmosphere was enhanced by the faint sound of a tantric chant in the background.

Senator Morzhan was fascinated by the curved chalk walls of the building which were devoid of pictures or markings and met in a high domed ceiling. Apart from the statue and vase at the far end of the temple, there were no other ornaments or artefacts to be seen, only slab benches positioned at intervals against the walls. On the Senator's last visit white-robed monks had been seated in a lotus position on these benches in a trance-like state.

The six high priests, all with long white beards and smooth shaved heads, and dressed in magenta-coloured robes, were seated at a large stone table in the centre of the room. One of the most revered priests, whose name was Tarq, was standing, holding out his arms in a friendly gesture and smiling.

"Greetings, my friend. It's been so long since we saw you last. Please sit down Senator Morzhan. I'll have your soldiers partake in some refreshments which they must need after their long journey." He waved his hand to the monk who had led the visitors into the temple. "Manku, show the soldiers to the eating hall and give them some food and drink."

"Yes Master," replied the assistant in a quiet, obedient voice, bowing slightly and clasping his hands in the prayer position before touching his forehead.

After the soldiers filed out of the room, the priest offered the Senator a goblet of fruit wine and spoke again in his soft voice. "Now Senator, what brings you to our humble home this time?"

"Thank you, Master Tarq, for your gracious welcome. And thank you for sparing the time to have an audience at such short notice."

As the Senator described the events of the last few weeks, the high priests sat in silence, eyes closed with blank expressions. They didn't react, but Senator Morzhan knew the priests were communicating their thoughts telepathically. Finally, Master Tarq spoke in a more concerned tone.

"We did experience a negative disturbance in the Universe which brought back memories of the Grekadian Wars and we understand the gravity of the situation. But there's nothing we can do to alter the fate of that which has been pre-ordained by the higher powers. We are not equipped to fight these rebels even though we are members of the Federation and have a peace treaty with the Tzuracians. What can *we* offer you, my friend, to help your cause?"

Senator Morzhan acknowledged the offer of assistance. "You have been our friends and have supported us in the past with your healing abilities by mending our wounded and curing our sick. Perhaps you can again support us in this way, using your psychic abilities if required. We must stop the rebels before they destroy everything we have struggled to achieve through the Federation Peace Treaty. If they take Terra Iota, there'll be no stopping them."

Master Tarq turned to face the other members at the table and, for some time, Morzhan sipped quietly on his citrus refreshment while studying the priests' open eye movements and subtle nods. No words were spoken, but the Senator could sense they were in strong psychic debate.

After some time, Master Tarq turned back to the Senator. "We agree to help the Tzuracians and their allies using our powers. Perhaps one of our high priests along with a medical healer could accompany each of your warships to assist your crew. Would this be of use to our allies?"

The Senator was pleasantly surprised with the answer. "Yes, yes, thank you for your support for the cause. We are most grateful. When can you arrange for this to happen, Master Tarq?"

The Chief Priest didn't hesitate. "We can accompany you when you depart."

"Excellent!" said Morzhan. "We would like to leave first thing in the morning."

"We will be ready Senator Morzhan."

The Tzuracians had gained the support of allies and were now better prepared for the onslaught.

COMRADES IN ARMS

TWO days after Zawkon landed on Terra Iota the fortifications were complete. Thompson and his engineers had finished burying the land mines, the cannons on the towers were in place and the force-field over the mine area had been activated. With the exception of a small company to man the towers, the rest of Zawkon's Regiment was deployed in the heavily-wooded forests and dense jungles in a half-mile radius of the mining complex. The only remaining strategic move was to position the Tzuracian warships in orbit around the planet after they delivered the much-needed troop reinforcements, including the Urgellans. Without these additional troops, Zawkon knew they would be outnumbered and outgunned, massacred in spite of their on-the-ground preparations.

Meanwhile, Captain Dakhar had landed back on Earth. Still on board his warcraft, he communicated with Lieutenant Montark by holographic transmission. "Lieutenant, report the current status."

"Yes Captain. The two emissaries have returned from Urgellan and Armonus with good news."

Captain Dakhar was in high spirits as Montark filled in the details. He was relieved to hear reinforcements of Urgellan super-soldiers were on their way to Terra Iota and with the support of the healing Armonusians.

"This is excellent, Lieutenant. Hopefully we'll now be able to defend Terra Iota against the rebels. Inform the Senate I'm remaining here on Earth with my one hundred Sentinels to combat Jackson and Khaneera. I'll keep you posted."

Dakhar saluted as the holograph dissipated.

***

Lieutenant Zawkon greeted the Urgellans warmly to Terra Iota, addressing them from a raised platform in the grounds outside the main building of the complex.

"Welcome friends of the Federation, and thank you sincerely for joining in our cause to thwart the Rebellion. We believe Terra Iota is about to be attacked by a rebel force including bloodthirsty Bladers, Kyroni and Diunons. We need to stop this scourge in its tracks before it spreads throughout the universe. Their sole purpose is to destroy the peaceful life we have built on our planets for over five hundred years.

"Although they've all been enhanced with Xytrinium, they have no idea you are here to combat them on an equal footing. We will take them by stealth and surprise. So stay hidden and make every arrow and every blade find its fatal mark. With courage and determination we *will* defeat these invaders.

"We believe the Diunons will bring with them an army of robots. Our 'Intel' has discovered that the Diutrons are controlled by computers on board their mother ships, making it difficult to shut down these mechanical monsters. However, my Sentinels will issue you with miniature Electro Surge Mines, ESMs, which can be attached magnetically to the robots if we can get in close proximity. When activated, these mines will send out a massive electrical charge, totally disabling the robots by frying their circuitry. It's our only option.

"Larger ESM land mines have been buried in a one-mile radius of the complex. My Sentinel troops are positioned in units on the eight main compass points in a half-mile radius. You need to position yourselves within five hundred yards around the complex, forming a tight inner circle. Any enemy making it through the first two barriers will come under another surprise attack from you. The rebels will be trapped between the Sentinels and you with nowhere to run or hide. The last line of defence is a unit of Sentinels at the complex supported by laser and pulse cannons on the towers. I emphasize again the need to maintain silence, limiting your communications to emergencies only. I wish you all success in the field and may the spirits of the Ancients protect you. Are we ready to do battle?"

The five thousand strong roared in unison, some with raised arms, thousands gripping their swords and others their bows. Standing before Zawkon was a sea of loyal soldiers, strong and dedicated to the cause, fired up ready to deal with enemies who might threaten their homeland and their families. They were willing to fight to the death to protect all that was dear to them.

Within minutes of Zawkon's address ending, the Urgellan troops silently formed into their respective units and paired off with a Sentinel to lead them to their allocated field positions. Having trained in the lush forests and thick jungles on their own planet for hundreds of years, the Urgellan soldiers were well suited for guerrilla warfare. Their uniforms of dark-green, suede jackets and trousers provided perfect camouflage, allowing them to blend in with their forest surroundings. Each of the two hundred clans had their own distinctive tartan which they proudly displayed on their regulation berets and their family coat-of-arms and crest was embroidered on their jackets.

The Urgellan weapon of choice was a compact version of the longbow made of high-tensile sprung metal, easily carried when slung on the back, and designed for shooting arrows at high speed over a long distance. The arrows of light-weight metal shafts were equipped with razor-sharp broad heads or hunting-heads made of armour-piercing Xytrinium. And the Urgellans were deadly marksmen. Urgellan soldiers also had a history steeped in sword fencing and short-blade, hand-to-hand combat, the blades of their weapons also strengthened by Xytrinium. Although every soldier carried a laser pistol, they much preferred their bladed weapons.

With the on-ground troops deployed, Zawkon boarded his flagship, ordering the other four ships in his fleet to take strategic positions within the planet's orbit. He requested they adopt battle-alert stealth mode, raise their shields and remain cloaked. They were to remain hidden until the enemy appeared out of hyperspace, then fire immediately on the invading rebel armada, bombarding each enemy vessel with photon cannon fire.

Zawkon directed his fleet to maintain their holding position, stressing that under no circumstances were they to pursue rebel spacecraft that managed to penetrate the barrier. Enemy ships that got through the aerial defence would be dealt with by troops on the ground and, breaking formation of the fleet would only present gaps of opportunity for other rebel ships entering Terra Iota's orbit.

Zawkon was satisfied all had been done to face the armada. Now the waiting game began. He felt mildly apprehensive sitting in the Commander's seat of his Destroyer. He was uncomfortable for two reasons. First, he had fought all his past battles on solid ground, face-to-face with his enemy. Despite his training under battle conditions in flight simulators back at the Flight Base on Tzurac, fighting in a spacecraft was outside his comfort zone. Second, he didn't know when, and from which direction, the rebel armada would attack. With his fleet of ships cloaked in invisibility and his crew on silent, the quietness was eerie.

***

In fact, the Rebellion's armada had departed the Planet Agorra for Terra Iota some four days earlier and were nearing the planet's orbit. Their armada comprised three Diunon ships containing three thousand Diutrons and one thousand Diunon soldiers, three Kyroni vessels carrying two thousand warriors, and three Blader warships with five hundred soldiers on board. It was a massive army.

Jackson in his battleship with his fifty crew and Khaneera with Yarron in their Class 10 Advance Destroyer had departed at the same time heading in a different direction towards Earth.

The battle was about to begin.

AERIAL DOGFIGHTS

A day passed in their holding pattern when suddenly flashes of light started to appear on the western horizon, directly above the mining complex. The armada had arrived.

Zawkon alerted his fleet to manoeuvre towards the enemy's flight path and lay in waiting as the invaders came closer and closer. As the lead ship came into range, Zawkon's craft fired, de-cloaking immediately to engage rapid assault. His fleet followed, surrounding the rebel armada, de-cloaking and opening fire.

Suddenly the dark void was ablaze with myriad flashes of laser fire and cannon blasts streaming between crafts as ships dived in all directions. Stunned by the unexpected attack from the Tzuracian fleet, General Dranz's ship took a series of major hits before it could raise its shields and take evasive action, recovering sufficiently to return fire. Nursing his own minor wound, Dranz could see on the ship's monitors some of his soldiers attending to more serious injuries, while others frantically dowsed flames in smoke-filled corridors. The other two Blader vessels also came under attack, zigzagging in different directions; trying to avoid repeated flak from the locked-on photon cannon fire, they returned fire.

Seeing the General's ships under attack, two of the Kyroni craft trailing behind them manoeuvred in a wide arc around the Tzuracian fleet, raising their shields and returning laser fire. The third Kyroni ship was not so lucky. Unable to raise its defences in time, it took the full blast of pounding strikes, exploding into fragments of twisted metal and shrapnel, annihilating all on board. The Diunon vessels also suffered the worst of the attack. Two of their craft took heavy blasts to their thrusters and, billowing smoke, spiralled out of control towards the surface of the planet beneath them. The third raised its shields and desperately returned fire. Nothing was going to plan.

Desperately, Dranz yelled orders to the other rebel ships over the Comms. "Abort the plan and head for the planet's surface. Land anywhere you can. Get your crew on the ground and out of the ships. We're just target practice up here and it's obvious they're not taking prisoners. Our shields won't hold for much longer. We'll regroup on the planet. Now move, damn it!"

On his tracking screens, Zawkon watched the rebel ships diving and weaving among his Tzuracian warships as they made for the surface of the planet. First, the two Kyroni vessels managed to break through the defences, landing approximately seven miles north of the complex in thick jungle. One by one the Bladers' damaged ships also made an emergency landing in one of the steep valleys west of the mining complex. The Diunon ship landed approximately ten miles south of the complex, not far from the resting place of its sister ships that had previously crash-landed.

Lieutenant Zawkon was satisfied with the outcome. His fleet had thwarted a full-scale air attack by the enemy, while sustaining little or no damage themselves. On the ground with their shields up, the rebel ships could fend off the Tzuracians for some time, but not indefinitely. And with the rebel armada pinned down on the planet's surface, the rebels would be unable to operate their laser cannons to fire upon the towers protecting the mining complex. If the rebels wanted to attack, they would have to stalk through the forests on foot, oblivious to what awaited them.

Zawkon communicated to the other fleet ships. "Commanders, we have succeeded in taking the rebels by surprise, inflicting heavy losses on our enemy. They have gone to ground. Stay in your holding pattern and monitor the rebel ships to prevent any from escaping. Do not use your open Comms except in extreme emergency. Zawkon, out."

Dranz was furious he'd been foiled and quickly contacted the Kyroni and Diunon leaders to assess the damage and revise his modus operandi. "General Grammik, General Marzon, report your status!"

The Kyroni were first to respond. General Marzon was extremely angry and seethed in his heavy accent. "General Marzon here. You've led us into a trap you fool! We followed you with your assurance this would be an easy victory – that we would take them by surprise. You've failed us, General."

Dranz knew he could not afford to lose the support of the Kyroni if he was to win this war. He had to regain their trust, knowing that without the support of the united tribes, they could not win this battle. Composing himself under pressure, he cleared his dry throat before responding.

"General, if I had known the Tzuracians would be waiting for us; do you think I would have placed myself in the frontline, positioning myself at the head of our armada to take the first confrontation with them? After months of preparation, I wasn't planning a suicide mission. I'm sorry for the loss of your men and understand your anger, but you need to channel your aggression on the enemy, not your ally. Remember, there is strength in unity. I need your military forces and loyalty to win this battle and our freedom from the Federation tyrants. Now, what's your status?"

There was a momentary pause while the Kyroni General digested General Dranz's words. "You're right General Dranz; we need to focus on the task at hand. We're about seven or eight miles north of the mine. I have two hundred warriors injured and eight hundred ready to fight. Although damaged, our two remaining ships can be repaired with time. What do you want us to do, General?"

Dranz spoke with urgency. "Forget about the repairs, General. Our priority is to take the mining complex. The Bladers are still four hundred strong and we're located on the western side of the complex. Mobilize your troops and start advancing towards the mine as fast as you can. By my estimation, if Grammik has sufficient numbers, we will be able to attack the mining complex simultaneously from three sides within two hours. Hitting them from different directions, we should still be able to capture the complex from the ground. Be on the alert for any military. We've already lost too many soldiers through unexpected surprises."

"Will do, General. Out."

The Diunons reported within minutes of Marzon signing off. "General Dranz, General Grammik here."

"What's your status, General?" asked Dranz.

Grammik opened with a tirade in Diunon dialect. "You've misjudged the Tzuracians, General, and under-estimated their firepower. So much for your planned air assault! Two of my ships crashed, five hundred of my soldiers were killed on impact, and a thousand Diutrons destroyed. You'd better get us out of this mess, Dranz."

Without waiting for Dranz to respond, Grammik continued with military details. "We're located about eight miles south of the mining complex. We still have five hundred soldiers ready for action. One thousand Diutrons are intact on the ships that crash landed and these can be controlled from my ship. We have a further thousand on my ship ready to be activated. What's your command, General?"

"I suspect there's a traitor amongst us, Grammik. Someone must have warned the Tzuracians we were coming. But I'm relieved at least half your unit of soldiers is able to fight and you have the remaining two thousand Diutrons at your command. Activate your Diutrons, General, and start the advance. We plan to attack the mining complex on foot from different directions within two hours. The Kyroni are already advancing and my troops are about to march."

"Very good General, we're on our way."

Dranz slammed his fist hard on the arm of his Command Chair, his mind racing with questions. *How did the Tzuracians know we were coming? All our communications on planets Steiros and Agorra were silenced to the outside world and no-one could have sent any messages.*

He searched for an answer. *It had to be Jackson or Khaneera who orchestrated this. While en route to Agorra they must have sent a message to alert the Tzuracians. The traitors! They have manipulated me into believing it was in our best interest to join forces and share in the Xytrinium once Planet Terra Iota was conquered. But they have sent me to be annihilated while they take control of Earth. There's no other explanation.*

Dranz was livid. *Damn, I knew I shouldn't have trusted a Tzuracian in league with a Terrestrial. If I survive this battle they'll be sorry they double-crossed me. I'll kill them both.*

DAY OF RECKONING

Aday after the rebel armada encountered the Tzuracians on Terra Iota, Jackson and Khaneera approached Earth. Although the radar at ASPECT signalled the entry of two UFOs into Earth's orbit, no sooner were the radar images detected over the Florida Gulf, than the signals disappeared, leaving their identity and trajectory unknown.

At nightfall, in stealth mode, Jackson and Khaneera made a swift reconnaissance flight over the MERIC Building and ASPECT complex before landing undetected. To their surprise, their screens showed the target buildings to be heavily fortified with cannons and crawling with guards.

Jackson turned to Stoltz in frustration. "What the #**? Have they brought out the welcoming committee just for us?"

Stoltz shook his head, bewildered.

Jackson suspected that MERIC had been tipped off by someone. But who? *It wouldn't be Khaneera. She wants nothing more than to personally annihilate Kyron and the Sentinels to even the score. And it wouldn't be one of my own men; they want the same spoils as me. The only one with designs on gaining total control is General Dranz. But surely he wouldn't jeopardize the mission and expose the surprise attack on Earth?* Jackson drew a blank. But this unexpected welcome wasn't going to interfere with his plans. He would have to find another way into the MERIC Building and he knew exactly how.

At their landing spot in deserted parkland on the east side of the MERIC building, Jackson, Khaneera and Yarron met in conference on board Jackson's craft.

"I think we've been tipped off, perhaps by Dranz, but we still need to enter the building without detection."

Khaneera fumed, "Damn them, Jackson! I don't trust the Bladers. I'll deal with Dranz later. But, for now, why don't we just blast the MERIC and ASPECT buildings and kill all those inside in one hit?"

Yarron frowned at Khaneera's cold-blooded statement, realizing how heartless she was. For a moment he was preoccupied thinking how much she had changed in his eyes. The sound of Jackson's voice interrupted his thoughts.

"Because, Khaneera," Jackson continued slowly and deliberately, "I'm not sure whether Kyron is in the MERIC Building, and I want to kill him *in person*. In any case, half the planet will be vaporized if the Xytrinium is still stored in these buildings and is ignited, and we'll go up with it. I want to keep the MERIC Building intact." He took a deep breath and added, "Patience, Khaneera, you've waited five years for this chance. Why not enjoy the slow, painful end to our nemesis? All will be ours in good time."

Khaneera was still agitated and snapped back at him. "Okay, Jackson, how do you intend to get into the building with both entrances heavily fortified?"

"Well," replied Jackson, "when I first joined my father's company he showed me the entire blueprint of the building, from the foundations up. There is a disused tunnel which was built to cart materials and equipment to a service transporter, or elevator, as they referred to it in past times. This is our way in. The elevator, on the other side of the corridor to the current transporter, was designed to carry weights of up to two tons and travels to all floors. My memories of the tunnel and elevator were refreshed five years ago when they investigated the death of my father in a so-called 'accident' in the transporter. At the time the power was still connected to the old elevator, though there were no security cameras in the tunnel or the elevator shaft. We can only hope they haven't disconnected the power or installed security. Are we good to go?"

Reluctantly, Khaneera nodded in agreement.

***

On Terra Iota the rebels were fast approaching. With their enhanced powers of strength and stamina, the Kyroni and Bladers were converging rapidly on their target from the north and west, respectively. The Diutrons with the Diunon soldiers, approaching more slowly from the south, were now three miles from the mining complex.

Running in pairs, one pair behind the other, the Kyroni were the first to encounter the ground mines. Suddenly there was an unexpected deafening explosion. The bodies of twenty of the lead rebels were flung into the air, lacerated and riddled with hot shrapnel. Stunned, the surviving Kyroni immediately behind them, froze in their tracks and dived for cover.

General Marzon, who was positioned ten ranks further behind in the line, quickly hand-signalled for the pairs behind him to fan out, the instruction passing like quicksilver down the line to the last pair of soldiers. Then Marzon signalled them to advance, slowly. As they did, they scanned the ground surface carefully with each step, the mangled dead warriors serving all too vividly as a warning. The Kyroni in front of Marzon nervously stepped out from hiding, crouching low in fear as they rejoined the march.

Before General Marzon could warn the Bladers to beware, two land mines in the Bladers' path from the west erupted violently, ripping apart thirty of Dranz's soldiers. Shocked and frustrated by this unexpected ground defence, Dranz feverishly directed his soldiers to spread out and keep low. As the invaders made their way nervously through the treacherous minefield, more of the hidden ESMs ignited without warning, with devastating effects on the Kyroni and Blader troops. Explosion after explosion, their numbers were rapidly being eroded.

The echo of distant blasts alerted the Sentinels and Urgellans hiding in wait in the forest, closer to the mining complex. They readied themselves for battle, the Sentinels drawing their swords and the Urgellans speedily stringing their bows and notching their arrows whilst remaining camouflaged. Scouts shimmied up the taller trees as lookouts. Using powerful binoculars, they spotted smoke from the explosions rising above the forest canopy less than a mile away, confirming the enemy were approaching from the north and the west.

An uneasy stillness came over the forest. There were no twittering birds and no noisy insects. Even Mother Nature was holding her breath in the quiet before the storm.

The Sentinels were the first to hear and see the Kyroni and Bladers stalking through the undergrowth towards them. Refraining from using their pistols, they moved rapidly towards the enemy, emerging suddenly from the thick foliage, taking the rebels by surprise. Sentinels usually faced their enemy openly, with dignity and pride, giving their opponents an equal chance to test their fighting skills. But, seriously outnumbered, the Sentinels now fought like powerful barbarians discarding their code of honour. The fate of the Universe depended on the outcome. So, with little resistance and silent blade work, the Sentinels struck, delivering quick, clean, fatal blows, before retreating to the cover of the forest, ready to strike again at each wave of the advancing enemy.

Despite the rebels' enhanced strength and agility, the attack was so sudden and the Sentinels' skills at swordsmanship so superior, there was no real battle. As his soldiers fell around him, General Marzon tried desperately to fend off three Sentinels who set upon him. His sword met its mark on at least one of the assailants, but when the General took a deep wound to his mid-section, blood gushed freely and finally, he too collapsed.

Wave after wave of rebels fell but, eventually, groups of Kyroni and Bladers, including General Dranz, broke through the sparse ranks of Sentinels, and continued their advance towards the mining complex. Dranz temporarily regained his confidence, thinking the Sentinels' defence of scattered landmines and a thin line of Sentinels without cannons was inadequate to protect the mining complex. He was sure the Diutrons coming from the south would take care of the remaining Sentinels while he and his soldiers, along with the Kyroni, seized the complex.

Then, as his men reached the five-hundred-yard line, thick, black clouds of arrows suddenly filled the sky ahead and rained down upon them. In waves, silent, armour-piercing metal shafts fired by Urgellans hidden in the next line of defence, found their mark. Rebels fell dead in their tracks and soon only Dranz and around a hundred and fifty soldiers remained.

In a quick change of tactics, Dranz ordered his remaining troops to head south to join the Diutrons, scouting around the mining complex in the corridor between the Sentinels and the hidden archers. Even before sighting the Diutrons, the rebels heard the noise of these heavy robotic machines crashing through the jungle, trampling the undergrowth, uprooting trees and blasting their pulse cannons at anything that moved. Dranz's unit fell in behind the Diutrons using them as cover as they advanced towards the mining complex.

Weighing over two tons, the Diutrons' suit of armour comprised a two-inch-thick, steel-plated exoskeleton fused onto another external layer of one-inch-thick Xytrinium. They were almost indestructible and only a handful of robots were blasted to smithereens by scattered land mines. The Sentinels and Urgellans were in awe of the robotic machines pounding towards them. Frantically, they shot their arrows and fired laser blasts at these monsters but their arrows shattered like matchsticks and their laser blasts had no effect on the robots' impenetrable metal shells.

In desperation some Sentinels and Urgellans tried to stalk behind the Diutrons to attach small magnetic ESM devices directly to the Diutrons' armour plates. But with their long and powerful mechanical arms the Diutrons easily swept them aside or hurled them like rag dolls into the undergrowth.

The army of Diutrons kept marching relentlessly towards the mine. And, as soon as they were in range, they began firing upon the towers, completely destroying two of the structures and knocking their cannons out of action. Sentinels in the remaining towers returned fire with their pulsar cannons, disabling a few of the mechanical robots, but making little impression on their numbers.

Behind the frontline, Dranz's marauders and some of the Kyroni who had now joined them, were caught in an attack from the rear. Sentinels from the half-mile line and Urgellans from the five-hundred-yard line swept up behind them, preventing any retreat. Both sides were relentless in their exchange of fire, laser pistols blasting in close combat.

As the battle raged, one of the Sentinel leaders, Sergeant Larzhan, opened direct communications to contact Zawkon. Clasping his left hand over one ear to drown out the excessive noise, he shouted into the transceiver above the battle sounds. "Commander Zawkon. This is Sergeant Larzhan, Ninth Infantry Battalion. Come in Commander, can you hear me?"

Zawkon responded immediately on his Comms, deafened by the electro-static of pulsar cannons and the sounds of the fierce battle. "I can just hear you Sergeant. What's the situation?"

Larzhan spoke quickly in a desperate attempt to try and stop the massive army of metal monsters that were storming towards the complex. "Commander, the Diutrons have almost reached the mine and have already destroyed two of the towers. There are well over a thousand of them and we're struggling desperately to hold them off. They'll soon overpower us. We've exhausted our supply of ESMs. We need your help. The Diutrons are being manipulated from a command post somewhere in close proximity, perhaps in one of the Diunon ships we saw crash land. Can you take this ship out?"

Zawkon responded immediately. "I'll do a reconnaissance over the Diunon ships. Hold on as best you can Sergeant. Zawkon, out."

Flying low in the vicinity of where the ships had crash landed, Commander Zawkon identified the wreckage of two Diunon crafts approximately a mile apart from each other. They appeared lifeless with no activity. But, a third ship nearby was emitting energy and, without warning, fired upon Zawkon's ship as it zoomed overhead, the impact absorbed by protective shields. Zawkon realised this was the source controlling the Diutrons. He gave an immediate order. "Lieutenant Sordahn, fire five EMI torpedoes at that Diunon warship. Now!"

Within seconds, the Diunon ship was immersed in a web of iridescent blue and white flashing electrical charges which lasted several minutes, before fading to reveal the outline of a black, dead hull.

On the ground, twenty yards from the mine, the Diutrons suddenly froze into lifeless statues, their energy source extinguished. Sergeant Larzhan tapped on his communicator, ecstatic. "Commander Zawkon, come in. You've done it Sir! The Diutrons are no longer active. You've killed the control switch."

Instantly, the battle for the mine was over. Without the protection of the mechanical robots, the Kyroni and Bladers were vastly outnumbered by the surrounding Urgellan soldiers and Sentinels. The invaders had no choice but to drop their weapons and surrender as Zawkon and his aerial fleet came in to land.

Cursing the outcome, the rebels were rounded up and escorted onto Zawkon's vessel while the Urgellans scouted the forest and jungles for stragglers. The Kyroni ships were found deserted but inside the burnt-out hulls of the Diunon vessels the Sentinels discovered remains, including those of the Diunon leader, General Grammik. He had obviously remained on board to direct the Diutrons remotely from his craft. The death of the Kyroni General in battle had already been reported. But, to Zawkon's disgust, the leader of the Bladers, General Dranz, remained unaccounted for. When they realised that his battlecruiser had miraculously disappeared, Zawkon was perplexed. Had Dranz managed to evade his fleet of warships and escape?

It was with mixed feelings that Lieutenant Zawkon sent a holographic communiqué to Dakhar back on Earth to report the battle victory, the capture of the rebels *and* the possible escape of General Dranz and some of his surviving Bladers.

"And what of the losses and injuries to the Sentinels and Urgellans?" came the concerned response from Dakhar, when Zawkon described the battle.

"I'm sorry to report Sir," said Zawkon, "twenty of our Sentinels were killed in the attack and more than a hundred were injured. The Urgellans lost seventy, and many sustained minor injuries. But, according to our Sentinels on the ground, the Urgellans are the bravest and most courageous fighters they've had the pleasure to serve with."

"Thank you for leading the Sentinels to victory Lieutenant. You are to be commended." Dakhar probed further. "And, how did our warships fair?"

Zawkon was confident about this. "Captain, every one of them remains intact. The ambush, which took the rebel armada of ships completely by surprise, prevented them from inflicting any serious damage to our fleet."

"Excellent. But we were lucky this time," said Dakhar. "If our informant had not forewarned us, we would have lost this war. The consequences are unthinkable."

"I agree Captain. There was a possibility of losing the Sentinels and our planet. But as it stands now, Dranz is potentially still a threat and the Federation will need to consider what action to take against the rebellious planets, Kyronis and Diunon."

Dakhar nodded. "I'll leave politics to the Senate, Lieutenant. Take the prisoners to Tzurac, but leave two of your warships stationed at Terra Iota; if Dranz and his Bladers have escaped, they may return when they believe it's safe. Can you also arrange to transport the Urgellans and the Armonusians home? I'll have Senator Volhardtz convey our gratitude to Queen Tarune and offer our condolences for the loss of her soldiers."

"Yes Captain, as you command. What do you want us to do with the one thousand plus Diutrons that are now out of commission?"

"For the time being they can remain on Terra Iota. But have Grant Thompson and his engineers remove their control circuitry as a priority. Store the mechanical units and keep the circuitry in a high security vault. We don't want the Bladers to get their hands on this technology."

"Very good, Captain. Any sign of Khaneera and Jackson Jensen?"

"No Lieutenant, we're still anticipating their attack."

"Well, may the Ancient spirits protect all of you, Sir."

Zawkon saluted and Dakhar reciprocated as his holographic image faded.

Taking a unit of ten Sentinels, Lieutenant Zawkon headed for the civilian complex to find Grant Thompson.

"Did we win laddy?" were Thompson's first words as he stepped onto the surface from the deep bunker where he and the mining families had taken shelter during the battle.

"Of course we did," said Zawkon with a smirk, the response bringing immediate relief to Thompson's face, "but only by removing the threat of the Diutrons. I need to ask a favour of you Grant."

As Zawkon explained what needed doing with the Diutrons, Thompson raised his eyebrows, threw his hands in the air with glee and blurted out his support in typical Irish accent. "No worries young fella, if that's all ya want fer savin' the Universe, oh, and us of course, we'll be delighted to oblige."

"Thank you, Grant. I'll be heading back to Tzurac first thing with my fleet as soon as we've collected our comrades who fell in battle. Two of our ships will remain in orbit around Terra Iota as a precautionary measure. Mining operations are still suspended for the time being. No-one from here is to send any messages to Captain

Dakhar or Kyron as they are still anticipating an attack by Jackson and Khaneera. You should retrieve any unexploded buried mines before the colonists venture into the mine field."

Grant responded more solemnly. "I'm very sad to hear about those brave soldiers who were killed and I'm very sorry for ya loss, Lieutenant. But their deaths will not be in vain."

As their warships accelerated to hyperspeed, Zawkon ordered the pilots to set a course for Tzurac. He asked the Armonusian healers to tend the wounded and organized for fallen comrades to be placed in cryonic capsules in preparation for a hero's burial in their motherland.

MERIC UNDER FIRE

B EFORE leaving his vessel, Jackson rounded up his men for a final briefing on the assault. The men stood before him muttering amongst themselves with excitement. Jackson remained silent for a moment. With piercing eyes he surveyed the congregation of misfits, murderers, and mercenaries who were out for blood and spoils. On first impressions they were looking rather dishevelled and somewhat older than he had recalled. But, he quickly put this down to his men being cooped up in confined quarters while on long-distance space travel. His men were itching for action and, with their enhanced powers, Jackson was confident they were a dangerous and deadly force. With an attack imminent, a mix of adrenalin and highly strung emotions made for a volatile cocktail.

As Khaneera and Yarron joined the group, Jackson raised his arms outward and spoke in a loud voice. "Listen up, everyone!" All went quiet. "I'm telling you what my strategy is before we commence our mission of massacre." Jackson sensed the rebels were restless and impatient and he needed to steer them into a well-timed, well-coordinated attack force that could strike quickly and mercilessly before the MERIC security officers knew what hit them.

He continued, sternly. "We'll start our attack from the basement up, using the internal transporter. As the transporter proceeds to the Penthouse, two of you will be dispersed on each floor. Khaneera and Yarron will issue each of you two gas grenades to activate as you enter the floor. The gas will stun the security officers but have no effect on you because of your enhanced senses. We will take no hostages.

Dispose of the security officers and then, until further orders, maintain your positions to guard against any intruders. Lieutenant Dawson, I need you to stay in the pilot's seat just in case something goes wrong and we need to make a fast exit. Are we clear on what has to be done?"

In unison Jackson's mercenaries raised their arms, pumping their fists in the air.

"Alright men, let's go and do our worst. And keep your mouths shut! For this operation to work, I need you to stay silent."

Under cover of darkness, out of sight from the security officers on the rooftop and travelling in single file, they reached the sealed entrance to the tunnel, some distance from where their ships had landed. The old steel door had been welded shut, but a laser cutter melted easily through the welding. Within minutes the four-inch-thick metal door was prized open, creaking painfully as it swivelled on its rusted hinges. Jackson and Khaneera cringed, hoping the sound wasn't loud enough to raise any alarms.

A strong pungent odour of stagnant, trapped air filled their nostrils as they entered the pitch-black tunnel. Clouds of fine, powdered dust sprayed out from underneath their heavy, leather boots with every step. Yellow beams of light from their mini-torches waved in all directions through the dust-filled tunnel. Jackson drew his Blader sword from the scabbard hanging at his side while using his other hand to point a guiding beam in front of him. Khaneera and Yarron copied his actions.

"This way," Jackson whispered, "and try not to fire your pistols. Remember, silence is our best weapon down here, so watch your step."

Just as Jackson finished issuing his warning, one of his men walked into a tangled mass of loose wiring and screamed instinctively, thinking it to be a thick spider's web. With lightning speed, in a clean slice across his throat, Khaneera silenced him with her razor-sharp blade. The others, including Yarron, watched in horror as the unfortunate mercenary slumped to the ground, dead, blood gushing from his throat. All were stunned but, although Jackson raised an eyebrow, not a word was said.

The group continued cautiously, Jackson's men nervously searching in all directions to avoid any other obstacles. Assorted cables and pipes of various thicknesses, coated in grey from years of gathered dust, ran parallel along the walls and ceiling and the men had to be careful.

After walking for what seemed an eternity they finally reached the dull stainless-steel doors of the old service elevator. On a side panel, flush with the frame, Jackson spied a small, rectangular, flat button the size of a keycard, illuminated in pale green. He depressed it with his right thumb and waited for a reaction. Nothing happened. Khaneera flashed a questioning look at him. Jackson pressed the button again, this time more forcefully. Still, there was no response.

Khaneera impatiently swept Jackson aside and executed a powerful front snap kick, smashing her heel accurately onto the button. Within seconds, came the groaning noise of machinery awoken from its dormant slumber. It was the sound of a rusted winching machine housed in a cobwebbed caged enclosure to the right of the doors. No sooner had it fired up, than the doors of the lift parted suddenly, coughing out a cloud of dust onto those standing nearby.

Glancing smugly at Jackson, Khaneera shrugged her shoulders, sheathed her sword and strolled confidently into the elevator. The others followed and the elevator door slammed shut behind them. Dimmed, red emergency lighting glowed eerily on their shadowy faces, giving them the frightening appearance of resurrected corpses.

Jackson whispered to his team. "Unholster your weapons and prepare to launch the gas grenades. Sergeant Stoltz, you take the first floor and stop anyone coming up from the ground."

"Aye, aye Captain," Stoltz replied quietly.

A pale green illuminated panel on the inside door frame displayed all thirty floors of the building. Jackson skipped the ground button and punched the first floor. The elevator jumped into life with a jolt. Travelling much more slowly than the building's internal transporter, the elevator passed the ground floor, heading for the first. Finally, it eased slowly to a standstill on the first level, the button glowing red. The doors sprang open from the middle, opening onto the first floor corridor. Stoltz and one of the other mercenaries quickly threw two activated gas grenades along the floor before roll-diving out of the elevator as the doors snapped shut behind them.

But, before Stoltz and his companion could identify their targets and fire their pistols, a Sentinel and a security officer appeared from the smoke-filled corridor wielding short staffs, knocking the pistols from the rebels' hands and clubbing them unconscious. While the MERIC security officer, protected by his gas-mask, hastily bound and gagged their captives, the Sentinel tapped the communicator secured to his left ear.

"Captain Dakhar, Corporal Tulghor. The rebels are in the building and on their way up in the old service elevator opposite the internal transporter. They're using gas grenades and attacking in two-man teams. We've secured the first floor. Out!" The message was relayed to the Sentinels on each floor who lay in waiting, poised ready to pounce.

Unaware their surprise entry had been foiled, Jackson and Khaneera continued confidently on their path in the service elevator, dispatching two of Jackson's mercenaries on each floor as planned. They had no idea their rebel soldiers were being ambushed. But Khaneera noticed Yarron becoming more anxious each time the elevator stopped and started on its journey. He had been very quiet since arriving on Terra Major and she sensed he was fearful of confronting Dakhar, a superior officer of his own race, an experienced soldier and a veteran of past battles. Not wanting this to jeopardise their victory, she whispered to him.

"Yarron, I want you to accompany Jackson's last man on the twenty-sixth floor. Continue up the stairs to the floors above as you take each corridor, joining us on the Penthouse level after you've dealt with the security officers."

Yarron seemed relieved, agreeing quickly, without question. "Alright Khaneera, if that's what you'd like."

"We're not sure what to expect when we get to the Penthouse and it would be good to have you as our surprise back-up."

"Good thinking Khaneera," said Jackson, cutting in on the conversation.

The lift halted on the twenty-sixth floor and Yarron saluted Khaneera just before the doors flew open. Tossing gas grenades into the corridor, Yarron and Jackson's henchman dived out into the smoke as the doors closed behind them.

Jackson's man was immediately knocked unconscious by a security officer who began cuffing him. But Yarron reacted quickly and was able to fend off his attacker. Surprised that his assailant was a Sentinel,

Yarron resolved to disarm rather than kill him. With their swords drawn, they lunged and parried, blow for blow, counter-strike for counter-strike, ducking, weaving, twisting, and back-flipping. They were equally matched. It was fast and furious, and there was no time to think, only to react. Through the smoke haze, the security officer who had subdued Jackson's mercenary, could only see sparks from the clashing blades. Doing a forward flip over the top of him, Yarron managed to pierce the Sentinel's right shoulder with the tip of his blade, landing behind him and brandishing a solid blow to the back of his head with the hilt of his sword. The Sentinel went down, landing on the floor, motionless.

As Yarron made his next move, turning and striding towards the security officer, the officer raised his handgun and fired off two laser rounds. But, with precision reflexes, Yarron pulled his cape in front of him in time to deflect the blasts. Spinning around, Yarron used his sword to knock the weapon from the security officer's hand and, with a powerful back-hand fist, swiped the jaw of the officer, laying him unconscious on the floor. He quickly tied both attackers up and, leaving Jackson's mercenary where he lay, headed for the stairwell.

CONFRONTATION

KYRON and Dakhar had positioned themselves on either side of the old service elevator doors in readiness to confront any invaders on the Penthouse level. So, as the elevator doors opened and Jackson and Khaneera stepped out, swords in hand, the intruders were surprised to encounter their arch enemies, poised to do battle. There was a momentary stand-off between the two pairs as they confronted each other again in the MERIC Building for the first time in five years.

Jackson and Khaneera were both dressed in black; Jackson in his leather jacket with matching cap and knee-high boots, toting two pistols, one on each hip; and Khaneera, with short, dyed, jet-black hair, her maroon cape draped over her athletic shoulders. She was like a black widow spider ready to pounce on her prey. Both appeared unfazed by the surprise welcome.

Back-to-back with Khaneera, and facing Kyron, Jackson spoke in a condescending manner. "So farm boy, still playing soldiers?"

Kyron knew that Jackson was goading him, hoping to throw him off guard by provoking his emotions. But Kyron ignored the bait, turning the tables with his reply. "You're looking worse for wear Jackson and so much older since I last had the pleasure of teaching you some manners. Obviously your confinement hasn't improved your attitude and I see you've picked up bad company along your wayward way. Well, you know what they say, 'If you lie down with dogs, you get up with fleas.' "

Infuriated, Jackson raised his sword and lunged at Kyron, while Khaneera dived defiantly towards Dakhar with pointed sword.

Kyron was startled by Jackson's speed. The Xytrinium infusion had definitely taken effect, forcing Kyron to apply all his skills to counter Jackson's every move by twisting, ducking, bending and weaving, while being forced backwards. Eventually, Kyron dislodged Jackson's sword from his hand by circling his own sword in a high forward arc, sweeping the blade in a downward motion and completing the circle. Kyron's sword sliced across Jackson's left thigh and Jackson winced in pain. The cut wasn't deep but it temporarily brought the fight to a standstill.

Jackson reached for the pistol at his side, unholstered it and fired at Kyron. But Kyron about-faced just in time to use his cape to block the blasts. Changing tactics, Kyron backward-somersaulted over Jackson, landed behind him and grabbed Jackson's pistol hand, simultaneously levelling his razor-sharp blade to Jackson's throat.

"I see you've been brushing up on your sword-play Jackson, but still trying to win unfairly. I'll take that."

Kyron wrenched the pistol from Jackson's hand and tossed it to one side. Reaching for the other pistol strapped to Jackson's thigh, Kyron pulled it from its holster and threw it aside as well. "Now, pick up your sword Jackson Jensen and we'll finish this duel on even terms, as gentlemen."

Withdrawing his blade from Jackson's throat and placing a foot on Jackson's back, Kyron pushed Jackson towards his sword. Jackson was livid. He retrieved his sword and, grasping the hilt in his right hand, turned to face Kyron once more, this time drawing a dagger from his boot. Storming towards Kyron, Jackson lunged at Kyron's heart with his sword. But Kyron stepped rapidly to Jackson's right, blocking the lunge with his own sword. The momentum allowed Kyron to turn on the spot and slice his sword blade across Jackson's back, slashing through his leather jacket and cutting deep through his soft flesh like a surgeon with a scalpel. Jackson winced again while arching his back, his contorted face expressing the pain. Kyron was getting the upper hand and Jackson's reactions were slowing. He felt his energy draining. *Was it just the injury?*

Meanwhile, Khaneera was locked in a sword battle with Dakhar. It was obvious Dakhar had the experience of a seasoned veteran, counter-blocking Khaneera's every thrust, slice, parry and lunge. But

Khaneera did not let up. Still on the attack, she combined her martial-art kicks and punches, executing these moves at a speed remarkable even to Dakhar. He was reeling backwards, being pushed further and further down the passageway on the defence. Dakhar knew Khaneera's skill in hand-to-hand combat was superior to most rank-and-file Sentinels, but it was clear that her isolation in confinement for five years had been to her advantage. *She must have used the time to sharpen her skills*, he thought.

In a move unnoticed by Dakhar, Khaneera drew her dagger as she ducked down to avoid a backhanded blade swipe. As she bobbed up, flaying her sword upwards towards Dakhar's head, Dakhar focussed to block the sword blade and did not see the dagger in her other hand targeted on his solar plexus. The sudden sharp pain stopped him in an instant, Dakhar collapsing limply to the floor. As Khaneera slowly withdrew the dagger, blood gushed from the deep incision. She smiled as she wiped the bright red fluid from the blade using Dakhar's cape. Turning to approach Kyron, her look changed from one of pleasure to one of hate. She had the taste of blood and was ready to kill again. But Kyron was oblivious to it all.

As Kyron stepped forward to attack Jackson once more, Jackson withdrew in a defensive position, waiting for Kyron to strike. But suddenly, Kyron hesitated. He had noticed a dramatic change in Jackson's appearance. Jackson's hair was turning silver and creases were forming on his face. He was literally ageing before Kyron's eyes. Puzzled by the transformation, Kyron raised his sword and turned side on, slowly circling Jackson with precision side steps. Then, raising his sword high above his head he moved forward and brought the sword down swiftly, aiming for Jackson's shoulder. Reacting more slowly than usual, Jackson barely managed to block Kyron's blade, using all his energy to swivel around and thrust his dagger at Kyron's solar plexus.

Kyron was too fast. He kept the pressure on his blocked sword with his left hand and used his right hand to stop the dagger by seizing and gripping Jackson's clenched dagger hand. With a fast reflex, Kyron raised his left leg and executed a powerful side kick to Jackson's mid-section. It sent Jackson flying backwards into a sprawled heap on the floor, his sword and dagger falling beyond his reach.

Kyron leaped with a forward somersault, landing with one foot on

Jackson's chest, and applying the other to hold Jackson's right arm on the floor. Jackson was firmly pinned down with Kyron's blade point now pressing on his throat. Kyron's eyes were fixed on Jackson's face, trying to comprehend what he was seeing. Staring back at him was an aged man, his hair white and his hands gnarled and wrinkled, his left hand gripping Kyron's blade.

"Well, what are you waiting for?" blurted Jackson, who was surprised by the sound of his now-frail voice. Then he saw his own withered hands. "What's happening to me?" His voice sounded weaker and more pathetic.

Before Kyron could respond, he heard a female voice calling angrily behind him. "Now it's your turn to die, son of Ahrmon!"

Kyron swung around to see Khaneera with a wild look in her eyes, holding a blood-stained dagger. Beside her, lying lifeless on the floor was Dakhar. His uniform was soaked by a large blood stain across his abdomen. *Was his close friend fatally wounded?*

Shocked momentarily and then livid with anger, Kyron stepped over Jackson and turned to face Khaneera. He wanted to charge at her with his full might and pierce her through her black heart. But inside his head, he heard his father's voice speaking to him, *'Calm yourself, my son. Dispel your emotions. Focus your energy on strategy. Use your power wisely to think and see clearly. Remember, battles are won with the mind, not with emotions.'* Kyron readied himself for confrontation, responding calmly to Khaneera's threat. "*I'm* not ready to die just yet, but I think it may be *your* turn."

As intended, these words provoked Khaneera into action. She returned the dagger to her boot, raised her sword, and charged madly towards Kyron. Kyron raised his sword in anticipation. Ten feet from Kyron, Khaneera sprang into the air, rolling into a ball above Kyron's head, and slashing out with her sword. Kyron blocked the sword and as Khaneera landed behind him, he whisked his blade in a fast backward motion, connecting with his attacker. He leapt upwards, twisted and landed five feet from Khaneera, now facing her. The sleeve on Khaneera's left arm was cut and Kyron could see blood seeping from a long, deep gash.

"Lucky strike, Tyros. You won't be so lucky next time," Khaneera cursed defiantly, springing forward and swiping her blade diagonally in an attempt to strike Kyron on his right shoulder. But Kyron moved side on, deflected her blade and followed through with a powerful right roundhouse kick to Khaneera's mid-section. Khaneera was temporarily winded, forcing her to double up in pain. But she recovered quickly, stood up and spun around, lashing out her blade in the direction of Kyron's head. Kyron was too fast. This time he ducked and lunged with his blade at Khaneera's leg, stabbing her in the left thigh before returning to a defensive position. Khaneera's anger overrode her pain and again, with incredible speed, she thrust her sword towards Kyron's heart. Kyron side-stepped to the right, deflected her blade and with the momentum, spun in a half circle, elbowing her in the left jaw which sent her stumbling sideways.

Khaneera steadied herself, tightly gripped the hilt of her sword and strode confidently towards Kyron, waving her sword rapidly in a continuous X-pattern as she closed in on her target. When she was within three feet of him, Kyron jumped high and somersaulted over Khaneera's head. His razor-sharp blade cut heavily across Khaneera's left shoulder and he landed in a defensive stance several feet behind her. Khaneera fell to her knees, dropping her sword and cupping her hand on the deep gash now oozing blood. With her back to him, Kyron did not see Khaneera reach for Jackson's pistol lying on the floor where Kyron had tossed it earlier. She stood up, turned and fired.

At that moment, Yarron, who had come from nowhere, flung himself in front of Kyron, taking the blast. The impact forced him backwards onto Kyron who grabbed hold of him, lowering him gently to the floor. Khaneera was horrified she had shot her own partner, but Yarron had protected the very person she had come to kill. In shock and in agonising pain from her shoulder wound, she turned and ran for the elevator, clutching her injured shoulder. She dived inside, the doors closing fast behind her.

"Stay still and I'll get help," ordered Kyron, realizing that Yarron's injury was painful, but not life threatening, the laser beam having only grazed the side of his neck.

"No, I'll be alright," responded Yarron wincing with the burning pain. "Just get me up. We've got to catch Khaneera."

Kyron holstered his sword and helped his rescuer to his feet. "Who are you? And how do I repay you for saving my life?"

Yarron was woozy but steady enough to stand. "I'm the fugitive the Federation has been chasing, Yarron Blandhar. But I'm also the one who alerted Dakhar to the rebels' invasion plans. I've got to stop Khaneera. Leave her to me."

Yarron wrenched himself from Kyron's hold and bolted to the elevator, disappearing as the elevator doors closed behind him.

Kyron rushed over to his friend Dakhar lying lifeless in a pool of blood. He knelt down and held Dakhar's head in his hands. Tears rolled uncontrollably down his cheeks until he heard a soft cry of pain from Dakhar's lips. Dakhar was still alive!

Kyron tapped his communicator, "This is Kyron Shield. Get me the Medical Healer immediately."

Kyron was instantly patched through to the Medic Ward on board Dakhar's ship and a voice responded calmly on the other end.

"This is Jarkor."

Kyron shouted frantically, "This is Kyron Shield. I have Captain Dakhar here with a serious stomach wound. He's bleeding badly and needs immediate attention. We're on the top floor of the MERIC Building. Come quickly."

"We'll be right there," replied Jarkor. "Stay with him and keep pressure on the wound"

Kyron used Dakhar's cape to stem the flow of blood and placed his flat hand over the deep cut on Dakhar's solar plexus, applying as much pressure to Dakhar as the pain would allow.

"Don't give up on me Ehrane. Stay with me my friend, they'll be here soon." Tears welled in Kyron's eyes; he was overcome with emotions, happy that his closest friend was alive but afraid he might still lose him.

Several minutes passed before Jarkor and his team of healers landed on the roof of the MERIC Building in a Tzuracian shuttle, arriving at the penthouse suite on the thirtieth floor with a hover-stretcher. Jarkor quickly administered emergency treatment.

"Will he be alright?" Kyron asked desperately.

"He'll need major surgery, but no vital organs appear to be damaged. Any longer and he would have bled to death. You've saved his life Kyron. We'll take him back to the ship immediately."

"I'll be there within the hour," said Kyron.

As Jarkor and his assistants transported Dakhar back to the warship, Kyron walked over to where Jackson lay. The decomposing corpse was almost unrecognizable and his skull had rotting skin trailing wiry, straw hair from underneath the black cap covering his head.

While gazing at Jackson's remains, the internal transporter doors suddenly drew open. Kyron spun around gripping his blade-staff, expecting Khaneera to re-appear. Instead, he saw Chief Hammond.

"Kyron!" Hammond exclaimed excitedly as he approached. "You'll never guess what's happened to Jackson's mercenaries we captured?" Then, seeing what was lying on the floor beside Kyron he went quiet. "Oh, I see you've already discovered what's happened. But there's one survivor from his crew, still alive and kicking strongly. We've got him under lock and key."

Without explanation, Kyron gave strict instructions to his Security Chief. "Richard, I want you to escort me along with the live rebel to Captain Dakhar's vessel. Ask your men not to touch the remains of the others. I'll have the Sergeant-in-Arms collect their remains. They need to be examined on board Dakhar's ship. Inform your security officers that Khaneera has escaped and she's being pursued by another Sentinel. They're both dressed in black and are either still in the building or heading for their spacecraft. Khaneera will stop at nothing, but the other Sentinel saved my life. Don't kill him. Okay? Let's go."

Hammond nodded in agreement.

***

Khaneera had managed to make it out of the service tunnel and into the park where the two ships were stationed. Knowing her injury would prevent her from flying the Advance Destroyer, she boarded Jackson's craft only to be confronted by Flight Lieutenant Dawson.

"What are you doing here and where's Jackson?" demanded the Lieutenant, concerned to see Khaneera injured and alone. "What's gone wrong?"

Khaneera collapsed into a chair in agony with blood spilling badly from her serious wound. "Jackson is dying."

Dawson stood momentarily paralysed and shocked at Khaneera's words. She burst into a rapid verbal assault. "What do you mean he's dying? Was he wounded? Couldn't you save him? Why did you leave him there? Who was the culprit? Where is he now? And where are Yarron and the others?"

Khaneera raised her bloodied hand, gesturing for the Lieutenant to halt her barrage of questions. She composed herself and cleared her throat, while collecting her thoughts. Both women cared deeply for Jackson. "I had no choice, Dawson. They were expecting us. I fought Captain Dakhar while Jackson attacked Kyron Shield. From what I saw of the fight, Jackson was combating Kyron on equal terms. But then I saw Jackson fall to the ground with Kyron standing over him. I finished off Captain Dakhar with my dagger and went after Kyron. When I reached him, Jackson was lying on the floor. He wasn't dead, he was just..." Khaneera paused before emphasizing her next words, "...he was just very, very old. He had aged so rapidly, within minutes. He looked at least ninety in Earth years."

Lieutenant Dawson said nothing. She just stared blankly, her eyes gazing into a void. She shook her head as if nothing made any sense, before blurting out a sudden thought. "My God! It must have been the infused Xytrinium. The stuff must have done something to Jackson's DNA to make him age so quickly."

Khaneera had reached the same conclusion. "Yes, I think you're right, Dawson. As I made my escape I saw some of Jackson's men who'd made it back to the service elevator. They were not only dead, but also decaying with old age."

Realising the possible implications, Khaneera was quick to ask, "Dawson, were *you* infused with the Xytrinium?"

Dawson shook her head in the negative. "No, thank God. I said I'd wait to see if there were any side-effects and I'm glad I did."

Khaneera was relieved – she needed a pilot. "Good, so am I. I need you to fly us out of here Dawson, and fast."

"But what about the others? What about Yarron?" Dawson was hesitant. "Khaneera, you can't leave them behind."

"I would say there *are* no others, if that's what Xytrinium does to Terranians. And as for Yarron," Khaneera said with hatred in her voice, "he's dead. The traitor tried to protect Kyron by jumping in front of my laser blast and he took the full brunt, point blank. Now let's get out of here!"

Realizing the urgent need to escape, Dawson contained her feelings, jumped into the pilot's seat and began frantically waving her hands over the control panels. The craft shook into life and started to lift with stealth and cloaking modes still in operation. The security officers on the rooftop of the MERIC Building were unaware of the activity thirty stories below.

Khaneera was still bleeding and in extreme pain as Dawson helped her into the co-pilot's seat. As Dawson strapped her in, Khaneera issued an unexpected order. "Turn this vessel in the direction of the MERIC Building!"

Dawson was confused. "Why? Aren't we heading for outer space?"

"Not before I blast that building into oblivion, hopefully with Kyron Shield still inside it."

Now Dawson was defiant. "I'm not going to start a war just so you can satisfy your obsession to kill Kyron. I'm getting the hell as far away from this place while I can."

Khaneera swiftly drew her pistol with her right arm and pointed the weapon at Dawson's head. "You'll do it, or else!" she threatened.

Knowing Khaneera's reputation for ruthlessness, Dawson complied. "Seeing as you have such a subtle gift of persuasion, Khaneera, I guess I have no choice." Dawson manipulated the controls and the ship was soon in position.

"Good, Lieutenant. Now arm your laser cannons," Khaneera ordered.

Dawson set the controls, her body language indicating silent protest.

"Now get ready to fire the weapons, Lieutenant," demanded Khaneera, brandishing her weapon again.

As Dawson raised her hand above the control panel ready to initiate the action, a Sentinel Destroyer suddenly de-cloaked and appeared in front of the MERIC Building directly in the line of fire. Immediately, it cloaked again to avoid being seen by Security on the rooftop.

"What in the name of the Ancients is this?" exclaimed Khaneera.

With a wry smile, Dawson replied, "It looks to me like what we call on Earth, a Mexican stand-off."

The Comms came to life. "Khaneera, this is Yarron. I suggest you abandon what I think you're about to attempt, before I open fire. All you have to do is point your craft upward and fly off. I won't let you start a war with Earth."

Khaneera couldn't contain her emotions. She screamed at Dawson. "This is the second time he's attempted to thwart my mission. This time I *won't* let the traitor live." She pressed the pistol barrel against Dawson's head and commanded, "Fire those cannons Lieutenant! That's an order!"

Dawson raised her hand nervously over the control, the vessel de-cloaked and the laser cannons fired. Yarron had anticipated her response and already had his laser cannons activated and ready. Seeing the flash from Khaneera's craft, Yarron returned fire, cursing Khaneera's reckless stubbornness.

There was a deafening sound as both crafts received blasts at point-blank range. Although the shields were active on each of the vessels, the close-range impact sent Yarron's craft spinning at high velocity past the MERIC Building and out to Earth's upper atmosphere. Khaneera's ship was sent spinning out of control into Earth's orbit, trailing black smoke.

The clash of battleships stunned rooftop security into action and, within minutes, General Blake's air force fighters at ASPECT scrambled in pursuit. DEFCON 2 swung into action.

DESPERADOES

SEVERAL hours after the confrontation, Khaneera awoke still strapped in her co-pilot's seat. Flight Lieutenant Dawson was seated at the controls, glaring at streaks of light flashing past on the main screen. Khaneera tried to move, but cried out as an agonising pain shot through her left shoulder. She saw a blue bandage strapped over her wound and her black leather jacket and black shirt had been removed and an arm sling placed around her bare neck and shoulders.

"Ah, you're awake, Sleeping Beauty," observed Dawson. With Jackson gone, Dawson realised Khaneera was now her only remaining ally. They were both deserters and fugitives and in spite of the fact that Khaneera had threatened her life at gunpoint, Dawson sensed an unusual bond between them.

"Yeh, I am Dawson. Where are we? And how long have I been unconscious?" Khaneera was still groggy.

"We're two light years from Earth, still in the Sideros-Hudor system and you've been unconscious for four hours."

"Where are you headed for Dawson? What have you done to my arm? And how come the ship is still operational after the blast we took?"

"Why don't I start from the beginning, Khaneera?" Dawson said gently. "But first, grab that bottle beside you and have a drink of water before you dehydrate. You passed out with the blast and have suffered significant blood loss from your shoulder wound.

"When your boyfriend fired on us at close range, the impact of the blast shook the ship violently, automatically triggering one of the defence mechanisms and releasing black smoke as a diversion.

It would have appeared as if the craft had been seriously damaged, but much of the impact was absorbed by the ship's shield.

"Righting the vessel, I punched in the coordinates to one of the isolated ASPECT fuel depots where ore transporters refuel and restock food supplies. We have enough fuel to get us there and I thought, from there, we could decide where we should escape to.

"I set the computer on auto-pilot while I attended to your wound. As pilots we're trained as field medics and this craft is equipped with medical facilities for just about every field injury, except of course for yours. I needed to administer a blood transfusion to a Tzuracian, improvising using a blood plasma and antibiotics usually designed for humans. I hope they will kill any possible infection. But I imagine you're still suffering the effects of the anaesthetic I used while I laser-sealed the deep gash."

"Thank you, I owe you," said Khaneera, gratefully. "And good thinking about the depot. How soon will we be there?"

"Assuming no trouble, we should arrive in just over a day. The depot is usually manned by a small unit of military personnel. I may be able to sweet talk them using my ASPECT credentials, if they're unaware of my desertion. But, if worse comes to worse, we'll take the depot by force. Any ideas on where we should go after we refuel, seeing as we'll be hunted by the Federation and their allies?"

"Yes, Dawson, I have."

Dawson interrupted before Khaneera could continue. "You can call me Pam now that we're partners in crime."

"Okay Pam. My plan is to get to Planet Terra Iota hoping General Dranz now has control."

Again Dawson interjected. "I hate to disappoint you Khaneera, but Dranz's attempt failed. He hasn't been seen or heard of since the rebels were defeated. I heard the conversations on the Comms while I was waiting in the ship."

Khaneera was shocked by the news. "How can that be? It should have been an easy victory given the number of soldiers and Diutrons he had at his disposal. Not unless the Sentinels on Terra Iota were forewarned too?"

There was a short pause. Dawson could almost hear the wheels turning in Khaneera's mind.

"Yarron! He must have let Dakhar know we were coming to Earth and Dranz to Terra Iota. He's deceived us all!" Khaneera was furious. "Alright, Pam, as soon as we've refuelled we'll head for the Bladers' hide-out on planet Steiros. Hopefully, you still have the co-ordinates? If Dranz is still alive, I want to join forces with him to organise another assault on Earth. I want to finish this mission and keep my vow."

Dawson was curious. "I never did find out why you're so intent on killing Kyron Shield. Jackson said it was something to do with avenging your father. Now we have plenty of time on our hands, do you want to tell me the reason?"

"Sure, why not. But I need another one of your pain killers."

Dawson reached for the medi-kit and pulled out a small pack of six tabs containing synthetic morphine. "I'll give you one of these. It should keep the pain at bay for another four hours. It works on humans but not so sure about the effects on Tzuracians."

After throwing a tab in her mouth and swallowing it with a swig of water, Khaneera enlightened Dawson. "I grew up on the planet Urgellan, one of the planets in the Grekadian star system. I was raised by my mother, a Tzuracian, and her husband, an Urgellan nobleman. He was a gentle man but much older than my mother. We lived on a country estate where all our needs were catered for. I played happily with the other children of nobility, mainly the boys. Now that I think about it, it's probably where I learnt the basic elements of becoming a Sentinel. I learnt how to ride a horse with and without a saddle, wield a sword and dagger, and use a bow and arrow – all with proficiency. I was always better at these things than the boys. I didn't have the same interests as the other girls, believing their interests were a waste of time and impractical. The girls disliked me because I always had the boys' attentions and the boys were jealous of my abilities, always wanting to compete with me. I was stronger, could run faster, jump higher, see and hear better, but never knew why, until my father passed away when I was ten years old."

Dawson was intrigued.

"Then, my mother thought it was time I learnt the truth about her and about my *real* father, and where my unique qualities came from. She told me she was once a Tzuracian Sentinel in love with the Chief of Security. Khane Zarkwin, my real father, had been training as a

Sentinel but was expelled from the Academy after losing his hand in a duel with another cadet, Ahrmon Tyros, bringing shame and disgrace to the Zarkwin family. He was transferred to the Security forces and eventually became Chief, but harboured a grudge because of his expulsion. After being thrown into prison for a conspiracy against the Sentinels and Ahrmon Tyros, he begged my mother to take herself and me, their unborn child, to Urgellan and start a new life.

"You see I had Sentinel blood and when I reached the age of sixteen, I had to join the Sentinels back on Tzurac, under my mother's maiden name, Penzark. She advised me never to divulge my Zarkwin heritage and, it was from that moment, I vowed to kill every member of the Tyros family for what they did to my real father."

"You mean the Sentinels never suspected you were the daughter of Khane Zarkwin?" asked Dawson inquisitively.

"No, they never suspected. For six years I waited patiently, channelling my hate into improving my blade techniques and other martial arts at every opportunity. I finally made it to the Sentinel Academy and eventually was able to track down the movements of Ahrmon Tyros. Frightened of my father's plans for revenge, the coward Tyros had escaped to Earth where he lived in secret for the rest of his life. I nearly got my wish to kill his only surviving son, Kyron Shield, five years ago and I could have killed him today if it wasn't for that damn Yarron getting in my way." Khaneera said, with hate in her eyes.

Dawson empathised with Khaneera's situation. "Perhaps it's not over yet. There might yet be another chance for you to face Kyron and I'm sure we haven't seen the last of the traitor, Yarron, if he survived the encounter as we did."

"I hope you're right Pam. I won't rest until I kill Kyron Tyros and also the traitor, Yarron."

Without allowing Dawson to pry any further into her background, Khaneera quickly changed tack. "So tell me, what's *your* story, Pam?"

For the next few hours, Flight Lieutenant Dawson told Khaneera her own history while checking the computer for the coordinates of Planet Steiros and showing Khaneera how to operate the controls of the ship. She also monitored the condition of Khaneera's wound, changing the bandages as needed.

The time passed quickly and, before long, they reached the small planet of Alkmene and the outpost supply depot. There, Dawson took charge. "I want you to remain hidden and quiet Khaneera while I land the ship and have it refuelled. Are you able to climb out of your seat and make your way down the passageway to the first cabin?"

Khaneera nodded her head and swivelled the co-pilot's seat around, slowly raising herself out of it. The wound was still very painful and she winced with every small movement, but she managed to reach the cabin, the pneumatic door automatically sliding closed behind her. From her room she could hear Dawson over the Comms negotiating with the ground staff on Alkmene.

"Ground control, this is Flight Lieutenant Dawson of DST thirty-niner requesting permission to land and refuel. Do you copy?"

There was no response. Dawson repeated the request and within seconds the speaker crackled and came to life.

"Copy that, Flight Lieutenant Dawson. This is Senior Flight Controller, Ben Morris. You have permission to land in Docking Bay 15. Can you see the guidance beacon flashing?"

"Affirmative."

Dawson guided the ship perfectly onto the landing bay and shut down the thrusters. After switching off the controls, she disembarked using the metal stairs from the hatch only to be greeted by a hostile party of six armed soldiers with their laser rifles aimed in her direction. She knew immediately she'd been identified as a deserter.

The seventh person in the party was non-military, dressed in a corporate-grey charcoal suit, looking every bit like a Company man with his slicked-back, short, brown hair, clean-shaven, baby face and shiny shoes. He stepped forward grinning as he spoke in a southern drawl.

"Welcome Flight Lieutenant Dawson, I'm Senior Administrator Ben Morris and I'm placing you in custody until the authorities arrive to escort you back to Earth for your court martial. Soldiers, take this deserter to her cell."

The soldiers surrounded Dawson and started to march her off when suddenly all six were struck in the back by a round of laser fire. Their smouldering bodies fell dead to the ground. In shock, Morris turned to see a female assailant dressed in black standing at the top of the ship's stairs holding two pistols. Both barrels were now pointed directly at him.

"What are you doing Khaneera?" cried out Dawson.

"What needed to be done, Pam. Don't do anything stupid Morris or you'll end up the same way."

Morris's face had turned pale in fear and without a moment's hesitation he raised his hands in total surrender. Khaneera quickly descended the ship's stairs and approached Dawson. "Okay Pam, so much for sweet talking them. Take this pistol and don't hesitate to use it. Now let's refuel and get out of here."

Dawson directed Morris into the flight centre and ordered him to commence the refuelling, which he did by giving orders over the Comms. She also ordered his two colleagues to take a seat, warning them of her very nervous trigger finger. Once they were seated, Khaneera held them at gunpoint while Dawson tucked her pistol into her belt, leaving her hands free to tie and gag them. Then, while Khaneera continued supervising Morris, Dawson headed off to pilfer supplies.

An hour later, Dawson and Khaneera were on their way. They were fully fuelled and stocked with supplies, leaving the ground crew, including Morris, tied up with their Comms console destroyed to prevent them sending out a distress signal.

Dawson punched in the coordinates for Planet Steiros, switching to auto-pilot and hyperspeed. Data flashed on the screen within nanoseconds displaying the planet's geological landscape and atmospheric conditions and their estimated time of arrival.

"Well, partner," remarked Dawson, "there's not much more we can do except catch up on sleep and work on battle strategies for your planned assault on Kyron and the Federation. I've done as much as I can for now."

"You've been great, Pam. Without you I would've probably been captured or dead. I'm in your debt. I don't know how to repay you, but I *will* make it up to you, I promise."

"Thank you Khaneera. There is one favour I'd like to ask of you."

"Name it and I'll do my best to provide."

"Well, I know you're in no condition to perform your martial art routines while you're healing, but would you at least be able to instruct me in the use of blades and other martial arts? I want to be more confident in protecting myself and you, if we encounter any attacks by would-be assailants." Dawson had come to admire Khaneera's strength and confidence.

"Yes, I'd love to, Pam. Besides, it'll take my mind off this annoying wound. Does this craft have a holograph program for hand-to-hand combat training?"

"Does it have a holograph program? This state-of-the-art ship is equipped with everything you need for battle conditions including weaponry, battle fatigues, training programs for all types of conditions, munitions and communications equipment."

"Good, we'll most likely need all of it. But, for now, let's view the holographic programs for hand-to-hand combat and find another blade for you to see what we can accomplish in the short time we have left."

"Okay, Khaneera, follow me to the combat training room."

Time passed quickly while Khaneera tutored Dawson in hand-to-hand combat and their friendship grew stronger by the day. Khaneera's injury had almost healed by the end of their flight, finally allowing her to replace the holograph program and partner Dawson personally.

"I'm surprised Pam at how well you've mastered the blade and how proficient you've become at martial arts."

"I've had a good mentor, Khaneera. Together, we make a good team."

"Together, Pam, we make good friends."

SANCTUARY

J UST as Khaneera finished speaking, the intercom sounded with the voice of the computer. *The ship is nearing the asteroid belt of Planet Steiros: Autopilot still active: Hyperdrive deactivated.*

"Better get back to the Bridge", said Dawson. "We need manual guidance through the asteroid field."

Within minutes, Dawson and Khaneera were fastened into their pilot seats. On the main screen the entire visual field was scattered with thousands of floating rocks ranging from the size of houses to football fields. The echoes of minor rock debris rumbled over the shielded hull like distant thunder.

Dawson took control. "Computer, switch off auto-pilot, raise shields to one hundred percent and reduce ship's speed to cruising level 3. Give me visuals to navigate the route to the planet."

On the right of the screen a holographic map instantly appeared displaying their pathway as a thin red line overlaying the grey planet. It was accompanied by a digital readout of the compass bearings.

"Good luck with the obstacle course, Pam," said Khaneera, realising what they were up against.

"Thanks, but it's more skill than luck that's needed," said Dawson without flinching. "I've done this before so I know what to expect." As giant asteroids hurled towards the ship at high speed, she was focused on navigating the craft around them, diving and weaving with near misses at every turn. "But now would be a good time to tell the Bladers we're approaching on friendly terms in case they mistake us for an enemy ship."

"Good idea," said Khaneera reaching hastily for the Comms control beside her. She switched it on with the translator button depressed and commenced broadcasting above the disruptive background noise.

"General Dranz. Are you there? This is Khaneera Penzark. Do we have permission to land our ship?"

There was no response.

"Maybe there's electrical interference coming from the asteroid belt," Dawson suggested. "Or, nobody's home."

Khaneera tried again. There was silence, and then a soft crackle on the Comms.

The voice was recognisable but faint and shrouded by minor static. "This is General Dranz. Do you hear me?"

"Yes," replied Khaneera, apprehensive at his stern tone, "I hear you General."

"How many on board your ship?"

"Just me and Flight Lieutenant Dawson."

There was a long pause before Dranz responded.

"You have permission to dock. We'll activate the traction beam when you're within range."

"Thank you General. Out."

Khaneera turned to Dawson with a concerned look on her face. "He doesn't sound too pleased to hear from us. Perhaps he's still angry at his defeat on Terra Iota and looking for someone to blame."

After safely navigating their course to Steiros, the ship finally came to rest in the cavern hangar. Before disembarking, Khaneera suggested precautionary measures for approaching their host. Although they had been in league together, she couldn't predict whether he would greet them as friend or foe.

"We'll leave our weapons on board until the General is more at ease with our presence. Much as I hate being unarmed amongst these cut-throats, I don't want to do anything that might provoke them. But be on your guard just in case they try anything."

"Alright, Khaneera, I'll follow your lead."

Walking down the gangplank stairs Khaneera and Dawson were confronted by Ramlok and half-a-dozen fully-armed Bladers, their pistols aimed at the intruders.

"Search for concealed weapons," yelled Ramlok, an evil smile appearing on his repulsive face.

"Is that any way to treat your comrades-in-arms?" taunted Khaneera.

"This is how we treat traitors," Ramlok replied roughly. "You follow. I take you to General and hope he let me torture you very slow before you die."

Khaneera and Dawson looked at each other apprehensively as they were marched off through the tunnel.

At the Command Room Dranz was seated at the far end of the table, his face contorted with a cold stare. Ramlok forced the visitors to sit in chairs at the other end of the table while he stood close behind them.

"You dare come here after what you and Jackson have done?" said the General aggressively.

Khaneera was puzzled. "What are we supposed to have done General? I don't understand."

Dranz was furious. He rose from his chair and slammed his clenched fist on the table, the force tipping over the metal goblet from which he had been drinking, spilling its contents.

"You led us into an ambush by warning the Sentinels we were coming to attack Terra Iota. My armada was destroyed along with most of my army. We were lucky to escape with our lives. But you'll pay for this with *your* lives."

Before the General could give the order for Ramlok to grab them, Khaneera acted. With incredible speed, she pushed herself out of the chair and somersaulted backwards over Ramlok's head, yanking the pistol from his holster. Gripping Ramlok tightly around his throat with her other arm, she pointed the pistol at Dranz and stepped backwards to lean against the wall, preventing an attack from behind.

She spoke with venom. "Now General, I want you to listen carefully to what I have to say before you make any more assumptions or sudden moves, or I *will* shoot you and then Ramlok!"

On hearing the scuffle the other Bladers from the escort party who had been waiting outside charged into the Command Room with their pistols drawn. Dawson froze knowing any sudden moves would start the trigger-happy Bladers blasting everything in sight.

But Dranz was quick to give an order. "Hold your fire and lower your weapons." They obeyed immediately. "Alright, Khaneera, you have my full attention," said Dranz, fearlessly. He was not one to be intimidated.

"It was Yarron," said Khaneera firmly. "He was the traitor. Not only did he betray you, but me as well. He must have used his pledge ring to communicate to Captain Dakhar and warn the Sentinels. I can't believe I didn't see it coming. They were waiting to ambush Jackson and me in the MERIC Building. Jackson didn't make it but I was lucky to escape with the aid of Lieutenant Dawson piloting us here. Yarron foiled my chance to kill Kyron Shield and then tried to destroy our ship by firing on us at point-blank range. I want revenge. I want to kill Yarron. I want to kill them all! That's why I'm here, to join forces with *you*. Would I come back here to find you, if *I* had set up the ambush against you?"

Dranz knew from the hatred in Khaneera's response that she was telling the truth. "Yes, I believe you. We have both been deceived. And, we *will* get revenge. My word is my bond. Come, sit down and drink to our renewed partnership."

Khaneera reluctantly released her stronghold on Ramlok and returned to her chair. "Okay, General, but I'll hang onto this pistol until I get back to my ship."

"As you wish, Khaneera. Ramlok, bring more wine and goblets for our guests. And good job, Lieutenant Dawson." Dawson acknowledged the General with a subtle nod as Ramlok stormed out of the room with a hateful look on his face. "So tell me, daughter of Zarkwin, where is Jackson and his bunch of misfits?"

"Jackson and his men died of old age," replied Khaneera, unemotionally.

Dranz stared at her in disbelief. "What do you mean old age? It doesn't take four hundred years to get to Terra Major."

"It appears Xytrinium, if absorbed by humans, has a fatal side-effect. Within hours of landing on Earth, while fighting our enemies, Jackson and his crew rapidly aged. They deteriorated to decomposing skin and bone."

"Well," said Dranz, "at least the non-humans haven't suffered the same fate. But how come you're still intact Dawson?"

"Good thing I'm afraid of needles," replied Dawson with a wry smile.

Ramlok returned with more wine and filled the empty goblets, giving a sideways glance at Khaneera, for his loss of face.

Dranz raised his cup enthusiastically and proposed a toast. "Here's to our renewed alliance and to the destruction of the Federation *along with Yarron*."

Khaneera and Dawson stood and raised their goblets in unison.

The General drained his goblet in one mouthful then wiped the back of hand across his mouth, before sitting back down. "You were lucky to have found us here. I'm not sure how many of my soldiers were taken alive on Terra Iota, but when they're interrogated by the Sentinels, they'll divulge the whereabouts of this base. It won't take long before the Federation hunts us down. I'm leaving in the next day or so for another sanctuary. The Federation may have won this battle, but we haven't lost the war."

"Any ideas General on where you're thinking of going?" interrupted Khaneera.

"Yes, I know exactly where to go and be welcome. Our hosts won't be too concerned about an Earth pilot," he said, looking at Dawson, "though I'm not sure how they'll treat a rogue Sentinel."

"I'll take my chances, General," said Khaneera, "if that's okay with you."

"Alright then, I'll send the co ordinates to you when we're ready to depart. You have a day to check your ship and do any maintenance in preparation for our voyage. Make sure you have enough supplies for a month." With a glint in his eye he added, "And before they slit your throats, I'd better tell my Bladers who the real traitor is."

"How thoughtful of you, General," responded Khaneera in good humour.

After the unsavoury ghetto of the Bladers' den, Khaneera and Dawson were relieved to return to the clean living quarters on board their ship. And as they retired for the evening, feeling somewhat more secure, Khaneera had time to reflect on her decision to rejoin the Bladers. Travelling further away from Earth and her nemesis was not what she wanted. But she had no choice. With Jackson gone and Yarron turned against her, Dranz was her last resort. Without his help, she could never hope to fulfil her mission.

The following day, as Dawson and Khaneera made preparations for their voyage, Khaneera pondered a destination and future as yet unknown.

YARRON IN PURSUIT

THE shock-wave from the blast had knocked Yarron unconsciousness and he awoke to find his ship spinning slowly without power, drifting silently in Earth's outer atmosphere. Feeling slightly drowsy and disorientated he forced himself to take control. He inserted the ignition code and the console jumped to life. Various coloured lights flashed and the panel beeped intermittently. Yarron waited for the console to stabilize and confirm the on-board computer had completed its auto-maintenance check of all systems. Within three minutes the lights stopped flickering and the noises ceased. A message in red flickered onto the console screen:

:All systems operational:
:No damage sustained:
:Ignition on standby:
:Two unidentified spacecraft approaching:

Yarron's reflexes kicked in with a command to the Comms, "Switch to cloaking, now!"

The computer obeyed the command instantly and on the main screen Yarron watched the two spacecraft change direction and veer to the left away from his ship. He recognised them as the battleships which had been docked at the ASPECT building on their initial fly-over when he first arrived on Earth with Jackson and Khaneera. Yarron needed to vacate Earth's air space immediately. But before departing, he needed to find out what had happened to Khaneera and her ship. The grogginess was starting to wear off and questions were racing through Yarron's head. *How long have I been unconscious? Was the other ship destroyed along with Khaneera and Dawson? Or did it survive the blast? And, if it survived, where would Khaneera have gone to escape from the Federation?* Yarron checked the time and calculated he'd been knocked out for close on half an hour. *There's still a chance of detecting the remnants of a heat-sink trail from Khaneera's ship.*

"Computer, scan for recent heat-sink signatures."

Within a minute the Comms responded, *'Three heat-sink signatures detected for Terranian battleships, two strong signatures bearing South-East; and one faint trail bearing West and fading.'*

Yarron was fast to react, knowing the last trail was most likely Khaneera's ship. "Computer, lock onto the West-bearing signature, de-cloak and fire up the thrusters."

Yarron needed to follow Khaneera for two reasons. He needed to destroy the copy of the Xytrinium infusion formula on the crystal memory rod he had given her. And, as much as he had once loved her, he needed to destroy her before she murdered more innocent lives. *I'll make amends for my crimes no matter how long or dangerous the mission and not rest until I'm absolved of my guilt. Once I've dealt with Khaneera, I'll hunt down the Bladers who also have the formula.*

Yarron checked the fuel reserves. "Damn, down to half capacity. Computer, plot the trajectory of the heat-sink to find its destination."

The Comms responded within seconds, *'Destination; unknown planet, five light years from Terra Major; no data; need to be in its orbit to extract detailed scientific specifications; fuel reserves barely sufficient to make the distance; estimated time of arrival at hyperspeed, two and a half days.'*

Yarron hesitated before deciding to take the risk. He didn't want to find himself stranded in deep space at the mercy of a distress signal to the Federation, but it was his only chance to deal with Khaneera. "Computer, take me to the unknown planet at hyperspeed."

The trip gave Yarron time to run systems diagnostics on his ship to check for damage. In spite of the close-range blast, most systems were intact, except for one power circuit that was now operating below standard. He had a supply of armoury and munitions as well as food and fresh water that would last several days, but Yarron was concerned about the depleting oxygen supply and the low fuel levels.

Two days later a sharp warning tone followed by a broadcast on the Comms interrupted his thoughts. *'Corporal Blandhar, the vessel is nearing the outer orbit of the unknown planet.'*

Yarron commanded promptly. "Disengage hyperdrive and reduce speed to one quarter pulse. Engage cloaking and stealth mode, raise shields to one hundred percent and magnify front screen tenfold."

Yarron made his way from the rear of the ship to the bridge and strapped himself into the Captain's Chair. On the screen he examined the lifeless orb, looking for signs of activity. "Computer, provide details on this planet."

'Force-field active two kilometres above surface; Terrestrial life forms detected; no natural water courses: Oxygen, carbon, nitrogen present but Tzuracian or Terranian life forms not sustainable: Large quantities of Xytrinium fuel identified; No spacecraft present.'

"Computer, search the area for a heat signature."

The Computer responded within seconds, *'Terranian battleship; heat-sink signature detected from three hours ago heading North-East.'*

Yarron was now deep in thought, realizing Khaneera must have landed on this isolated planet, presumably to refuel at what must be a Terranian depot. He desperately needed to refuel too if he was to pursue her. But, while Tzuracians would usually be welcomed by Terranians, he was a Tzuracian fugitive and, following a visit from Khaneera, the depot would be on high alert. Discarding his black outfit and slipping back into his maroon Sentinel uniform, Yarron prepared for contact.

"Lock onto those coordinates and retain them in the data base. Maintain shields, hold ship on cruise-speed in the planet's orbit and de-cloak. Patch me into the communications on Alkmene with Terranian translation."

Instantaneously, the image of a Terranian appeared on the front screen and began to address Yarron in a hostile tone. "This is Senior Flight Controller Ben Morris. Identify yourself and your reason for being here."

Yarron had to think quickly without appearing suspicious. "Greetings, Senior Flight Controller Ben Morris. This is Lieutenant Brahn Ludhar, Western Quadrant Patrol. I'm in pursuit of the fugitive, Khaneera Penzark, under orders to capture her and bring her before the Tzuracian Senate for crimes against the Federation. I have tracked her to this isolated planet and need your assistance to continue my mission. Do I have permission to land?"

There was a brief moment of hesitation before Morris responded. "You have permission to land, Lieutenant. Continue to Bay 15 and we'll activate the traction beam when you are within range."

"Thank you Sir, will do."

Within thirty minutes, Yarron had docked at Bay 15, shut down the engines and disembarked from his ship, his blue cape swept back over both shoulders. Like Dawson, he was met by a reception party of six armed soldiers with guns at the ready and Morris giving the orders.

"I'm Ben Morris and, if you don't mind, I need you to hand over your weapons as a precaution. We were surprised recently by your fugitive, Khaneera Penzark, who murdered some of my soldiers."

Not wanting to provoke the situation Yarron obliged, feeling apprehensive not knowing whether or not they realized he too was a fugitive. "Yes, of course. I would be on-guard as well, especially after encountering a cold-blooded killer like Khaneera. Here, take my weapons."

Yarron handed his blade-staff as well as his pistol from the holster on his hip to one of the soldiers who stepped forward to collect them. "All I'm asking for is any information you have as to where Khaneera might be going. I've been hunting her since her escape from Tzurac but she always manages to outwit me. My Senate wants her dead or alive, preferably alive, before she destroys the alliance we have with the planets in the Federation."

"Sorry for the tight security measures," Morris apologised, "but after what she did here a few hours ago, I can't trust anyone arriving unannounced."

Yarron played naïve, faking surprise, "What, Khaneera was here that recently? You mean to say I only just missed her?"

"Yes," replied Morris. "She killed six of my soldiers, forced me to refuel her ship, and destroyed my deep space communications so I was unable to send a distress signal to alert the authorities on Earth. And we're also unable to receive incoming communications long-range. Khaneera was travelling with one of the ASPECT pilots and that's how she got the drop on us."

Yarron breathed a sigh of relief. Obviously, Morris had not recognised him as a fugitive. "I'll tell you what I can do to help both of us out. If you refuel my ship and provide the coordinates of Khaneera's ship as she departed, I'll contact ASPECT and ask them to send out the Comm technicians and more soldiers to increase security at your station. But we need to act fast if I'm to catch up with that conniving bitch. Can you do this?"

"It's a deal," said Morris.

Yarron knew he had only a small window of opportunity to refuel and disappear into deep space before he was discovered. ASPECT would be in contact with Dawson's father, an experienced deep-space pilot, who would have a good idea of where his daughter had taken the battleship to refuel before leaving the Sideros-Hudor System. The Federation could be hot on their trail.

While his ship was being refuelled, Yarron retreated to his Pilot's seat, pretending to alert the authorities on Earth. He emerged, nodding in the affirmative to indicate the message had been sent. Fulfilling his part of the bargain, Morris returned Yarron's weapons and gave the coordinates of Khaneera's trajectory. They shook hands to acknowledge the mutual assistance.

Blasting off from the planet, Yarron set his ship to cruise control in a north-easterly direction while interrogating the navigation charts. He was trying to determine which particular star system Khaneera might be travelling towards for sanctuary. And there it was, on the second chart he examined on the screen. Located in the Northern Quadrant, Planet Steiros in the Erémos System was their obvious destination. She was headed for the Bladers' hideout.

Yarron commanded the computer to set the coordinates for Planet Steiros and hold, the coordinates having previously been provided by General Dranz. "Computer, what is the estimated time of arrival at full hyperspeed?"

'ETA ten Tzuracian days,' was the response.

Yarron needed a plan of action. Was Khaneera simply going to Planet Steiros to hide? Or, was it possible she was going there to team up with the Bladers after their defeat on Terra Iota, ready to make another attack? If so, his arrival there would inevitably end in his death, both parties knowing he was the one who had betrayed them.

He couldn't fight both Khaneera and the Bladers alone; it would be a suicide mission. He had to tell Captain Dakhar where Khaneera was headed and leave the hunt for her to the Sentinels. Knowing his contact with Dakhar would intensify the Federation's search for him, he decided he would head to Planet Agorra instead, destroying the Bladers' other base and infusion equipment and Xytrinium formula that he had recklessly given them through Khaneera.

"Computer, reset coordinates to Planet Agorra and power to hyperspeed."

'Affirmative,' responded the computer as Yarron tapped his pledge ring to activate his holographic image to Dakhar.

REHABILITATION AND RECOVERY

ON board Dakhar's warship at the ASPECT building, Kyron holographed the Tzuracian Senate to report the attack by Jackson and Khaneera. He reported the deaths of Jackson Jensen and his mercenaries, Captain Dakhar's injury, and the disappearance of Khaneera Penzark and Corporal Yarron Blandhar.

Kyron then made a call on his secure communicator to Torri. "Hello my darling. How are you and the children?"

"Kyron, it's so good to hear your voice," Torri said, excitedly. "Are you alright? We've missed you so much and we're all very worried for your safety. I keep telling the children you'll be home soon."

"I can't tell you how good it is to hear your voice too, Torri. Are the children there and can I say hello to them?" Kyron was relieved to hear Torri's voice and to learn all his family were safe and sound.

"Yes, here they are. Say hello to your father children." Torri didn't know her husband had just survived a life-and-death struggle with Jackson and almost lost his life at Khaneera's hands.

Zuri and Ehrana spoke together. "Hello Daddy, we love you."

Then Zuri said, "When are you coming to Grandma's place, Daddy?"

"I love you too and miss you both very much. I'll be there in a couple of days after I finish helping Captain Dakhar. Have you been good for your mum and grandma?"

"Yes," they said in unison.

"I'm very happy to hear you've been behaving yourselves. Love you both."

Torri resumed talking on the communicator. "Do you want us to stay here for a little longer, Kyron?"

"Yes, if you don't mind Torri. I'll fill you in later, but we don't need to worry about Jackson or his men any more. Jackson's dead but I'm at the bedside of Ehrane who's on the mend after being badly wounded by Khaneera. Unfortunately, Khaneera managed to escape again."

"Oh my God, Kyron, is there no end to this woman? And Ehrane is badly injured? Are you sure *you're* alright? Shouldn't I come straight away?" Torri was anxious.

"No Torri, the danger has passed and I'm perfectly fine," Kyron said, reassuring her. "I just need to sort out some issues here and then I'll come straight to my mother's place to bring you and the children home. I'll be able to tell you more when I see you."

"Alright, Kyron. Send our love to Ehrane and wish him well for a speedy recovery. Bye for now. Love you."

"Love you too, Torri. Bye for now."

Kyron stayed close by Dakhar's bed while he lay, still unconscious, in the recovery room. The room had subdued lighting and the familiar scent of orange blossom and it was quiet, save for the soft, meditative background music. Over the next twenty-four hours Jarkor called in regularly to check on the patient's progress. On one such visit he stopped to talk with Kyron.

"Kyron, I know how close you and Ehrane are as friends and you saved his life by calling me when you did; any further delay and he would have bled to death. He was lucky there was no serious damage to his vital organs, but it will take time for him to heal fully, internally. The surgery and healing process we administered will help his recovery, but he'll be on light duties for quite a while."

"Thank you Jarkor for all you've done," were the only words Kyron could muster. He was overwhelmed by the thought that his friend had come so close to death.

On the second day, Dakhar awoke. He opened his eyes slowly, trying to focus on his surroundings. As his filmy vision slowly cleared he could make out Kyron still in his Sentinel uniform with a two-day stubble, sleeping awkwardly on a visitor's chair. As Dakhar tried to raise himself in the bed, he felt a sharp twinge to his mid-section. Lifting the white thermo-blanket he saw azure-blue healing bandages wrapped tightly around his torso. He called to Kyron in a faint voice. "Hello, my friend."

Startled from his sleep, Kyron sat rigidly upright and stared at Dakhar. "Ehrane," he exclaimed excitedly, "you're awake. I'm so happy to see you're alright. You gave me a scare for a while. I thought I'd lost my best friend."

Before Dakhar could answer, Jarkor appeared at his bedside and activated a holograph of Dakhar's medical records, suspended above the bed. After taking time to carefully examine the charts and symbols, Jarkor extinguished the image and turned to his patient, expressing his thoughts in Terranian out of courtesy for his vigilant visitor. "You're recovering well, Captain. What sort of liquids would you prefer for breakfast?"

"Liquids?" Dakhar queried, raising his eyebrows.

"Yes Captain, you'll be on liquids for at least ten days until your digestive system heals."

Dakhar pulled a distasteful look and winked at Kyron. "Okay, I'd like some fermented fruit wine."

"No intoxicating beverages for you for a while," Jarkor replied in good humour, "and you won't be out of bed or walking for another forty-eight hours."

Dakhar leaned back slowly on his upright pillow which was now pinned against the wall with his elbow. Even without telepathy, Kyron sensed Ehrane was feeling mildly depressed and sought to cheer him up, by reminding him of their success.

"Ehrane, thank you for your help in fighting off Khaneera and Jackson. They would have killed me if you hadn't been there to help."

This motivated Dakhar to ask questions. "Yes Kyron, tell me what happened? Were you injured at all? I haven't even thought to ask if you were hurt. What happened to Jackson and Khaneera? Did we defeat them? Where are Jackson's men? Did we win the battle or are we still under siege?"

"Slow down my friend, before you raise your blood pressure or have a heart attack," Kyron laughed. "I'll tell you how it all went while you *drink* your breakfast."

While Dakhar sipped slowly on coloured liquid listening with keen interest, Kyron explained in detail all that had happened since Dakhar was rendered unconscious on the Penthouse floor. "The last I saw was Yarron racing off in pursuit of Khaneera after saving my life. We believe Yarron confronted her in one their battleships as she tried to escape, but after firing at each other's craft both disappeared. We don't know whether or not they survived."

Dakhar nodded slowly, piecing together the events as Kyron continued, "I've kept the Senate informed and they'll wait to hear from you when you've recovered. In the meantime I'll need to return to MERIC to restore order, talk to General Blake at ASPECT and inform the World Assembly. You'll be in good hands with Jarkor. Oh, and Torri and the children send their love and wish you a speedy recovery. Do you want me to contact Tajhira to let her know you're alright?"

"Thanks Kyron and thank Torri for me. You're a true Tzuracian and a good soldier, as well as a great friend. But I'll contact Tajhira as soon as you're on your way."

Kyron was about to depart when Dakhar's pledge ring suddenly vibrated and a holographic image of Yarron dressed in full Sentinel regalia shot into the room.

"Captain Dakhar. I have some vital information to tell you about Khaneera and there isn't much time to act."

Dakhar and Kyron were astonished to see Yarron alive and well, despite a severe laser burn to his neck.

"Alright Corporal Blandhar, we're listening," said Dakhar, leaning forward with keen interest.

"Khaneera survived and I've been pursuing her ship. She refuelled on Planet Alkmene, killing six of their guards and destroying the fuel depot's communications. She's heading for Planet Steiros in the Northern Quadrant of the Erémos System to meet up with the surviving Bladers at their remote hideout."

Both Dakhar and Kyron were furious to hear Khaneera was at large and still menacing the Universe.

"You'll understand I won't be pursuing Khaneera and her partners-in-crime to Steiros alone," Yarron continued. "I'll leave that task to the Federation forces – with numbers, you have a much better chance of bringing Khaneera to justice. But you'll need to move quickly if you want to catch them because they may not stay on Steiros for long. I'll send you the co-ordinates of the planet and a map of the pathway through the surrounding asteroid belt."

Dakhar nodded with thanks. "We appreciate the information Corporal and I'm grateful to hear you saved Kyron's life, almost at the expense of your own. You've shown your true loyalty as a Sentinel." Dakhar hesitated for a moment. "I wish I could guarantee you a full reprieve, Corporal, but I can't. I assume you'll try to outrun our forces and find a safe sanctuary for yourself. But if you are caught, I'll attest to all you have done to make amends."

"Thank you Sir. May the Ancients forgive me," said Yarron, setting his coordinates for the far-flung Hiera Domain. "Blandhar, out!"

The image disappeared as suddenly as it had appeared, leaving Dakhar and Kyron in silence. They felt for the Sentinel who had made a grave error of judgement in trusting Khaneera, but now was doing everything possible to atone for his sins.

Dakhar turned to Kyron. "There's nothing I'd like more than to capture Khaneera again personally. But there isn't enough time. We need immediately to divert Lieutenant Zawkon and two of his ships to Planet Steiros. He's *en route* to Tzurac and much closer to the Northern Quadrant. I'll holograph him now, instructing him to destroy everything in sight but to capture Khaneera and the Bladers alive. They know the whereabouts of the formula and blueprints and we have to reclaim them. Kyron, can you inform the Senate of our intentions?"

"Will do."

***

Next morning, without his two day-old stubble and attired in a clean, pressed Sentinel uniform, Kyron visited Dakhar to check on his progress. "Good morning my friend, how are you feeling today?" he asked as he seated himself in the visitor's chair beside Dakhar's bed.

"Hello Kyron," said Dakhar, pleased to see him. "I feel much better than yesterday. The pain has subsided and this morning I was able to get out of bed to walk around for a while."

"Sounds promising. You'll be back in uniform in no time."

"But Kyron, I have some news that will interest you." Kyron pulled his chair closer to the bed to listen more intently. "Jarkor came to see me last night. He had the results of the tests on the remains of Jackson and his men, as well as on the survivor who's still alive and well."

As Dakhar continued, Kyron leaned forward, with interest. "The test results on their DNA indicate why their bodies aged prematurely and deteriorated at such a rapid rate. In simple terms, Terranian DNA has a double helix of chromosomes whereas Tzuracian DNA has a quadruple helix. When Sentinels are infused with Xytrinium, the chromosome structure is modified in only one set of the helix strands, giving them their enhanced qualities, including longer life. However, when Terranians are infused, the Xytrinium excites the chromosomes in the double helix affecting the entire structure, reducing their life span. The release of adrenalin excites the chromosomes, speeding up the ageing process. The greater the adrenalin rush, the faster the ageing."

Kyron thought for a while before responding. "I understand, but how do you account for one of Jackson's crew not being affected, unless he's not Terranian?"

"He's definitely a Terranian, Kyron. Jarkor thinks he probably has a protective gene. But he'll need to do more research and testing when we return to Tzurac." Dakhar paused for moment. "You know what the good thing is about this?"

Kyron shook his head blankly, waiting for the answer.

"If our alchemists can identify the protective gene, Kyron, perhaps genetic engineering could make Torri immune to the negative side-effects of Xytrinium infusion. Then her life could be extended to match yours."

Kyron's eyes lit up. He couldn't contain his thoughts. "You're right, Ehrane. This is good news."

"Kyron, my friend, there's something else I would like you to think about."

Kyron calmed himself and relaxed back in his chair. "Okay, I'm open for more good ideas. What is it you'd like me to consider, Ehrane?"

"We hope Zawkon captures her, but while Khaneera is still at large, you remain in grave danger. She's a killer and, if she manages to join forces with the callous Bladers she may be back for another assassination attempt. Being here on Earth leaves you vulnerable. I know we previously agreed you would stay here as Tzuracian Ambassador until your children are older, but circumstances have changed. Jarkor tells me I'll be on light duties for a very long time to come and might not be returning to my post as Captain of my Regiment. If this is the case, I would like to have you living with my Regiment on Tzurac where you and your family would be better protected."

Dakhar paused to allow Kyron some time to absorb his suggestion. "Promise me you'll consider this seriously Kyron and talk it over with Torri before I leave."

Kyron reflected for some moments on what his friend had suggested. The plan seemed feasible. It would be a safer environment for his whole family, his children might be happier playing with other Sentinel children, and there would be relatives to meet. There would also be opportunities to advance in the ranks under the tutelage of Dakhar and other senior officers.

Kyron replied philosophically. "I think you're right, Ehrane. Perhaps it *is* time for me to return to my real home and my heritage. I'll talk this over with Torri and give you my answer before you depart. I'll see you in two days' time and leave knowing you are fast recovering." Kyron offered his arm to Dakhar in a Sentinel handshake and saluting, turned to march out of the room.

At the World Assembly Kyron addressed the crowded hall from the podium. "Good afternoon Senators and honourable members. I'm here to inform you about an attack by the Rebellion on Terra Iota and Earth … " After several minutes, Kyron finished his report with confidence. "You may stand down on your security protocols for the moment as the battle has been won. And we have a lead on Khaneera's whereabouts. The Tzuracians are now in pursuit of her."

A round of spontaneous applause erupted in the House.

"I commend the Sentinels and the Urgellans for their valiant efforts in thwarting the enemy," Kyron continued, "and I suggest the World Assembly pays a formal tribute to those loyal soldiers who were killed protecting the Federation of Planets."

As the words 'Hear! Hear!' rippled throughout the audience, the Senior Senator had to slam his hammer down three times to regain their attention. "On behalf of the Senators of the Assembly," he proclaimed, "I would like to thank Ambassador Sentinel Kyron Shield for his leadership in winning the battle against the rebels. We hope he continues as Tzuracian Ambassador to Earth."

The Senators all stood to applaud Kyron and Kyron acknowledged this with a Sentinel salute before making his way from the dais and out of the hall.

FAREWELLS

D EPARTING from Washington on the shuttle, Kyron was soon back in his penthouse office at the MERIC Building discussing his future movements with Miss Blake.

"Lauren, I'm leaving this afternoon to visit Torri and the children and bring them back to New York. Tomorrow morning I'll be taking my family to see Captain Dakhar aboard his ship. In the meantime, can you arrange to have that old service lift and service tunnel demolished immediately? I don't want anyone else gaining access through the disused entry."

"Sure, Kyron, I'll fix this in your absence. And give Captain Dakhar my well wishes."

"Thank you Lauren, I will. You'll be in charge while I'm gone and I'll see you in two days."

***

When Kyron arrived at his mother's place his children were very happy to see him. "Daddy! Daddy!" cried Zuri and Ehrana, as they raced up and hugged their father at the doorway.

Kyron picked them up and carried them inside, one under each arm. "You've both grown *so* tall since I last saw you. Zuri, you've become even stronger and look at you my little princess, Ehrana; you're even more beautiful with your golden hair so long."

"Hello my love," said a soft voice from behind him. Kyron turned his head to see Torri, smiling warmly. Kyron stood up from the couch where he had plonked himself and the children, walked over to Torri and, without a word, took her tightly in his arms. The children giggled as their parents kissed.

The embrace lasted for some time, breaking only on hearing Zelda's voice. "Hello, my son. It's good to see you. Would you like some tea?" Kyron's mother was carrying a tray of treats, china cups and a teapot of freshly brewed tea. She set the tray down carefully on the table in front of the couch and began to pour.

Before Kyron had the chance to tell Torri how much he missed her, Kyron felt obliged to go over to his mother, give her a hug and kiss her gently on the cheek. "It's good to see you too mum. The tea looks very inviting."

Zelda fussed as only a mother could. "Come and sit down, son. You must be very tired after what you've been through and travelling out here as well."

Kyron glanced at Torri with a knowing expression and winked to indicate they would soon be alone together to catch up on lost time. Torri nodded and smiled, acknowledging his thoughts, and strolled over to sit on the couch beside him.

Kyron's mother handed Torri and Kyron a cup of tea and a piece of chocolate cake; the children sitting upright on the floor waiting patiently to receive their delights.

"How long will you be staying this time, my son?" she asked, hopefully.

"Unfortunately, not long enough, Mum. I need to return tomorrow before Captain Dakhar leaves for Tzurac and I'd like him to see Torri and the children before he goes."

Seeing the sadness in his mother's eyes Kyron added, "But don't be too disheartened Mum. I'd like you to come back with us to stay for as long as you'd like."

His mother's expression changed instantly, but before she could respond, Ehrana burst out, her mouth covered in chocolate icing, "Yeh, Grandma Zelda, come and stay with us in *our* house."

"Well it's unanimous then, Mum," said Kyron, chuffed at Ehrana's comment. "You're coming with us."

"Yes," agreed Torri, "it's settled. We'll pack tonight for an early start in the morning."

"Thank you everyone, I'd love to stay with you for a while," said Kyron's mother, elated.

After dinner, Kyron and Torri helped Zuri and Ehrana pack their bags and retired early to their room after bedding down the children. Kyron's head was spinning and he was anxious to tell Torri what was on his mind. "Torri, I need to talk to you."

Torri curled herself up on the bed with crossed legs, hugging a pillow to her chest to make herself more comfortable. "Alright, Kyron, you have my full attention."

"Ah, where do I begin? You know how Ehrane was seriously injured and is recovering?" Torri nodded. "Well Ehrane will be on light duties for a very long time. He'll be unable to lead his Regiment and wants me to be with him so he can mentor me during his recovery. He realizes the agreement we had was for me to come to Tzurac when our children are in their teens, but circumstances have changed."

Torri was concerned and responded in a more serious voice. "Are you saying you may need to leave me and the children here on Earth while you go to Tzurac?"

"No, no, sweetheart," said Kyron, quickly reassuring her. "I would never leave you and the children by yourselves. I love all of you too much to ever think of doing such a thing. No, Ehrane believes we may still be in grave danger from Khaneera. We would all be more protected living on Tzurac.

"There's more. Although it's confidential, I need to tell you that Jackson and his men all died of premature ageing after being infused with Xytrinium, with one exception. Terranians obviously suffer fatal side effects from infusion. But if the Tzuracian alchemists can identify the protective gene that saved this one mercenary, it's possible they can discover a safe means to help *you* be infused so we could grow old together."

Torri sat in silence for some time, her eyes fixed while her mind processed the information. She had many questions. "What about your mother and the MERIC Company? What about not being able to visit *my* parents? What about the children, their friends, and their schooling? How will Zuri and Ehrana feel about living on a strange planet with strange beings who speak an alien language? We really need to think about this carefully, Kyron, before you give your answer to Ehrane. And let's be cautious about the other possibility until the scientists know that Xytrinium infusion can be made safe for humans."

Kyron knew she was right. "Maybe there's a solution to satisfy all our needs. But, for now, Torri, we need to get some sleep. We have an early start in the morning."

They prepared themselves for bed, turned off the lights and snuggled up close. While lying close to Torri in the darkness, Kyron thought to himself how good it felt to be close to Torri's warm body again. Her hair was soft and silky with a faint perfume of roses and her skin was smooth. He whispered in her ear. "I missed you so much. I love you Torri."

"I love you too. It's so good to have you back close to me again, Kyron."

They kissed passionately while caressing each other's bodies and when their lips finally parted, they fell asleep wrapped in each other's arms.

Next morning, as the splinters of light from the early sunrise crept through the narrow window shutters in their bedroom, Kyron woke surprised to find Torri sitting next to him in a lotus position.

"Good morning, darling. Did you sleep well?" he inquired in a slow voice while stretching out his body to shake off the effects of a well-rested sleep.

"Good morning, my love. Yes, it was the deepest sleep I've had in a long while. I felt safe and secure knowing you were safe as well."

Kyron smiled contentedly, leaning over and gently kissing Torri's hand that was resting on her folded knee. With her other hand, Torri ran her fingers slowly through Kyron's thick hair. "I was awake before the sun rose, thinking about what you said last night, Kyron, and trying to find a solution to please everyone. I have a suggestion."

Kyron was now wide awake and propped himself up against the wooden bed-head. "Okay, I'm curious."

"Alright, but hear me out before jumping in with an alternative." Kyron nodded.

"Instead of joining Ehrane and his Regiment on Planet Tzurac, why can't Ehrane perform his light duties here on Earth and bring his Regiment here with him? This way, we'll have more protection, you will still receive your mentoring, and the children can play with

Sentinel children from the families of Ehrane's Regiment. I'll be able to continue working at MERIC and the Xytrinium storage will be well guarded.

"Of course Ehrane would need to seek permission from the Senate, and the families of the Regiment would have to agree to living on Earth for a time. When Ehrane completes his light duties, we could join him on his return to Tzurac. And, by then, they may have developed a safe method for Xytrinium infusions for humans."

Kyron raised his arms above his shoulders and clasped his hands behind his head. He thought deeply for some time, before eventually responding with enthusiasm. "You're such a clever woman, Torri. It's a big ask but, if Ehrane agrees and the Senate approves, it will benefit both Earth and Tzurac by creating closer relations with the Tzuracians. I might retain my position as the Tzuracian Ambassador or, better still, Ehrane could replace me in my role while on lighter duties."

Kyron kissed Torri and sprang out of bed enthusiastically to begin preparations. "Let's pack and get back to New York."

Later that morning, Kyron and his family went directly to see their friend to present their case. No longer bedridden, Dakhar was freely walking around his ship making last minute arrangements for his return voyage when Kyron and Torri appeared on the scene.

"Torri, it's so good to see you," Dakhar said, kissing her on the cheek and exchanging hugs.

"It's good to see you too, Ehrane. How are you feeling?"

"Much better thank you, Torri, and you're looking as beautiful as ever." Torri blushed.

Before Dakhar could utter another word he was attacked by the children.

"Uncle Ehrane, Uncle Ehrane," cried Zuri and Ehrane's namesake, Ehrana, rushing towards him and clutching their arms around his legs.

"Hello, my little ones. It's so good to see you both. Look how tall you've grown. Come and say hello to Jarkor, my healer, and he'll show you some interesting things while I talk to your mum and dad."

Jarkor, who was standing nearby, glared at Dakhar, communicating how he felt about inquisitive children who want to touch everything they see. Forcing a smile, he took the children's hands gently in his own and led them from the room.

"Come and join me in the conference room and we'll have some refreshments," Dakhar said warmly to Kyron and Torri.

While enjoying Tzuracian beverages, Kyron and Torri suggested their alternative plan to Dakhar. Dakhar seemed impressed.

"This suggestion has merits and I like the idea of being here on Terra Major with my closest friends while I recuperate. I'm reasonably certain the families of the Regiment would enjoy a change of scenery too. Kyron, I know it's a hard choice for you to leave your home and to take Torri away from her family. So I hope, for all our sakes, the Senate sanctions your proposal."

They toasted the idea, Ehrane saying, "So, stay here in your role as Ambassador, Kyron, and manage MERIC until you receive word of the Senate's decision. I'll be departing for Tzurac tonight."

After collecting the children, Dakhar escorted them from his ship and offered his farewell. "Stay well my friends and may the Ancients guide and protect you."

Torri hugged Dakhar and with a tear in his eye, Kyron offered Ehrane a Sentinel handshake, stepped back and finished with the Sentinel salute. "You stay well too, my friend, and may the Ancient spirits also protect you."

"Bye Uncle," yelled Zuri and Ehrana in their high-pitched voices, waving goodbye as Dakhar re-entered the craft.

That night, in the western quadrant of the Universe, the faint light of a lonely spacecraft departing Earth could be seen fading into the void, the population of Terra Major oblivious to the recent events which could have destroyed their planet.

THE ENEMY'S CAMP

WITHIN a week of receiving his orders and travelling at full hyperspeed, Zawkon's fleet reached the asteroid belt of Planet Steiros. His instruments detected no other craft in the vicinity. But Zawkon, cautious and always alert for traps, tested the area for heat signatures. He was unsurprised when his ship's sensors detected a day-old heat signature of a Terranian battleship. *Must be Khaneera's,* he thought.

Before ordering his battleships to enter the mapped pathway, he signalled them by holograph to silence their communications, be prepared for encounters with the Bladers or Khaneera, and switch to stealth mode with cloaking and shields at full capacity. He also emphasized the need to capture their enemies alive, if possible.

Slowly and quietly, they manoeuvred their ships to avoid shards of meteorites spinning out of their orbital pattern. Large rock splinters continuously ricocheted off the crafts' raised shields, echoing deeply through the hulls like the sound of drums being fiercely hammered. Creeping through the treacherous rocky maze the crew spotted ill-fated, ship-wrecked spacecrafts from different worlds, floating lifeless amongst the scattered debris. They travelled through a haunted graveyard of ghost ships that conjured up uneasy feelings amongst the troops.

Emerging safely from the perilous asteroid belt and hovering just above the planet's surface, Zawkon's hunting party was confronted with huge, rusty, metal doors sealing the entrance to what appeared to be a large cave. All three ships hovered at a short distance from the entrance.

This side of the planet was in semi-darkness but no moons were visible. Zawkon realised the grey blanket over the landscape was in fact dust blocking out the full sunlight and creating an uninviting, scorched planet. Atmospheric samples indicated unbreathable air combined with toxic fumes.

Zawkon sent a holograph to the other pilots. "We're going in. We'll blast the doors with laser cannons and land inside the cave. Have your men don their breathing masks and full battle dress. We need to be prepared for anything."

In a matter of seconds, Zawkon's ship decloaked and fired, the impact of the blast tearing the metal doors apart. He waited in expectation for return fire. There was none. The enemy had either been caught off-guard or had already left the planet. He signalled for his ships to advance cautiously. Shields still active, the ships entered the cave in single file, finding themselves inside an enormous hangar.

Suddenly, they were hit by a hail of fire from remote-controlled laser cannons positioned strategically on the side walls of the cave. The rapid laser fire was intense but the shields withstood the impact. Without hesitation Zawkon's three ships returned fire, instantly knocking out the cannons and allowing a safe landing.

The ships touched down in a triangular pattern behind two craft housed further inside the hangar; a distinctive, black-scorpion Blader warship and an Assault-class Terranian battleship.

"Disembark and assemble," ordered Zawkon. "And stay alert. There could be more surprises in store for us."

On the ground, Zawkon directed twenty of his Sentinels to stand guard over the ships and the others to accompany him. Approaching the second set of smaller metal doors inside the rudimentary hangar, Zawkon punched a large, dome-shaped button at the side of one of the doors. Instantly, the doors rolled apart revealing numerous dark tunnels leading off in different directions.

Passing quickly through the opening, his soldiers crouched in defensive positions, their weapons covering attack from all directions and their eyes searching frantically for hidden enemy. Zawkon hit another dome-shaped button on the cave wall near the frame and the heavy metal doors screeched closed behind them, the sound of worn metal on metal torturing the Sentinels' sensitive eardrums.

Lieutenant Zawkon ordered his soldiers to attach their Comm earpieces and set their pistols on stun. He divided the eighty soldiers into units of ten and directed them to advance into the tunnels, with care.

Leading one of the units, Zawkon entered the larger tunnel. It was dead quiet and very dark. There was barely enough light to see, even with a Sentinel's keen eyesight. Black algae covered the clay walls which glistened with water seeping from the ceiling. With pistols at the ready, the group moved cautiously, heading towards a large room at the end of the tunnel.

Ten paces from the exit Zawkon heard the familiar sound of metal clicking on a gun. He stopped in his tracks, turned to his soldiers, and with hand signals, indicated a possible trap. By example, he detached two smoke grenades from his utility belt. The rest followed his lead. He signalled them to arm their grenades and toss them into the large room ahead. As veterans, they were familiar with this tactic which created a smoke screen, momentarily affecting the enemies' vision.

Allowing thirty seconds for the smoke to fill the void, the lieutenant signalled his Sentinels to charge and fan out into the room. His suspicions of an ambush were correct. The Bladers were positioned strategically around the large hall and could easily have killed the unprepared Sentinels one by one as they entered from a single point. But now, the Sentinels had the advantage. While the Bladers fired haphazardly, the Sentinels' breathing and sight were unaffected by smoke. They stunned the Bladers in their hidden positions and, by the time the smoke had cleared, fifty Bladers lay unconscious on the floor of the hall.

"Bind the Bladers' wrists and legs," said Zawkon quietly. "We don't want them going anywhere until we return."

He waved his soldiers forward to the entrance of another tunnel on the other side of the room. There, Zawkon drew his blade-staff from his belt with his free hand and activated its blue light. The others again followed their leader's action. Apprehensive, they continued without a word down the dark tunnel, kicking open the doors on either side of the tunnel, one by one, expecting Bladers to leap out. There was no reaction.

Then, as they neared the tunnel's end, they heard a loud exchange of laser fire. Zawkon eased the remaining door ajar to see his other

Sentinel units at the far end of the room pinned down by the Bladers' fire power. He hand-signalled his group to spread out as they entered the room and whispered an order in his Comms, "Fire at will."

As his unit filed out from the tunnel discharging their weapons, the Bladers, caught in a cross-fire, blasted their laser weapons wildly in all directions. They were an easy target for the Sentinels and fell like flies, landing unconscious on the cold, hard floor.

"Bind them securely and continue to search all areas of this tunnel maze," commanded Zawkon. His Sentinels disappeared quietly into the dark tunnels, the Lieutenant following about twenty paces behind one of the units.

Within fifty paces of the entry, the tunnel Zawkon was in divided into a fork and Zawkon veered into the left tunnel, thinking he was still following his soldiers. The tunnel continued for some distance before leading into a dimly-lit, smaller room where Zawkon realised he was quite alone. The sparsely furnished room contained a wooden table surrounded by half-a-dozen roughly-carved, wooden chairs. Several navigation charts of various star systems were pinned to the walls. Zawkon was inspecting his surroundings when all of a sudden he was startled by a familiar, threatening voice. He turned in an instant with his blade drawn to confront the intruder standing behind him.

"Lieutenant Zawkon. Come to meet your death and join your beloved Captain Dakhar in the after-life?"

Zawkon responded in a fearless and confident tone, his glaring eyes fixed on a woman dressed in tight-fitting, black leathers, brandishing a sword and with a pistol holstered at her side. "Khaneera Penzark, what a pleasant surprise. No. Captain Dakhar and I are not yet ready to meet our Maker. Nor are you. I have orders to bring you back alive, though I'd rather dispose of you permanently."

Khaneera had not expected to hear Dakhar was still alive and raised her sword ready to strike. "You're lying Zawkon," she shouted, "I killed Dakhar back on Earth. I gutted him with my dagger and watched him bleed out."

"No Khaneera, you ran away and he was saved by Kyron Shield. So put down your blade before you do any more harm to yourself and come with me, quietly."

Khaneera was riled. "I could have shot you in the back, Zawkon, but I prefer to carve you up slowly, to dispel the legend of the great Kal Zawkon."

"Well, so far you've *failed* to kill Dakhar, *failed* to defeat Kyron and *failed* in love. I've heard how your boyfriend Yarron betrayed you. You should quit while you still can. Surrender your weapons or face the consequences."

Khaneera was infuriated. Without another word, she charged ferociously at Zawkon, waving her long blade rapidly in criss-cross fashion. But Zawkon's reflexes were too fast. He jumped, somersaulted in mid-air and landed on the table behind her. Khaneera turned on the spot and sprang onto the table with her blade outstretched, the tip pointing inches from Zawkon's throat.

Zawkon forcefully blocked her weapon to his right with his blade and, at the same time, swung a powerful punch with his left fist to Khaneera's head. The blow sent Khaneera flying backwards off the table, but her sharp reflexes enabled her to perform a back-flip and land on her feet. Zawkon also leaped off the table with a sideways twist, landing three feet from Khaneera and facing her raised blade. Khaneera lunged forward with her blade. Zawkon side-stepped to his left and, with his clenched left fist, hard-punched her to the right side of her jaw, knocking her to the ground and landing her in a sprawled out position.

"You know," he said in his gruff voice, "I don't usually hit ladies, but seeing as you're no lady, I've made an exception."

Khaneera reached for the dagger in her boot and quickly scrambled to her feet, holding the long blade in her right hand and the dagger in her left. She was bleeding from her cut lip and wiped the blood from her mouth with her sleeve. Zawkon could see the fire in her eyes and the determination on her face.

"Lucky punch Zawkon," she said, sneering. "Let's see how you handle two blades."

Zawkon reached for his boot dagger just in time to defend against Khaneera who raced towards him with both blades waving in a figure-eight pattern. Blades clashed with every thrust, blocked and counter-blocked, with both of them ducking, weaving, flipping and twisting. Zawkon, the more experienced of the two, made several cuts on

Khaneera's torso. But her fierce determination didn't slow her down and she kept at him with a feverish pace. Zawkon recognised her skills at hand-to-hand, close combat had greatly improved. She fought well above the level of the other Sentinels and her stamina was remarkable. He was finding her quite difficult to contain.

But Zawkon also combined his other martial art skills, using front snap kicks, sidekicks and reverse roundhouse kicks to foil Khaneera and slow her down, knocking her to the ground several times. Each time her sharp reflexes allowed her instantly to regain her footing and continue her vicious attack. Zawkon had several opportunities to kill her, but his orders were to capture her alive. If he couldn't take her out, he would have to knock her out.

Finally, with her last onslaught, Zawkon managed to block both her simultaneous blade thrusts by pinning her arms at her side and head-butting her heavily enough to knock her unconscious. Zawkon let her slump to the ground, concussed. Cuffing her hands behind her back, he searched her for the precious crystal memory rod and found it in her boot, tucked into the empty dagger sheath.

Just as Zawkon completed his search, several of his soldiers burst into the room, surprised to see Khaneera sprawled on the ground.

"Well done sir," said one of them.

"Yes, good job Lieutenant," said another soldier behind him.

Zawkon acknowledged his success, before asking, "Have you found General Dranz and any more of his Bladers?"

"Yes Sir," replied the Sergeant, the third Sentinel to enter the room. "We found the rest of the Bladers, including General Dranz, who was wounded when he drew his sword against Lieutenant Kruzak. He should have known better than to challenge the Lieutenant. General Dranz was soon on his knees, a wound to his right arm, begging for his life. The Bladers have been rounded up and taken to the main room, the one we first entered. What do you want us to do with the instruments and the computer containing the infusion blueprints?"

"Good work Sergeant. Put them in the Bladers' ship ready for destruction. Make sure the Bladers are cuffed and secure them in the cells on our ships. Get Khaneera on her feet and keep her well-guarded as you escort her to my ship."

Two of the Sentinels dragged Khaneera to her feet. She was now conscious but drowsy as they started to walk her out of the room.

"Hold fast soldiers," commanded Zawkon to the two escorts. He confronted Khaneera, who was displaying a large, bruised swelling on her forehead. "I want to know the whereabouts of your pilot, Flight-Lieutenant Dawson."

"Why would I tell you anything?" Khaneera slurred bitterly, spitting in his face.

"Take her away soldiers and Sergeant, take a small party and search both the Blader and Terranian ships for any more rebels, including Dawson. But be very cautious. I'll be right behind you after I have a final look around."

"Very good sir!" The Sergeant saluted and marched out.

As the Sentinels vacated the room, Zawkon began examining some of the navigational star charts on the wall in an attempt to identify more rebel hideouts. With his back still to the entrance, he sensed another presence enter the room without warning. In a reflex action, he quickly drew the blade-staff from his belt and turned sharply in a defensive position, half expecting to find another Blader. Instead, he was confronted by an anaemic-looking entity with short, roughly-cropped, dark hair matching his dark eyes, dressed in a fawn hessian robe and wearing simple leather sandals.

"Greetings friend," said the stranger, speaking softly in Treldarian dialect, with his arms outstretched and his palms facing upward, "I come in peace with no harm intended."

"Who are you and what are you doing here?" demanded Zawkon.

The stranger let his arms fall slowly to his side and began to speak in a humble voice. "We are the race that live on this planet and have done so since time began. My name is Rému and I am chief of the Glandels. We are a peaceful people and possess no weapons of war or flying craft as we have no need or desire for them. Being isolated on this desolate planet is our only defence against unwelcomed visitors. Unfortunately, the Bladers accidentally stumbled on our planet and decided to stay, enslaving my people and taking advantage of our women and our resources. The reason I am telling you all this is in hope you'll not destroy our home thinking it to be a Bladers' base. We would prefer everyone to leave us in peace and never return."

Zawkon was perplexed to find another race living on the planet and he was sympathetic to their cause. "I am Zawkon, a Sentinel officer in the Tzuracian armed forces. We're only here to capture the Bladers and take them back to our Planet Tzurac for punishment. The Tzuracians are the peacekeepers of the Universe and it is our pledge to prevent wars and disruption. We mean no harm and will leave you to your peace, undisturbed. If you like, I will give you a distress beacon which can be activated if your people should ever need our help in the future."

"Thank you Sentinel Zawkon for your compassion and understanding. Yes, please leave us your distress beacon which we hope never to have to use. You and your soldiers are welcome to share our table for the night before you depart to your own world."

"Thank you for your hospitality, Rému, but we must return immediately. We'll be departing within the hour. But there is one other favour I would ask of you. Can you tell me if you have seen the whereabouts of a Terrestrial who goes by the name of Pam Dawson? She's also a fugitive and we've been unable to locate her. I know she came here with one of our fugitive Sentinels."

Rému shook his head. "I know of her from a previous visit, but I'm sorry to say we have not seen her this time. We'll certainly be vigilant and let you know using the beacon if we find her."

"Thank you Rému. I must go. My troops are waiting."

Zawkon headed for the hangar, assuming all the captives were now on board ship as he passed through the empty main hall. As he did, he was approached by Lieutenant Kruzak.

"Lieutenant Zawkon, we searched the Blader ship and there's no-one aboard. However, we found Flight-Lieutenant Dawson hiding in the storage bay on the Terrestrial craft. She came out fighting and disarmed two of our Sentinels before we managed to restrain her. We're not sure where she got her fighting skills from, but we've placed her in a cell on board your ship."

"Thank you Lieutenant, but it's her pilot skills I'll need to fly the Terranian battleship back to Tzurac. So, keep her in restraints with several of our Sentinels guarding her. As for the Bladers' vessel, I want it totally destroyed so there are no records left of the formula or Xytrinium infusion process. We'll haul the scorpion ship into space using a traction beam and then torpedo it. Are we ready to depart this planet?"

"Yes Commander."

The Tzuracian fleet accelerated through the twisted, metal doors that once hid the Bladers' cave hangar and into space. Behind them, the explosion of the Bladers' warship could be seen illuminating the skies above Steiros, leaving the peaceful Glandels to celebrate the end of their persecution.

Travelling at hyperspeed to Tzurac with the rest of his fleet and the Terrestrial battleship flown by a reluctant Dawson, Zawkon activated his pledge ring to send a holographic message to Dakhar, reporting their success.

The battle-scarred Lieutenant Zawkon appeared to Dakhar, looking triumphant, displaying in his hand the crystal rod that held the Tzuracian secret to Xytrinium infusion. "We've got it Captain! And we've got Khaneera, Sir, as well as Dranz! Mission accomplished."

"Well done, Zawkon," said Dakhar. "I'm relieved and I know someone else who will be too." It gave Dakhar great pleasure to relay the good news to an anxious Kyron.

In her isolated cell on board Zawkon's ship, Khaneera was restless; her mind racing with a kaleidoscope of images from her initial escape through to her recapture. She was obsessed with her hate for Kyron Shield and she cursed the fool who had thwarted her attempt to kill him. She had added to her collection of vendettas, the young Sentinel, Yarron, who had stirred her passion for love and given her the freedom she longed for, only to betray her to her enemies. The fire that roared inside her was intense and her desire for revenge fanned the flames of her fury. She was in captivity again, but she was determined that, one day, she would finish what she had started, fulfilling the oath she made to avenge her father and the injustice he suffered at the hands of Ahrmon Tyros and the Sentinels.

REASSESSMENT: REASSIGNMENT

WHEN Captain Dakhar arrived back on Tzurac from Earth, still slowly recovering from his almost-fatal wound, the remaining ships from his fleet had already arrived. They had come from Terra Iota and Steiros with their captives, who had been placed in high security cells. The Bladers were initially resistant to interrogation, cursing the Tzuracian interrogators, refusing to answer questions, and protecting their trade secrets even under threat of death. But, when the Tzuracian scientists employed powerful mind probes, the Bladers slowly revealed information, piece by piece. Dakhar began to consolidate information about their hideouts and sanctuaries, scattered throughout the galaxies as well as about those who harboured them.

Discovering this information, the Senate ordered immediate action, instructing the Sentinels to capture any Bladers and collaborators remaining at these locations using whatever force was necessary. They were to destroy all bases, except for sanctuaries that had been home to indigenous tribes who had been subjugated by the rebels.

Special hearings were arranged to discuss the future of the other planets involved in the conspiracy, Kyronis and Diunon, and to re-assess security throughout the Federation. Captain Dakhar was summoned to appear before the Senate to submit his report on the battle and was privileged when also asked to contribute to the Senate's decision making on these matters.

Within days of his return, Dakhar rose earlier than normal one morning and dressed in his formal Regimental uniform wearing the midnight-blue sash of his rank and carefully pinning his service medals to it. He ate a hearty breakfast with his family; Tajhira, his beautiful Urgellan wife of noble blood, and his young son, Kyrah. All the while he was bombarded with a never-ending barrage of questions from the inquisitive four-year old about his father's latest adventures. It was good to be home, knowing his family was safe and happy and that he had survived his near-death encounter to be with them. Dakhar had suggested to Tajhira the possibility of living temporarily on Earth with the families of his Regiment and she was open to considering the idea if the Senate sanctioned it.

Arriving at the Senate Chambers, Captain Dakhar was ushered to a seat in the front row. He was used to escorting prisoners into the Chambers but this time he was a special guest. Nerves mixed with anxiety contributed to his mildly unsettled stomach.

Finally, all six senior Senators arrived, seating themselves in readiness. They wore their distinguished purple robes and matching tasselled caps, representing their status in the legal fraternity. The select members were the law makers; legal scholars of senior rank who had the knowledge, experience and wisdom to administer and protect the citizens of Tzurac and the Federation. Today, in a closed court, they were to adjudicate on the fate of the planets that had conspired with the Bladers in their attempts to destroy the Sentinels and the Federation. They were also to discuss security arrangements to ensure nothing like this would ever happen again to endanger the peace which had reigned throughout the Universe for centuries.

The Elder, Senator Ghalbrak, the head of the Senators, was the first to speak. "Captain Dakhar, thank you for attending the Tribunal this morning." Dakhar rose from his seat and acknowledged the Elder with a respectful nod. "Please sit down, Captain. This will be a long hearing. I know you were badly wounded. Are you well enough to speak with us?"

Dakhar re-seated himself before answering. "Thank you, Senator. The wound is almost healed and I'm anxious to report to you."

"Fine, Captain. We've read your written summary, but we would like you to tell us again, in detail, exactly what happened."

For the next hour, Captain Dakhar relived the chronological events and decisions he had made. He described how he had strategically organised his fleet; requested permission for the emissaries to visit the Tzuracian allies to enlist the armies of Urgellan and help from the Armonusians; the outcomes of the battles; the encounter with Khaneera and Jackson Jensen; as well as the escape of General Dranz and Khaneera.

He explained to the Senators that if it were not for Corporal Yarron Blandhar's guilty conscience and forewarning of the invasion, the outcome would have been devastating to the Tzuracians and the Federation. He praised Blandhar for his attempts to make amends and for putting his own life at risk to save Ambassador Kyron Shield. Dakhar also praised the courage and loyalty of his Sentinels and of Kyron, as well as the bravery of the Urgellan soldiers in supporting the cause.

The Senators sat in silence for some time after Captain Dakhar finished reporting, reflecting on all they had been told. Then the Elder spoke again. "Thank you, Captain for your thorough narration. In light of this, what do you believe we should do in order to improve our security? You may speak freely."

"Thank you Senator Ghalbrak. First, I recommend the planets Kyronis and Diunon be placed under martial law and the leaders who sanctioned involvement in the rebellion imprisoned. Obviously we need to tighten security here on Tzurac, particularly at the Science Academy, our prisons and our Air Base. To protect Earth and its reserves of Xytrinium, we should consider expanding the size of our small Sentinel barracks there into a major Academy housed in a large Citadel, complemented with full Fleet support. If General Dranz and his Bladers had attacked Terra Major and not Iota, the planet would have fallen. And, on a more personal note, I would like your permission to be re-assigned with my Regiment to the base on Terra Major at least for the foreseeable future. This will help us establish tighter security there and build closer relations with our allies, the Terranians."

After finishing his recommendations Dakhar sat quietly, feeling awkward in the dead silence, watching the Senators confer amongst themselves. He started to question whether he had overstepped his invitation to speak freely.

Then the Elder spoke again. "It is agreed unanimously by the Senators of this Tribunal to accept your recommendations Captain, with one condition on your personal request for reassignment to Earth."

Dakhar's heart sank on hearing the word 'condition'.

"We have been monitoring your distinguished career for many years and we consider you are worthy of a new Commission. We recognise your length of service and loyalty, your military astuteness, your strong leadership in battle and your concerns for the safety of your Sentinels. Lieutenant Dakhar, we are promoting you to the rank of General, First Class." All the Senators nodded affirming their decision.

"The condition on your reassignment is that you take charge of the entire Western Quadrant, administered from Earth. In this position you will be the Commanding Chief of Military Operations situated in a new Sentinel Academy within a Citadel on Earth. If you take on this responsibility, you may request volunteers from your Regiment to accompany you with their families. Do you accept our offer General Dakhar?"

Dakhar rose from his seat and cleared his throat before speaking. He had not anticipated such an honour. "I am humbled by your praise Senators and I'm grateful to serve Tzurac to the best of my ability with the Commission bestowed upon me. I relish the opportunity to demonstrate my worthiness as a General."

"Thank you, General. We are grateful for what you've already done to protect and save Tzurac and the Federation. We'll hold a formal swearing-in ceremony within the next few days and you should prepare to depart for Terra Major assuming the Terranian World Assembly agrees we can establish a permanent Tzuracian base there. Is there anything else you would like to say to the Senate, General?"

"Yes, Senator there is. I would like to recommend Lieutenant Kal Zawkon for promotion to Captain for his outstanding service and leadership in the field. He has proven on many occasions his worth as a lieutenant and his ability to be a good captain. He is a brilliant battle strategist and a dedicated, loyal officer who shows consideration for the safety of his troops."

The Elder nodded his immediate agreement. "We'll make the arrangements, General. Both promotions can be recognised in the one ceremony. Now if this concludes our hearing, the Tribunal will adjourn."

Waiting at home, Tajhira was anxious to hear all that had happened. "Well, my husband, how did it go at the Chambers this morning?" she asked, as Dakhar arrived.

"I have good news, my love."

"Before you tell me anything, Ehrane, come and sit down while I bring you a drink."

As Dakhar made himself comfortable on the padded lounge, Tajhira returned with a tall glass of iced aromatic tea.

"Thank you Tajhira. This is just what I need. The session with the Senators this morning was exciting, but tiring."

Tajhira was delighted to hear of her husband's success, but apprehensive about leaving Tzurac so soon. It was all a little overwhelming. "What about Kyrah?" was her first response. "He'll miss both his friends and teachers."

"All going well, my love, a lot of his friends will be coming with us if the Regiment volunteers to join me. We'll make it work. You and Kyrah and your happiness, are the most important things to me."

"Well, let's see if Kyrah likes the idea. I'm sure he will, as he is so much like his father," she said, smiling affectionately.

The response from young Kyrah as well as from Dakhar's Regiment was enthusiastic. Kyrah was excited at the suggestion and over two thirds of the Regiment – two thousand Sentinels including the newly-commissioned Captain Kal Zawkon – volunteered to accompany their leader.

Following a formal promotion ceremony attended by the entire Sentinel Academy, Dakhar prepared for his Regiment's departure. This time, he was going to make Terra Major his home.

NEW BEGINNINGS

KYRON was there to welcome the Regiment when they arrived at the ASPECT building in three warships and to escort the Regiment to the temporary Citadel. He invited Ehrane and his family to stay with him and Torri but Dakhar declined the offer, not wanting to desert his soldiers while they were trying to adapt to a strange new world and a different race.

A week passed while the Regiment settled into their temporary accommodation, their families being housed in buildings outside the Citadel amongst the Terranian military community. The Tzuracian children with Sentinel DNA began classes at the Sentinel school. Kyron asked Zuri and Ehrana, who'd been students there for over a year, to show the new children the rules and help them settle in. Strong friendships soon developed between the Tzuracian and Terranian children and Zuri and Ehrana quickly became best friends with Dakhar's son, Kyrah.

At the end of the first week Dakhar and his family were invited for dinner at Kyron and Torri's house, a beautiful sandstone mansion on the outskirts of New York City. The home overlooking the now-green pastures and surrounded by tall, lush, oak trees was well away from the skyscrapers and madding crowds of the city. Torri prepared a Tzuracian meal especially for the occasion.

When their visitors arrived, Kyron and Torri were quite taken by the Urgellan beauty of Tajhira. She had angelic features with wispy, flaxen hair, violet eyes and a slender body. Kyrah had been blessed with his mother's violet eyes and fine bone structure.

After dinner, the children played in their bedrooms with Tzuracian games and toys which Kyrah had brought with him to Earth. Torri gave Tajhira a tour of the mansion while Dakhar and Kyron retired to the homely lounge, immersing themselves in close conversation. Ehrane had much to tell Kyron of what had been happening since his last visit to Terra Major. Relaxing in comfortable dark, leather lounge chairs and sipping single malt whisky, Ehrane spoke in a more laid-back fashion, dropping his military guard.

"Kyron, I missed the nice beverages you Terranians drink and I also missed your company."

Dakhar was keen to tell Kyron about his promotion and his new responsibilities until Kyron interrupted. "Sorry, Ehrane, that's excellent news. But can you fill me in on what happened after Captain Zawkon was sent to capture Khaneera and the Bladers on Steiros? I wished I could have been there."

"Yes, of course …" Dakhar related the story, finishing by explaining that Khaneera was back in a cell under high security, that Dranz and his Blader rebels had been executed and Corporal Yarron Blandhar was still a fugitive-at-large.

"You'll be aware that Flight Lieutenant Dawson piloted the Terranian battleship back to Earth under guard and the World Assembly decided her fate. And, the captured Kyroni and Diunons underwent a procedure to neutralize the Xytrinium enhancements and were transported to prison farms on other penal settlements within the Federation."

Kyron was intrigued. "I didn't know the infusion could be reversed?"

"Yes, Kyron, it can be reversed with what we call a 'diffuser'. Our alchemists have manufactured synthetic bacteria which rapidly break down Xytrinium in the DNA. The side-effect of this bacterium shuts down adrenalin production and reduces aggression. This helps to control DNA-enhanced prisoners without losing their ability to perform manual labour tasks."

"Fascinating," responded Kyron. "Well, I guess you've covered everything, Ehrane, and it sounds like it's all under control."

"Not everything my friend. I have some news you may not have been expecting. Your position as the Tzuracian Ambassador has now been bestowed upon me."

"Oh," exclaimed Kyron while searching Dakhar's eyes for some answers. "What happens to me now that I'm no longer performing those duties? What role will I have in the Regiment?"

Dakhar leaned back in his chair and with a warm smile offered a proposal to Kyron. "You, my friend, are invited to attend the Officers' Training Academy under my recommendation and tutelage. Kyron, you have the potential to become a fine officer and a strong leader of soldiers. If you accept, you will be instructed in the ways of a Sentinel, steeped in tradition, honour and pride. You'll learn of your heritage and that of your forefathers. It will be hard work, but I'm sure you'll thoroughly enjoy the privilege. What say you, son of Ahrmon Tyros?"

The worried look on Kyron's face dissolved into a broad grin and he responded without any hesitation. "I'm honoured to be invited and I accept your offer. When do I start, Ehrane?"

"As soon as it can be arranged. Will Torri be able to manage MERIC while you're undertaking officer's training?"

"Yes, of course. With the assistance of Miss Blake, she'll manage very well."

Just as they finished their conversation, Torri and Tajhira returned from their tour of the expansive home.

"How do you like the house, Tajhira?" asked Kyron.

"You and Torri have a beautiful house with lovely furniture. And it's such a large place."

"Thank you Tajhira. The house was built by Samuel Jensen and bequeathed to me, and I'm most thankful. There's plenty of room for you and the children to stay here with us if you like until Ehrane has sorted out your permanent accommodation. I'm sure Torri would enjoy your company and the children play so well together. What do you think?"

Torri nodded her agreement with Kyron's suggestion as Tajhira looked pleadingly towards her husband. Dakhar spoke on behalf of his family. "Thanks Kyron for your kind offer. I think it's an excellent idea. Tajhira and I will need to sort out some things first, but it's an arrangement to everyone's liking."

"It's settled then," said Kyron with a pleased expression. "Just let us know when you decide to come and I hope it's soon."

After their guests left to return to the Citadel, Kyron and Torri sat in the lounge to talk about the night's events.

"Thank you for cooking a lovely meal Torri and for making Tajhira and her son feel so welcome."

"I hope they enjoyed the dinner. You know Kyron, Tajhira and I get on very well. I'm glad you asked them to stay with us until they organise their own accommodation. She'll be good company and we'll be able to share our different worlds and customs. I'll learn more about Tzurac and it will be nice to have a close female friend for a change."

"Yes I agree totally, my love. It will work out well in view of what Ehrane told me about his plans for my future."

Torri looked concerned. She had more thoughts of Kyron undertaking a cadetship back on Tzurac. "You're not going anywhere in the near future are you?"

"No, Torri. No need to be alarmed. Ehrane has been given the role of Tzuracian Ambassador and has invited me to become a cadet in the Officers' Training Academy in the new Citadel here on Earth, to be trained under his direct tutelage."

"Oh, I'm so pleased for you. You must accept his offer, Kyron. Your mother will be so proud, as your father would have been. This is wonderful news." She walked over and kissed him, proudly.

"Of course, this means you will need to manage MERIC full-time Torri, while I attend the Academy. How do you feel about this?"

"I think it will work out just fine. And, when is all this happening?"

"It will take at least three months to establish the Academy so we have plenty of time to organise ourselves."

"Good," said Torri with a grin. "Just to change the subject, did Ehrane mention anything about Khaneera?"

"She's locked up again and, with heightened security on Tzurac, I don't think we have to worry about *her* anymore."

Torri breathed a sigh of relief on hearing that Khaneera was again behind bars. But secretly she wished the cold-hearted killer was no longer in the picture at all.

"However, there's one other thing I need to mention Torri before we retire for the night... Have I told you lately that I love you?"

Torri smiled devilishly, reached for Kyron's hand and led him to the bedroom.